BOOKS

Simply Learning, Simply Best!

Simply Learning, Simply Best!

蘇瑩珊◎著

倍斯特出版事業有限公司
Best Publishing Ltd.

Learning English Grammar with **Hollywood Stars** ☆

跟著大明星學英文文法

70 位Hollywood Stars領銜主演英文文法！

大明星強勢登台，變身英文文法實力派！

☆Stars Quotes☆-----睿智名言揭幕單元文法重點!!
☆Grammar Show☆--Easy英文文法登台演出!!
☆Life Story☆---------閱讀大明星的精采故事練語感!!
☆Sentence Show☆--從句子再練習一次文法!!

最**星光熠熠**的英文文法書，公開大明星們不為人知的**小故事**
看英文文法如何與Super Stars擦出**精彩火花**！

We come to love not by finding the perfect person, but by learning to see an imperfect person perfectly.
我們談戀愛並不是要找完美的人，而是要學習如何看到不完美的人完美的一面。

---Angelina Jolie 安潔莉娜．裘莉

Preface 作者序

對於追星或是蒐集愛好品這一類的行為，在以前都很容易被長輩們視為「玩物喪志」。但在今時今日，「喜好」卻往往成為學習最大的動力；比如，因為喜歡韓星而研讀韓語，或是熱愛蒐集工藝品而學習相關知識等的例子比比皆是。而我有幸執筆倍斯特出版社這本有趣的英語學習書，從明星的名言來探討英語的文法，感覺這個企劃讓枯燥的文法學習頓時多了幾分的趣味。

此書的完成，除了家人的支持外，也有賴於許多語言學習專家及外籍友人的協助。在此感謝我的家人和 Tony Benson, Miroslav Fizel, Felicia Hose, Sandy Wang。同時，也謝謝審稿老師 Wendy 老師、Matt 老師的用心校稿，以及辛苦的編輯瑞璞和協助本書完成的編輯們。

期望本書能帶給讀者們學習英語的樂趣。

蘇瑩珊

Preface 編者序

在學英文的時間，你是否有默默當過某西洋明星的粉絲與追星族呢？

第一次用英文來了解自己偶像的第一手資訊時，感覺一定是雀躍的吧！

眾星雲集的文法書登場

本書特別邀請 70 位來自 Hollywood 的 Super Star 們，一一領銜主演一個文法小劇場。有在關注西洋流行文化的您，一定會知曉他們。這裡有他們高低起伏的人生故事以及獨特睿智的人生哲學。

文法小劇場—文法好簡單

每一個文法都由大明星們的一句名言開始說起，並搭配輕巧的文法說明。並有眾星的精彩生平故事來練習「閱讀」與「文法觀念」。有時，為了配合人物與文法，在名言選材有時有做必要性的修改。但是在編輯時盡力保持大明星的迷人風采。

追星也是在學英文的，好嗎！

希望讀者在看完本書後，文法與閱讀能力大幅提升，將來瀏覽英文娛樂版新聞或是明星最新動態都很 easy，而這一切都因英文而「打開」很多！

好了，馬上要開演，趕緊入場囉！讓大明星用他的故事與人生智慧陪你學習英文文法吧！

選自於大叔 Will Smith 威爾史密斯的名言：

The first step is you have to say that you can.

（第一步是你必須說你辦得到。）

倍斯特編輯部

Contents 目錄

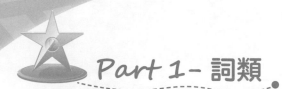

Part 1- 詞類

Part 2- 時態、助動詞、動狀詞

Part 3- 句型

Part 4- 語態與語氣

Instructions 使用說明

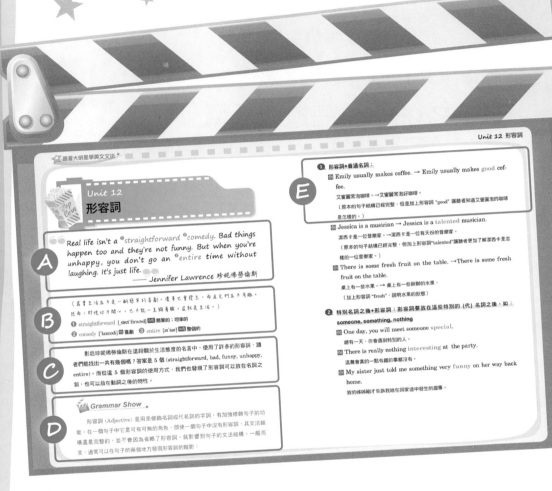

翻著大明星學英文文法

Unit 12
形容詞

Real life isn't a °straightforward °comedy. Bad things happen too and they're not funny. But when you're unhappy, you don't go an °entire time without laughing. It's just life.
—— Jennifer Lawrence 珍妮佛勞倫斯

（真實生活並不是一齣簡單的喜劇，還事也會發生，而且它們並不有趣。但有，即使你不開心，也不致一直開著嘴，這就是生活。）

❶ straightforward [‚stret`fɔrwəd] 形 簡單的；坦率的
❷ comedy [`kɑmədɪ] 名 喜劇　❸ entire [ɪn`taɪr] 形 整個的

影后珍妮佛勞倫斯在這段關於生活態度的名言中，使用了許多的形容詞，讀者們能找出一共有幾個嗎？答案是 5 個（straightforward, bad, funny, unhappy, entire）。而從這 5 個形容詞的使用方式，我們也發現了形容詞可以放在名詞之前，也可以放在動詞之後的特性。

Grammar Show

　　形容詞 (Adjective) 是用來修飾名詞或代名詞的字詞，有加強修飾句子的功能。在一個句子中它是可有可無的角色，即使一個句子中沒有形容詞，其文法結構還是完整的，並不會因為省略了形容詞，就影響到句子的文法結構。一般而言，通常可以在句子的兩個地方發現形容詞的蹤影：

❶ 形容詞+普通名詞：
Emily usually makes coffee. → Emily usually makes good coffee.
艾蜜麗常泡咖啡。→ 艾蜜麗常泡好喝咖啡。
（原本的句子結構已經完整，但是加上形容詞 "good" 讓聽者知道艾蜜麗泡的咖啡是怎麼樣的。）

Jessica is a musician. → Jessica is a talented musician.
潔西卡是一位音樂家。→ 潔西卡是一位有天份的音樂家。
（原本的句子結構已經完整，但加上形容詞"talented"讓聽者更加了解潔西卡是怎樣的一位音樂家。）

There is some fresh fruit on the table. →There is some fresh fruit on the table.
桌上有一些水果。→ 桌上有一些新鮮的水果。
（加上形容詞 "fresh"，說明水果的狀態）

❷ 特別名詞之後+形容詞：形容詞要放在這些特別的 (代) 名詞之後，如：someone, something, nothing
One day, you will meet someone special.
總有一天，你會遇到特別的人。
There is really nothing interesting at the party.
這舞會真的一點有趣的事都沒有。
My sister just told me something very funny on her way back home.
我的妹妹剛才告訴我她在回家途中發生的趣事。

A　Hollywood stars大明星的精彩語錄，從裡面來學習文法

B　翻譯來自星星的語言，不再隔著語言

C　説明名言和文法之間的關聯，更好進入文法要點

D　文法小劇場，文法説明不多也不少，這樣份量剛剛好

E　列點舉例説明，容易學習容易記起來

Ⓕ 藉由閱讀有趣的大明星人生故事來增進英文理解力

Ⓖ 文章中出現的單字補充，學習很自然

Ⓗ 與單元文法觀念相關的句子我們再聚焦學習一次，也看看文法在文章中怎麼展現

Ⓘ 兩題小練習 驗收一下學習的成果，是否有學通

☆ 跟著大明星學英文文法 ★

Life Story

As the breakout star of the popular movies, *The Hunger Games* and *X-Men: First Class*, Jennifer Lawrence is the name the whole world is talking about.

The beginning of her story may be no different from other Hollywood stars. Lawrence earned her career by herself. She first decided to be an actress at the age of 14. In order to start her acting career sooner, she graduated from high school two years early even achieving GPA 3.9 (the full marks are 4). Even though she is no longer considered as a starlet, she still works hard every day. Once in an interview with Glamour magazine, she mentioned she has never understood why some people have to stop working when they become successful. She thinks these people should work harder when they become successful because others are expecting more from them. For her, success doesn't mean she is allowed to work less. It is actually the other way around.

在熱賣電影《飢餓遊戲》及《X 戰警：第一戰》中展頭角的珍妮佛勞倫斯，已成為一個全世界都在談論的名字。

她的故事的開始也許和其他好萊塢明星並沒有不同。勞倫斯自己爭取了她的事業。她在 14 歲時就決定成為演員。為了早點開始她的演藝事業，她以 GPA3.9 的成績（GPA 的滿分為 4 分），提早兩年從高中畢業，即使她現在已經不再被視為是初出茅廬的新人，她每天仍努力不懈。她在一次《Glamour 雜誌》的專訪中提到，她不瞭解為何有些人在成功之後便停止工作，她認為這些人應該在成功後更努力，因為別人會對他們有更多的期望。對她而言，成功並不代表她可以少努力一些；而是恰恰相反。

* recognize [ˋrɛkəgˌnaɪz] ⅴ 認出
* brand [brænd] ⋒ 品牌
* mention [ˋmɛnʃən] ⅴ 提到
* well-known [ˋwɛlˋnon] ᴀᴅᴊ 知名的
* unrealistic [ˌʌnrɪəˋlɪstɪk] ᴀᴅᴊ 不切實際的

Sentence Show

Unit 12 形容詞

❶ As the breakout star of the popular movies, *The Hunger Games* and *X-Men: First Class*, Jennifer Lawrence is the name the whole world is talking about.

這句話的兩個形容詞分別為"breakout"（突然竄紅的）和"popular"（受歡迎的），用來修飾"star"（明星）和"movies"（電影）。這裡也可以清楚看到形容詞可有可無的特性，即拿掉的兩個形容詞後"As the star of the movies"仍為一個合文法的句子。

❷ The beginning of her story may be no different from other Hollywood stars.

"nothing"（沒有）為這句話裡的特殊代名詞，所以它的形容詞"different"（不同的）在此處就要擺至"nothing"後方做修飾，中文翻譯為：「沒有什麼不同的」。

Practice Time

Q1：珍妮佛勞倫斯是個聰明的女孩。

Q2：珍妮佛勞倫斯總是期望她能認識某個特別的人。

Q1 Ans：Jennifer Lawrence is a smart girl.

Q2 Ans：Jennifer Lawrence always hopes she can meet someone special.

Part 1

詞類

Unit 01
一般動詞

❝ Just keep moving ❶forward and ❷ignore what anybody thinks. Do what you need to do, for yourself. ❞

—— Johnny Depp 強尼・戴普

（持續向前，不管任何人怎麼想。做你需要做的，為你自己。）

❶ forward [`fɔrwəd] adv 向前　❷ ignore [ɪg`nor] V 忽視

　　個性巨星強尼・戴普這兩句話都是祈使句，所以主要動詞均使用現在式。這裡要注意的是動詞後面接動詞時，後方的動詞會依前一個動詞做不同的改變，如："keep" 後面的動詞需為動名詞形式 (Ving)，"need"之後則為不定詞形式 (to V.) 等。（關於動名詞和不定詞是什麼請閱 Part 2，Unit 21&Unit 22）

🎬 Grammar Show ★

　　動詞 (Verb) 是用來表示動作、行為和狀態的詞。在本書中將動詞歸納為三大類：一般動詞，be 動詞及助動詞。現在我們就先從一般動詞來介紹吧！

　　一般動詞：泛指一般動作的詞，通常來說，如果一個動詞既不是 be 動詞，也不是助動詞，那通常會被歸類到一般動詞裡。例如: 看 (watch) 聽 (listen)，跑 (run)，游泳 (swim)，玩樂 (play) …等等。一般動詞有可以細分及物動詞 (Transitive Verbs) 和不及物動詞 (Intransitive Verbs)。

1 及物動詞：是指這個動作有碰及或接觸物品或事務。及物動詞後面一定要接
受詞，整個語句才會完整

例 I **drink** coffee every morning.

我每天早上喝咖啡。

例 When he **has** free time, he likes to **read** novels.

當他有空時，他喜歡閱讀小說。

2 不及物動詞：指動作本身並不會或是不需要接觸其他的物品或事務，即可完
成

例 In winter, it usually **snows** in Europe.

歐洲冬天通常會下雪。

例 Grandmother's apple tree is **growing** so fast.

祖母種的蘋果樹長得很快。

此外，一般動詞又需依人稱及時態而做不同的變化。例如：

人稱	動詞與時態
I（我→第一人稱單數）	eat（吃→現在簡單式） ate（吃→過去簡單式） am eating（吃→現在進行式）
he（他→第三人稱單數）	eats（吃→現在簡單式） ate（吃→過去簡單式） is eating（吃→現在進行式）
they（他們→第三人稱複數）	eat（吃→現在簡單式） ate（吃→過去簡單式） are eating（吃→現在進行式）

Life Story

①Some people say he is weird. Others say he has a strong personality. As for Johnny Depp himself, he agrees with the later one more. "I was not the kind of person that easily fitted in," he once revealed in an interview. "When I was a student, the school divided students into three categories: rich kids, good kids and bad kids. However, my appearance has created the fourth type—weird kids."

Although people said the choices he made were strange, Depp knew exactly what the career path he wanted to pursue was. He dropped out of high school at the age of 16. He first joined a band, The Kids, but had to sell pens to support the band. ②By the time The Kids broke up in 1985, Depp had been acting for a year. After several small roles as a film extra, Depp landed his first big role in the horror film-Nightmare on *Elm Street*. Later, Depp continued to flourish and popularity increased for his work. He won many film awards and has become the highest paid actor in Hollywood.

有些人說他很有奇怪；而有些人說他很個性。對強尼・戴普自己來說，他比較同意後者。「我不是那種容易適應環境的人，」他在某次訪問中說道。「當我還是學生時，學校將學生分為三類：『有錢的孩子』、『好孩子』和『壞孩子』。但我出現後，則多了第四類—『奇怪的孩子』。」

雖然人們說他總是做奇怪的決定，但戴普很清楚自己想追求的職業。他在 16 歲時從高中輟學。一開始他加入了一個叫 The Kids 的樂團，但他必須靠賣筆來維持樂團。在 1985 年樂團解散時，他已經開始他的演藝事業一年了。在演過許多小配角後，他終於在恐怖電影《猛鬼街》裡演出要角。之後，他的事業持續發光，也因電影作品增加了知名度。他獲得了許多電影獎項，並且成為好萊塢片酬最高的男演員。

● weird [wɪrd] **adj** 奇怪的　● reveal [rɪ`vil] **V** 顯露出　● pursue [brænd] **V** 追求

 **Sentence Show**

❶ Some people say he is weird. Others say he has a strong personality.

這裡前兩句話中的主詞"some people"和"others"均為複數第三人稱，故兩者的動詞"say"均需使用一般式。又"say"在這裡做為及物動詞「指明」，所以兩者後面均需要有受詞（到底說了什麼），語句才會完整。

❷ By the time The Kids broke up in 1985, Depp had been acting for a year.

這句話說的是強尼‧戴普在年輕時所發生的事，屬於已經過去的事情，所以時態使用過去式。又"broke up"（解散）屬於不及物動詞片語，故後方不需要受詞便可完整表達句子的意思。

★ 註：『片語』簡單來說就是一群字組，沒有像句子有主詞與動詞。

 Practice Time

Q1：強尼‧戴普喜歡彈吉他。

_____

Q2：當強尼‧戴普贏得獎項時，他哭了。

_____

Q1 Ans：Johnny Deep likes to play guitar.

Q2 Ans：When Johnny Depp won the award, he cried.

Unit 02
be 動詞

"People ❶react to ❷criticism in different ways, and my way is ❸definitely to come out fighting."
—— David Beckham 大衛•貝克漢

（人們面對批評的方法不盡相同，而我的方法絕對是正面迎擊。）

❶ react [rɪ`ækt] **v** 反應　❷ criticism [`krɪtəˌsɪzəm] **n** 批評

❸ definitely [`dɛfənɪtlɪ] **adv** 肯定地

　　在貝克漢的這句話裡面，用連接詞"and"連接了兩個句子；而兩個句子中則各有一個動詞。聰明的讀者們，你們能指出是哪兩個嗎？答案揭曉！前一句的動詞為"react"，屬於一般動詞；而後一個句子的動詞則是"is"，屬於 be 動詞。你知道差在哪嗎？

Grammar Show

　　be 動詞通常是用來表示「主詞狀態」或是「陳述事實」。be 動詞的中文翻譯一般為「是」或「在」，而位置通常放在主詞之後（即主詞+be 動詞）。be 動詞的使用還會因為主詞的人稱和句子的時態不同，而有以下變化：

	現在式	過去式
第一人稱單數 (I)	am	was
第二人稱單數 (you)	are	were
第三人稱單數 (he/she/it)	is	was
各人稱複數 (we, you, they)	are	were

有了初步的認識後，現在就讓我們來看如何正確使用 be 動詞在句子裡吧！

1 陳述狀態、現象或概念/想法

例 He **was** very exhausted, so he fell asleep so soon.

他非常的疲勞，所以很快就睡著了。→說明他的狀態是疲勞的

例 We **are** excited about our upcoming holiday in Barcelona.

我們對於即將來到的巴塞隆納假期感到非常興奮。→說明我們是興奮的

例 The pollution **is** worse than before.

污染程度每況愈下。→說明污染的事實是比以前糟的

例 Art **is** the expression of people's emotion and affection.

藝術是人類情感的表現。→說明藝術的事實是表達情感的方式

2 陳述事實，如：歷史事件，關係職稱或人格/事務本質⋯等等

例 My mother **is** a gardener.

我媽媽是園藝家。→媽媽的職稱是園藝家

例 Her housemate **is** very picky about her living environment.

她的室友對於居家環境非常挑剔。 →室友對特定事物是很愛挑剔的

例 World War II **was** from 1939 to 1945.

第二次世界大戰是從 1939 到 1945 年。→說明第二次大戰的歷史事實

Life Story

For girls who aren't interested in sports and don't recognize any football players, they must know one name — David Beckham. (Or at least they know David through his famous wife, the former member of Spice Girls, Victoria Beckham.) In fact, he is not only a well-known football player but also the face of many international brands.

❶Beckham decided to be a professional footballer while he was still at school. At the time, most of his teachers and classmates thought his football dream was unrealistic. His teacher even asked him to say something for real instead. However, he answered being a professional footballer was the only thing he ever wanted to do. He later mentioned the above story in a 2007 interview and encouraged his audience to dare to dream. "**❷Impossible is not a fact. It's an opinion.** If you have dreams and you believe in yourself, your dream can come true," he said."

對那些對運動不感興趣、也不認識任何一個足球員的女孩來說,她們一定知道一個名字——大衛‧貝克漢。(或者,至少她們會透過他有名的妻子,前辣妹合唱團團員維多利亞‧貝克漢而認識他。)事實上,他不僅是位知名的足球員,還是許多國際品牌的代言人。

貝克漢在讀書時就決定要成為一個專業的足球員。當時,大多數的老師及同學們都認為他的想法很不切實際。他的老師甚至要求他改說些實際的夢想;然而,他回答專業足球員是他唯一想做的事。他之後在 2007 年的一個專訪上提起上述這個故事,並鼓勵聽眾們要勇於做夢。『不可能』並非事實,只是一個表述。如果你有夢想並且相信自己,你的夢想就會實現。」他說道。

● recognize [`rɛkəg͵naɪz] **V** 認出　● well-known [`wɛl`non] **adj** 知名的
● brand [brænd] **n** 品牌　● unrealistic [͵ʌnrɪə`lɪstɪk] **adj** 不切實際的
● mention [`mɛnʃən] **V** 提到

Sentence Show ★

❶ Beckham decided to be a professional footballer while he was still at school.

由於這句話說的是貝克漢讀書時的事情，是已經過去的事，所以 while 連接詞所連接的兩個句子裡的動詞"decided"和"was"都是過去式（現在簡單式分別為"decide"和"is"）。又因為 while 子句裡的主詞是第三人稱單數，所以使用"was"。

❷ Impossible is not a fact. It's an opinion.

這個句子的句型為「A 不是 B 是 C」，故動詞需使用 be 動詞。這兩句話的主詞都是第三人稱單數，所以需使用 is。此外，這兩句話表達的是「普遍認知的事實」，所以時態使用現在式。

 Practice Time ★

Q1：貝克漢不是籃球員。他是足球員。

_____

Q2：貝克漢是他那個時代最偉大的足球員。

_____

Q1 Ans：Beckham is not a basketball player. He is a footballer.

Q2 Ans：Beckham is the greatest footballer of his day.

Unit 03
連綴動詞

❝ No matter what you look like, I think the key is to be happy with yourself. ❞

—— Adele 愛黛兒

（不管你看起來是什麼樣子，我想關鍵是你要對自己感到滿意。）

　　句中的動詞"look"翻譯為「看起來」，在文法裡稱為「聯綴動詞」（Linking verbs）。「聯綴動詞」和一般常見的「動作動詞」（Action verb）在用法上不太相同。就讓我們來看看到底有什麼不同吧！

Grammar Show

　　一般常見的「動作動詞」後面常有用副詞修飾該動詞的情況，如："walk slowly"（緩慢地走路），"talk loudly"（大聲地說話）等。然而，在「連綴動詞」之後多使用形容詞來做說明，如："look funny"（看起來很好笑）。

❶ **"be 動詞/look (看起來) /smell (聞起來) /taste (嚐起來) /sound (聽起來) / feel (感覺起來) /seem (似乎) /get (變得) /become (變成)"+形容詞**
一般「動作動詞」是用副詞來修飾動詞；而「連綴動詞」之後是用形容詞且並非用來修飾動詞，而是修飾該句的主詞。

　例 This bag **is big**.

　　這個包包很大。（形容詞"big"和動詞"is"無關，而是說明主詞"this bag"）

例 The sky **looks** very **blue**.

天空看起來很藍。（形容詞"blue"說明主詞"the sky"的情況）

例 Their music has **become** quite **commercialized**.

他們的音樂變得很商業化了。

2 **"be 動詞/look/smell/taste/sound/feel/seem/become" + like + (a/an) 名詞/名詞片語**

這裡的**"like"**是介系詞，是「像」的意思。

例 She **is like an angel.**

她像一位天使。

例 The weather is so cold. It **feels like winter** now.

天氣太冷了。感覺像是冬天到了。

例 After taking acting courses for two years, Peggy **seems like a professional actress**.

在上了兩年的表演課程後，佩琪似乎就跟專業的女演員一樣。

3 **be 動詞/become + (a/an) 名詞/名詞片語**

例 Henry **is a math teacher**.

亨利是名數學老師。

例 My brother **became a doctor.**

我的弟弟成了一名醫生。

Life Story

One thing you should know about Adele is she is one of the most effortlessly funny people you will ever meet. Every second thing she says, on stages or in interviews, is hilarious. Back to the days when she released her first album, her producer asked her to lose some weight because fans might be more interested in seeing a singer having a model figure. "❶I like looking nice, but I always put comfort over fashion. I don't find thin girls attractive; be happy and healthy. I've never had a problem with the way I look," she claimed. "I would rather have lunch with my friends than go to a gym."

That producer could never have guessed how successful Adele was to become. Following her debut album "19", her second album "21" also received huge success and thus made her a multi-millionaire. Right now, ❷she has met her Mr. Right and become the mother of a lovely boy.

關於愛黛兒，有一件事你應該要知道：她是那種你曾見過的，說笑不需要太費力的人之一。無論在台上或受訪，她每秒鐘說的話都讓人捧腹大笑。在她出第一張專輯時，她的製作人要她減肥，因為歌迷大多較有興趣看到擁有模特兒身材的歌手。「我喜歡看起來好看，但我總是覺得舒適比潮流重要。我不覺得瘦女孩比較吸引人；重要的是保持開心和健康。我不在乎我看起來怎樣。」她提到。「我寧願和朋友們一起午餐而不是去健身房。」

那位製作人可能從未想過愛黛兒今天會如此的成功。緊接於她第一張專輯 "19" 之後的，是同樣獲得極為成功的的第二張專輯 "21"，這張專輯也讓她成為了鉅富。而現在，她已經遇到她的真命天子，也生了一個可愛男孩當了媽媽。

- effortlessly [ˈɛfətlɪslɪ] **adv** 毫不費力地
- hilarious [hɪˈlɛrɪəs] **adj** 極可笑的
- figure [ˈfɪgjə] **n** 體型
- debut [dɪˈbju] **n** 首次露面
- millionaire [ˌmɪljənˈɛr] **n** 百萬富翁

Sentence Show ★

❶ I like looking nice.

like 為一般動詞，like+Ving 表示喜歡做某事。故 like 後面的 look 需要寫成 looking。而 look 剛好是「連綴動詞」所以後面加一個形容詞 nice。修飾主詞 "I"（我），表示是「我」喜歡看起來「好看」。

❷ She has met her Mr. Right and become the mother of a lovely boy.

此句話中使用連接詞"and"連接了兩個句子，讓我們將重點放在有本單元重點「連綴動詞」的後面一個句子。句中的"become"為「連綴動詞」，後面接「名詞片語」"the mother of a lovely boy"，說明主詞"she"的狀態是「成為了一個可愛男孩的媽媽」。

 Practice Time ★

Q1：愛黛兒是一位英國歌手。

_____.

Q2：愛黛兒的音樂聽起來很美。

_____.

Q1 Ans：Adele is a British singer.

Q2 Ans：Adele's music sounds beautiful.

Unit 04
名詞

Many women think they need large ❶breasts. But I am the living ❷proof that you can go far with small ones.

—— Cameron Diaz 卡麥蓉・狄亞茲

（許多女人覺得她們需要大胸部。但我是活生生的證明，讓你知道小胸部也可以光芒四射。）

❶ breast [brɛst] **n** 胸部　❷ proof [pruf] **n** 證據

　　這句話裡共有 3 個名詞，依序是"women"（女人），"breast"（胸部）和"proof"（證明）。此外，從這句話也可看出名詞的一些特性，如複數型與單數型的不同，以及名詞前面可以有數量詞（如：many）或形容詞（如：large, living）做修飾。

🎬 Grammar Show ★

　　名詞 (Nouns) 是用來泛指人事物地點抽象概念的名稱，又可區分為「普通名詞」(Common Nouns) 及「專有名詞」(Proper Nouns)。

❶ 「普通名詞」用來泛指一般性的人事物

　　例 secretary (秘書)，job (工作)，table (桌子)，wisdom (智慧) 等。（第一個字母通常為小寫，但如果是放在句子的開端，第一個字母則需大寫。）

2 「**專有名詞**」，顧名思義就是具有「唯一、獨一無二」的性質

例 Mozart (莫札特)，Mars (火星)，California (加州)，World War II (二次世界大戰)。（專有名詞不管是放在句中、句首或句尾，第一個字母永遠大寫。）

3 普通名詞與專有名詞又可區分為五大類：

集體名詞 (Collective Nouns)：由相同或類似性質的個體，組合而成的集合體名稱。如: army (軍隊) , crew (船員) , family (家庭)。

--複合名詞 (Compound Nouns)：兩個或兩個以上的單字所組成的一個名詞。如: laptop (筆記型電腦) , washing machine (洗衣機) , mother-in-law (岳母)。註：有些字沒有連字號-。

--具體名詞 (Concrete Nouns)：可以看得到見，摸得到的實體物品。如: picture (圖片) , television (電視) , Danube River (多瑙河)。

--物質名詞 泛指無法分為單獨個體的物質名稱，通常也有具體名詞的特性。如: soap (肥皂) , meat (肉類) , milk (牛奶)

--抽象名詞 (Abstract Nouns)：與具體名詞相反，泛指那些看不見、摸不到的性質、感情、概念等的抽象概念。如: love (愛) , passion (熱情) , space (空間)。

Life Story

You have got to love Cameron Diaz. Not just because this 41-year-old actress is probably the only woman left in Hollywood who eats properly, but also ❶she is a smart and modern-day feminist who wrote a lifestyle guide called *The Body Book*. Also, even though she is "of a certain age", she doesn't want to settle down and have kids now. In her opinion, what women need to do is not worry about what they don't have but just love what they do have.

If you watch Cameron's recent films, you may find some tiny wrinkles crinkle up at the corner of her eyes when she laughs. ❷Unlike so many Hollywood stars who are addicted to Botox, she looks like she has lived. She doesn't even mind getting older roles as she thinks those are actually the best roles for a woman. She laughs, makes faces, and is not afraid of looking ugly for a second or two. Cameron is really the down-to-earth woman we wish we knew from our neighborhood.

　　你一定會喜歡卡麥蓉‧迪亞茲。並不只是因為這位 41 歲的女演員可能是好萊塢唯一飲食正常的女性，還因為她是一位聰明的現代男女平權主義者，寫了一本名為《The Body Book》，暢談生活方式的書。同時，即使她已到了「特定年齡」，她並不會因此想要安定下來或是生孩子。她認為，女人真正需要的，不是煩惱所沒有的，而是熱愛所擁有的。

　　如果你有看卡麥蓉近期的電影作品，你也許會看到她大笑時眼周出現的皺紋。不像許多好萊塢明星有對肉毒桿菌的沉迷，她看起來就像她是經歷過歲月的。她甚至不介意接演年紀較大的角色，因為她認為這樣的角色對一個女人來說才是最好的。她大笑、扮鬼臉，不害怕有一、二秒的時間看起來是醜的。卡麥蓉真的是我們會希望在鄰里間認識的一個樸實的女孩。

- properly [ˋprɑpɚlɪ] **adv** 恰當地
- feminist [ˋfɛmənɪst] **n** 男女平權主義者
- crinkle [ˋkrɪŋkl̩] **v** 起皺
- addict [əˋdɪkt] **v** 使成癮

Sentence Show ★

❶ She is a smart and modern-day feminist who wrote a lifestyle guide.
主要子句中形容詞"smart"（聰明的）和"modern-day"（現代的）修飾名詞
"feminist"（男女平權主義者）。而 who 子句的部分，"lifestyle"（生活方
式）和"guide"（指南）均為名詞，前者為"life"、"style"兩個名詞所組成的複
合名詞。

❷ Unlike so many Hollywood stars who are addicted to Botox, she
looks like she has lived.
此句除了"stars"（明星）外，"Hollywood"（好萊塢）和"Botox"（肉毒桿菌）
亦屬於名詞的一種，稱為「專有名詞」。此外，本句在"Hollywood starts"這
個名詞組合前，還有用數量詞"many"（許多的）做修飾，這也是名詞的特性
之一。

 Practice Time ★

Q1：卡麥蓉・迪亞茲是一位很棒的女演員。

_____.

Q2：卡麥蓉・迪亞茲在她主演的電影裡扮演過多重角色。

_____.

Q1 Ans：Cameron Diaz is a great actress.
Q2 Ans：Cameron Diaz has played multiple roles in movies.

Unit 05
名詞的複數

I hope you don't ❶mind that I ❷put down in words. How wonderful life is while you're in the world.
—— Elton John 艾爾頓‧強

（我希望你不介意我用文字記下來，這世界有你真好。）

❶ mind [maɪnd] Ⅴ 介意　❷ put down ph 寫下

　　首先先找出這句話的名詞，第一個是 "words"（文字），第二個是 "world"（世界）。此時讀者們應該有發現前者是個可數名詞，因為其後有加上表示複數的 "-s"；而後者為不可數名詞，所以雖然是單一個，也不可使用冠詞 "a"，而是使用 "the"。

Grammar Show

❶ 當我們要表達名詞的單複數形式時，通常會依名詞的「可數」(Countable Nouns) 和「不可數」(Uncountable Nouns) 性質做判斷

可數名詞是指可以很清楚的把份量區分開來或數出來的名詞，如:一顆蘋果（an apple），兩張桌子（two tables）等等。不可數名詞則是指那些無法細數或分割的實質物體或抽象概念，如: 頭髮（hair），冰淇淋（ice cream），幸福（happiness）等。

❷ 冠詞 a/an & the

在數算單數可數名詞，我們通常會依該名詞的發音選擇在其前加上冠詞 "a/an"，如:

"a dog"（一條狗）或"an apple"（一顆蘋果）；而單數的不可數名詞，則通常在前面加上冠詞 "the"，如：the sun（太陽）。那麼，對於兩者的複數變化，又該如何表達呢？

❸ 可數名詞的複數型變化，一般依字尾的變化判斷在其後加上"-s"，"-es"，"-ies"或"-ves"，如：

單數	複數
bottle （瓶子）	bottles
bus（公車）	buses
candy（糖果）	candies
thief（小偷）	thieves

而還有部分可數名詞的複數形式則呈現不規則變化，如：

單數	複數
foot（腳）	feet
child（孩子）	children
man（男人）	men
woman（女人）	women

❹ 計算不可數名詞時："a/an/數字 + 單位量詞+ of + 不可數名詞"

而此「單位量詞」指的是盛裝該物品的容器或該物品呈現的形式，如："a glass of water"（一杯水）或"a piece of paper"（一張紙）。此外，如果單位量詞前的數字超過 1，則該單位量詞需加上 s 或 es："three glasses of water"（三杯水）或 "five pieces of paper"（五張紙）。

 Life Story

Even if you don't know Elton John, you must have listened to his works such as "Can You Feel the Love Tonight", a song from Disney's 1994 animated film The Lion King or "Candle in the Wind", the song as a tribute to Princess Diana.

Ever since he came out in 1973, he has devoted himself to raise awareness of gay rights. ❶He has been associated with many AIDS charities and raised large amounts of money by recording and selling his singles. In 1992, John founded the Elton John AIDS Foundation to support research into different HIV/AIDS prevention programs. ❷Other goals of this Foundation are to help eliminate discrimination and prejudice against HIV/AIDS-affected individuals, and to provide every possible assistance to these people. He recently made a speech at a fundraising event and asked people to remove the stigma of the disease. He also encouraged people living with or at risk of contracting HIV/AIDS not to be ashamed and to face the disease positively.

即使你沒聽說過艾爾頓‧強，你也應該聽過他的作品：1994 年動畫電影《獅子王》插曲《今夜你感覺到愛了嗎？》與紀念戴安娜王妃的作品《風中之燭》。

自從在 1973 年出櫃後，他便一直致力於提倡同志權利。他的名字一直與許多愛滋病慈善機構連在一起，而他也靠錄製與販售單曲為這些機構募了許多款項。之後，他在 1992 年創立了艾爾頓強愛滋基金會，目的是為了對不同愛滋病防治法進行研究。而基金會的其他目標，則是幫助化解人們對於愛滋病患的偏見和歧視，並對於這些患者提供必要的幫助。他最近在一場愛滋病的募款活動上演講時要求人們去除對該疾病的污名。同時，他也鼓勵愛滋病患者或處於感染愛滋病風險的人不要感到羞恥，而是應該對該疾病抱以積極面對的態度。

- tribute [`trɪbjut] **n** 敬意
- eliminate [ɪ`lɪmə,net] **V** 消除
- discrimination [dɪ,skrɪmə`neʃən] **n** 歧視
- prejudice [`prɛdʒədɪs] **n** 偏見

Sentence Show ⭐

❶ He has been associated with many AIDS charities and raised large amounts of money by recording and selling his singles.

這句話裡有三個名詞，依序是：“charities”（慈善機構），“money”（錢）和 “singles”（單曲）。「慈善機構」和「單曲」皆為可數名詞，故前者單數形 “charity”去“y”加“-ies”，後者則直接在字尾加“-s”。「錢」為不可數名詞，故 要很多錢時，不可直接在其後加“-s”，而是要像此處使用“large amounts of”表 達。

❷ Other goals of this Foundation are to help eliminate discrimination and prejudice against HIV/AIDS-affected individuals, and to pro- vide every possible assistance to these peole.

這句話我們重點來看“individuals”（許多人）這個名詞。「個人」的單數形為 “individual”，複數直接在其後加上“-s”。而句尾的 “people” 是複數名詞。

 Practice Time ⭐

Q1：艾爾頓・強發行過多張專輯。

_____.

Q2：艾爾頓・強經常在早晨吃一片烤吐司和喝兩杯咖啡。

_____.

Q1 Ans：Elton John has released many albums.

Q2 Ans：Elton John usually has a slice of toast and two cups of coffee in the morning.

Unit 06
代名詞

"
Books have always helped me ❶make sense of things.
With any life experience, you can find someone who
has documented it in a ❷poetic way. "
—— Kate Beckinsale 凱特•貝琴薩

（書本幫助我了解事物的意義。有了書裡有各種人生經驗，你就會發現他
們記錄的方式多麼詩意。）

❶ make sense `ph` 頗具意義　❷ poetic [po`ɛtɪk] `adj` 詩的

　　這句話裡有一個代名詞"it"，這個 it 代指的是什麼呢？通常要找代名詞所代
指的人事物，就需要往它之前的句子裡找尋。順著"it"往前，發現它是可被記錄
(documented) 的事物，再往前閱讀，就會發現這裡"it"代指的是"any life experience"。

Grammar Show

　　代名詞 (Pronoun) 也是名詞的一種，故可用來代替名詞。在句子中，代名詞
的功能和名詞一樣，可當主詞、主詞補語、受詞、受詞補語和受詞補語。

❶ **在一個句子中，為了避免重複提到之前已經提過的名詞，即可使用代名詞**
　　所以當我們看到一個句子裡使用了代名詞，而不知道這個代名詞代指的是什麼的時
　　候，就可以從這個代名詞往前找找我們要的答案，因為通常一定是前面已經提過的

了，後面才會使用代名詞！事實上，代名詞的種類非常的多，本單元首先就最常見的「人稱代名詞」來為大家進行解說：

❷ 人稱代名詞 (Personal Pronoun)：用來代替"人"的名詞：

當主詞時: I, you, he/she, we/they

當受詞時: me, you, him/her, us/them

表示所有格時: my, your, his/her, our/their

例 Mary lives next door, and **she** is also my classmate.

　　Mary 住在我隔壁，而她也是我的同班同學。→ she 代指前面的 Mary

例 Mike is seeking my suggestions on **his** career.

　　Mike 正在向我詢問我對於他職涯規劃的意見。→his 指的是 Mike 的

例 Some men were following me, and then **we** all jumped onto the same train.

　　有一些男人緊跟著我，然而現在我們都跳上了同一列火車。

　　→we 代指的是一些男人和我（some men and I）

★ 在介系詞後面接當受詞的人稱代名詞

I'll speak **to them**.

我會跟他們說。

I'll get it **for you**.

我會幫你拿那個。

希望大家現在對人稱代名詞有初步認識。在接下來的單元裡，我們還會一起看不同的代名詞形式，如：指示代名詞、反身代名詞等。

 **Life Story**

❶People usually relate the elegant and well-spoken British actress image to Kate Beckinsale. Admittedly, she is a woman's woman through and through. As for the topics which concern women most, beauty and ageing, she has her own perspectives.

❷While most people link their self-worth to youth and beauty, Beckinsale thinks they might lose their marked individuality. She says she loves being pretty as much as everybody else. However, she doesn't think this is the only thing a woman should focus on. Needless to say, the pursuit of beauty shouldn't become the culture of a nation. She always thinks ageing is going to happen and it should. "There is nothing that serves my soul in wondering how crow's feet are going to affect my life." Since her father died when she was 5, she has even considered ageing as a blessing because it means she has lived another day. When she turned 40 in 2012, she still remained positive. "I am so much happier in myself these days. I prefer what I look like. I prefer what I feel like now."

人們通常將優雅與談吐文雅的英國女星形象和凱特・貝琴薩相連結在一起。無可否認的，她從裡到外都是女人中的女人。對於「美和老化」這兩個女人最關心的話題，她一直有自己獨特的看法。

當許多人認為自我的價值就是擁有年輕美貌時，貝琴薩認為這些人很有可能失去自己的獨特性。她說，她就像大家一樣愛漂亮；然而，她並不覺得這應該是女人唯一關注的事。更不用說，追求美貌也不該成為國家的文化。她一直覺得年老終將會發生，而是應該發生的一件事。「關心魚尾紋如何影響我的生活對於我的心靈沒有任何好處。」當她的父親在她五歲時去世後，她認為老化是一種祝福，因這表示又多活了一天。即使她在 2012 年時年屆不惑，她仍積極看待這件事。「這些日子以來，我心情更好。我喜歡自己的樣子，也喜歡我現在的感覺。」

- elegant [ˈɛləgənt] **adj** 優雅的
- perspective [pɚˈspɛktɪv] **n** 觀點

Sentence Show ★

❶ People usually relate the elegant and well-spoken British actress image to Kate Beckinsale. Admittedly, she is a woman's woman through and through.

這裡有兩句話，代名詞"she"出現在第二句話中。光看第二句無法知道這個 she 代指的是誰，但如果從前一句看，就會知道 she 代指凱特‧貝琴薩。

❷ While most people link their self-worth to youth and beauty, Beckinsale thinks they might lose their marked individuality.

這裡貝琴薩認為「他們可能會失去他們的獨特性」，閱讀整句後，會知道「他們」指的是一開始的「大多數人」；而這些「大多數人」是什麼人呢？就是那些將「自我價值」和「年輕貌美」連結在一起的人。

 Practice Time ★

Q1：她是凱特‧貝琴薩嗎？

_____.

Q2：凱特‧貝琴薩是個很好的媽媽，因為她很愛她的女兒。

_____.

Q1 Ans： Is she Kate Beckinsale?

Q2 Ans： Kate Beckinsale is a great mother because she loves her daughter very much.

Unit 07
名詞與代名詞的所有格

I think most of us are ❶raised with ❷preconceived notions of the choices we're supposed to make. We waste so much time making decisions based on someone else's idea of our happiness – what will make you a good ❸citizen or a good wife or daughter or actress. Nobody says, "Just be happy – go be a ❹cobbler or go live with goats."

—— Sandra Bullock 珊卓、布拉克

（我想我們之中多數都曾被先入為主的觀念教導該做什麼樣的選擇。我們浪費許多時間做那些別人覺得是為我們好的決定—例如：該成為怎樣的好公民、好妻子或好的女演員。從沒有人說：「去做個修鞋匠或是去和山羊一起住——只要你活得開心就好。」）

❶ raise [rez] **V** 養育　❷ preconceived [ˌprikən`sivd] **adj** 先入為主的

❸ citizen [`sɪtəzn] **n** 市民　❹ cobbler [`kɑblə-] **n** 修鞋匠

　　在珊卓布拉克這句較長的名言中，我們看到了名詞與代名詞不同的所有格表現方式。"preconceived notions of the choices" 和 "our happiness" 你知道用法差在哪嗎？

Grammar Show

　　所有格 (possessive) 簡單來說，可以翻譯為「…的」，可用來表示某人或某物的歸屬。

❶ 有生命的名詞，如：**girl, Peter** 等；在表示其所有格時，大多以 **A's B（A 的 B）**顯示。然而，各名詞的所有格表示法，還需視其單複數形式及字尾做不同的變化

	名詞	所有格形式	說明
單數名詞	Peter	Peter's	在字尾加"-'s"
	the girl	the girl's	在字尾加"-'s"
	the boss	the boss's	在字尾加"-'s"
複數名詞	girls	girls'	字尾已有 (e) s 時，僅加"'"即成所有格
	people	people's	字尾沒有 (e) s 時，仍需在字尾加"-'s"

例 **Peter's** bag 彼得的書包

例 **the boss's** pen 老闆的筆

例 **girls'** outfits 女孩們的外出服

例 **people's** right 人們的權利

❷ 無生命的名詞，如：**table, book** 等，在表示其所有格時，需使用 **B of A（A 的 B）**的方式表達

例 the legs **of** the table 桌子的腳

例 the cover **of** the book 書本的封面

❸ 代名詞，如：**I, you, they** 的所有格表示法：

代名詞	所有格形式
I（我）	my（我的）
you（你）	your（你的）
he（他）	his（他的）
she（她）	her（她的）
it（它）	its（它的）
we（我們）	our（我們的
you（你們）	your（你們的）
they（他們）	their（他們的）

例 **my** life 我的生活

例 **his** pet 他的寵物

例 **your** cars 你們的車

Life Story

Academy Award-winning actress Sandra Bullock first became widely known for her leading role in the 1994 hit *Speed*. She has since starred in many more movies, and has quickly become a popular face on the big screen. ❶Her latest work is the blockbuster movie *Gravity* in which she starred alongside George Clooney. She was subsequently nominated for a second Academy Award for Best Actress and named *Entertainment Weekly*'s 2013 Entertainer of the Year.

To be honest, she is definitely not the most beautiful actress in Hollywood. However, ❷her generosity, great personality and sense of humor have definitely made her many people's favorite Hollywood actress. To date, Bullock has donated one million dollars to the American Red Cross organization at least four times. Moreover, she also sent large amounts of money to support the victims of the 2004 Indian Ocean earthquake and tsunami, Haiti earthquake, and the 2011 Japan earthquake. No wonder people call her America's sweetheart.

曾獲得奧斯卡最佳女主角獎的珊卓‧布拉克，是在 1994 年賣座電影《捍衛戰警》中擔任女主角後開始廣為人知。接著她開始接拍更多的電影，並很快地成為大銀幕裡受歡迎的臉孔。她最新的作品是與喬治‧庫隆尼一起演出的《地心引力》，並因此再次獲得奧斯卡最佳女主角提名，以及《演藝週刊》點名的「2013 年最佳演藝人員」。

事實上，她並不是好萊塢最漂亮的女演員。然而，她的慷慨、絕佳的人格特質與幽默感，絕對讓她成為大家最喜愛的好萊塢女演員。至今，珊卓‧布拉克已捐款四次給美國紅十字會，且每筆捐款均為一百萬美元。此外，她也捐了多筆大額款項給 2004 年發生在印度洋的地震和海嘯、海地地震，以及 2011 年日本地震的受災者。難怪大家叫她是美國甜心。

● blockbuster [ˈblɑkˌbʌstə] **n** 院線強片　　● nominate [ˈnɑməˌnet] **v** 提名

Sentence Show

❶ Her latest work is the blockbuster movie *Gravity* in which she starred alongside George Clooney.

Her 是代名詞 she 的所有格，這裡"Her latest work"表示「她最近期的作品」。

❷ Her generosity, great personality and sense of humor have definitely made her people's favorite Hollywood actress.

這句話裡有三個不同的所有格表示方式：1. "her generosity"，her 是代名詞 she 的所有格，這裡表示「她的慷慨」；2. "sense of humor"，humor 不是 "人"，不能直接在後面加上所有格"…'s"，所以使用 A of B（B 的 A）這種表達方式，表示「幽默的意識（幽默感）」；3. "people's favorite actress"，"people"是"大家"，所有格為直接在其後加上"…'s"，這裡表示「大家喜歡的女演員」。

 Practice Time

Q1：珊卓‧布拉克的母親是德國人。

_____.

Q2：珊卓‧布拉克的快樂來自對每日生活的熱情。

_____.

Q1 Ans：Sandra Bullock's mother is German.

Q2 Ans：Sandra Bullock 's happiness comes from the passion of everyday life.

Unit 08
反身代名詞

❝ Sometimes, you can't see yourself ❶clearly, until you see yourself ❷through the eyes of others. ❞

—— Ellen DeGeneres 艾倫、狄珍妮

（有時候，你無法看清楚自己；直到你看見別人眼中的自己。）

❶ clearly [`klɪrlɪ] adv 清楚地　❷ through [θru] prep 憑藉

　　"you"加上"self"成為反身代名詞，表示前面動詞（see）的動作反歸於行為者 "you"的身上。那麼，其他人稱（I, he, them 等）的反身代名詞又是如何表示呢？單數型和複數型有沒有不同呢？

 Grammar Show

　　反身代名詞 (Reflexive Pronoun)，是由代名詞演變而來。具有代名詞和「…自己（的）」的性質。以下是反身代名詞的單複數型：

	單數型	複數型
第一人稱	myself	ourselves
第二人稱	yourself	yourselves
第三人稱	himself / herself / itself	themselves
無人稱	oneself	

　　反身代名詞用途可分為以下四類：

1 在一個句子中做為動詞的受詞，且句子的受詞和主詞指的是同一個對象時，受詞則需變化成「反身代名詞」

例 My sister likes to talk to **herself**.

我姊姊喜歡自言自語。

例 He almost cut **himself** when cooking in the kitchen this afternoon.

他今天下午煮飯時差點切傷自己。

2 亦可加在及物動詞之後，如：**enjoy, dress, kill, teach, hurt, cut, devote** 等

例 Please be careful when using the knife, you may cut **yourself**.

使用刀子時請務必小心，你很有可能會割傷自己。

例 Let's enjoy **ourselves**!

讓我們好好享受吧！

3 反身代名詞也可用來強調語氣，尤其是用來強調主詞，有「就是單獨一個人或事物」的意味

通常緊接在主詞後或是句尾。事實上，在這種情況下，反身代名詞扮演可有可無的角色，換句話說，即便刪除了反身代名詞，也不會對句子的結構產生影響，文法還是正確的。

例 I **myself accomplished** this mission.

我獨自完成了這個任務。

例 She **herself** finished the homework.

她自己完成了作業。

4 **"by oneself"**是慣用法，有「獨自一人的」之意：

例 She went to the cinema **by herself**.

她獨自一人去看電影。

例 He doesn't like to study **by himself**.

他不喜歡自己念書。

 **Life Story**

It was not until the twins Zony and Yony appeared on her talk show that most Taiwanese started to know Ellen DeGeneres.

Ellen DeGeneres is introduced as a stand-up comedian under her *Wikipedia* profile. Indeed people who watch The Ellen DeGeneres Show she hosts are attracted to her funny but witty language. For example, once she talked about why cruel wild animal hunting should be banned. She said, "You ask people why they have deer heads on the wall. They always say, 'Because it's such a beautiful animal.' There you go. I think my mother is attractive, but I have photographs of her." As a homosexual, ❶DeGeneres always suggests people accept themselves no matter what other people think of them. ❷ "Stay true to yourself," she said. In her opinion, people should never follow someone else's path unless they are in the woods and lost.

　　直到雙胞胎左左右出現在她的脫口秀後，艾倫・迪珍妮才開始被大多數的台灣人所熟知。

　　在她的維基百科檔案中，她被介紹為單人相聲喜劇演員。而人們在看過她主持的「艾倫・迪珍妮秀」後，也受她有趣但又充滿智慧的言語所吸引。某次在談論殘忍的野生動物獵殺應該被禁止時，她說：「你問那些人為什麼要掛鹿頭在牆上，他們總是說：『因為牠們是很美的動物。』你看吧！我覺得我媽媽很迷人，但我只會擁有她的照片。」而做為一個同性戀者，迪珍妮總是建議人們接受他們自己，無論其他人怎麼想他們。「維持真實的自己」她說。她認為人們不該只是跟隨別人的腳步，除非他們是在樹林裡迷了路。

- twins [twɪnz] **n** 雙胞胎
- comedian [kə`midɪən] **n** 喜劇演員
- homosexual [ˌhoməˋsɛkʃʊəl] **adj** 同性戀的
- stand-up **ph** 單人喜劇表演的
- ban [bæn] **V** 禁止

Sentence Show ★

❶ DeGeneres always suggests people accept themselves no matter what other people think of them.

「迪珍妮建議人們應該接受他們自己…」所以這裡的反身代名詞「他們自己」代指的是「人們（people）」，是一個複數的第三人稱，故需使用複數的第三人稱反身代名詞形式：themselves。

❷ Stay true to yourself.

首先，這句話因為沒有明顯的「主詞＋動詞＋受詞」形式，所以如果是要從中文「維持真實的自己」進行翻譯時，可能會有點困惑。到底句末的「自己」該用哪個人稱的反身代名詞？然而，再次閱讀後，可能會發現這是一個命令句的形式，故使用第二人稱"yourself"。

 Practice Time ★

Q1：艾倫自己主持節目。

_____

Q2：艾倫認為自己是單人相聲喜劇演員。

_____

Q1 Ans：Ellen hosts the show by herself.

Q2 Ans：Ellen thinks of herself as a stand-up comedian.

Unit 09
指示代名詞

> And if you don't ❶reach for the moon, you can't ❷fall on the star. This is what I have told myself.
>
> —— Jessie J 潔西 J

（如果你沒有達到月球，你就不會跌落在星星上。這是我一直告訴自己的。）

❶ reach [ritʃ] Ⅴ 到達　❷ fall [fɔl] Ⅴ 跌倒

　　指示代名詞類似之前提到的代名詞，都是用來代指某些已經確定的人事物。而找尋所代指的內容的方法也和代名詞相同，就是由該字往前去尋找已提過的內容。這裡的指示代名詞是"This"，代指的是前面"And if you don't reach for the moon, you can't fall on the star"這句話。

Grammar Show

　　指示代名詞 (Demonstrative Pronoun) 主要功能是代替某些已經確定或特定的人事物。指示代名詞在句子裡的角色就跟名詞一樣，可當主詞或是受詞。用法如下：

❶ 依照主詞/受詞的單複數及離說話者的距離遠近，指示代名詞可以細分為下：

	距離遠（離說話者）	距離近（離說話者）
單數	that（那）	this（這）
複數	those（那些）	these（這些）

例 She told me **that** was annoying.

她告訴我那 (件事) 很煩人。

→在說話者跟聽話者同時知道是「哪件事」的情況下。

例 Ben doesn't like **this**

Ben 不喜歡這個 (物品)。

例 Those are grapefruits and **these** are oranges.

那些是葡萄柚，這些是柳丁。

② 指示代名詞可用來取代之前已經提過的名詞，避免重複

例 This boy is very hard-working, but **that** one/boy is not.

這個男孩非常努力工作，但那個男孩不是。

→that 代替之前提過的 boy。

例 Those books are the best-sellers, and **these** are too.

那些書是暢銷書，這些也是。

→these 代替之前提過的 books。

③ 指示代名詞的**"this/that"**可用來取代之前提過的句子，讓句子看起來更清楚簡單

例 David didn't tell the truth. **This** made his teacher angry.

David 沒有說實話讓他的老師非常生氣。

→this 代替"David didn't tell the truth"這件事。

例 She speaks up for all the students. **That** is very brave of her.

她為全部的學生發聲，這是非常勇敢的事。

→ that 代替之前提過的 "She speaks up for all the students."

 **Life Story**

Jessie J, whose birth name is Jessica Ellen Cornish, is a famous British singer and also a girl who has always been unstoppable.

Jessie just turned 26 this March, but this young woman has had full control of her life and her look. ❶She never thinks of being second best because her goal is to be number one. To achieve this, she always works very hard without stopping for a minute to expect or presume. ❷Of course she sometimes wants to have an easy life such as having a day under the duvet and watching films. However, she knows she has to work hard if she wants that. In order to look more like herself, she has done her own styling for a long time because she doesn't think there should be anyone telling her how she is supposed to look. With this hard-working attitude and ideas of her own, perhaps this is why she has 15 million in record sales and 6.4 million Twitter followers.

潔西 J 的本名是潔西卡.艾倫.柯妮許，她是一位有名的英國歌手，同時也是一個無人能擋的女孩。

潔西在今年三月剛滿 26 歲，但位年輕的女子已經完全掌握自己的生活與容貌。她從沒有想過當第二好的，因為她只想當第一名。為了達到這個目標，她沒有一分鐘停下來預想或是猜測。當然她也想要輕鬆的生活，比如躲在被窩看電影。但是，她知道如果要過這樣的生活，就必須要努力。而為了看起來更像她自己，她已經很長一段時間自己做造型，因為她覺得不該由其他人來告訴她該怎麼打扮。認真工作的態度和擁有自己的想法，也許這就是為什麼她有 1500 萬張專輯銷量成績，以及 640 萬的推特追隨者。

- unstoppable [ʌnˋstɑpəbļ] **adj** 擋不住的
- expect [ɪkˋspɛkt] **V** 預料
- presume [prɪˋzum] **V** 假設
- duvet [djʊˋve] **n** 被子
- suppose [səˋpoz] **V** 認為應該

Sentence Show ★

❶ She never thinks of being second best because her goal is to be number one. To achieve this, she always works very hard without stopping for a minute to a minute stopping to expect or presume.

第二句開頭 "To achieve this"（要達成這個），到底要達成「哪個」呢？答案就是上一句的"Her goal is to be number one"，也就是潔西 J 要達成的目標。

❷ Of course she sometimes wants to have an easy life such as having a day under the duvet and watching films. However, she knows she has to work hard if she wants that.

第二句話最後的"if she wants that"（如果她要那個），又是要「哪個」呢？答案依舊出現在前一句中，即"an easy life"（一個不費力的生活）。

 Practice Time ★

Q1：人們稱潔西 J 為典範，但她不喜歡被這麼認為。

_____.

Q2：潔西 J 非常努力工作，但那些和她同年紀的人通常並非如此。

_____.

Q1 Ans： People call Jessie J a role model but she doesn't like to be thought of like that.

Q2 Ans： Jessie J works very hard but those of the same age as her often don't.

Unit 10
不定代名詞

"Remember that there's always someone ①fighting for you."

—— Lady Gaga 女神卡卡

（記住總有人為你戰鬥。）

① fight [faɪt] V 戰鬥

女神卡卡說，總有人 (someone) 會為我們戰鬥，但到底是什麼人呢？是你？是他？還是隔壁的劉媽媽？雖然總有這麼一個人，但因為女神卡卡不知道為你戰鬥的會是誰，所以這裡所說的「有人」(someone)，只是一個未定的人物，我們稱為「不定代名詞」。

 **Grammar Show**

不定代名詞 (Indefinite Pronoun) 直接從字面上解釋是「代替某些不確定或不特定的人、事、物」。

① 我們首先從它所代替的數量來做分類，可分為：**none, one, ones, any, both, most, some, few (little) , many (much) , another, others, each, either, neither**

如果再依照所代替名詞的性質下去細分，則可再分為以下：

	人	事/物
some	someone / somebody	something
no	nobody / no one	nothing
any	anybody / anyone	anything
every	everybody / every one	everything

2 不定代名詞可當一個句子的主詞和受詞：

例 My sister took this pen and also that **one**.

　　我姊姊拿了這支筆，還有那隻。→one 用來代替 pen

例 **No one** can change his mind once he decides **something**.

　　一旦他決定事情後，沒人可以改變他的心意。→No one 當主詞，something 作為

　　decide 的受詞

例 Only **few** are going to the concert, **others** will stay at home.

　　只有少數人要去參加那場音樂會，其他人將留在家裡。→few 與 others 皆為主詞

3 不定代名詞除了有名詞的功能外，有時也可當形容詞來修飾名詞，而此時又

　　可以可數名詞及不可數名詞來區分：

many (很多), a few (一些), few (幾乎沒有), some (一些), a lot of, lots of (很多)	+ 可數名詞
much (很多), a little (一些), little (幾乎沒有), some (一些), a lot of, lots of (很多)	+ 不可數名詞

例 How **many** cats do you have?　你有幾隻貓？

例 Is there **much** work to do?　還有很多工作要做嗎？

例 Cindy saves **a little** money every month.

　　Cindy 每個月都省一點錢。

例 He wanted was **a few** days on his own.

　　他希望有幾天屬於自己的時間。

例 They had **little** money to spend.　他們幾乎沒有錢可花。

例 He has **few** friends.　他幾乎沒有朋友。

例 I have **lots of** questions.　我有很多問題。

例 Rita has **a lot of** money.　Rita 有很多錢。

 **Life Story**

She is talented and famous. She has travelled around the world to perform in front of millions of fans. Every time she appears in the spotlight, her costumes always have a wow effect on people. At this point, you must have guessed I am talking about the singing and song-writing sensation, Lady Gaga.

Before she gained fame, Lady Gaga struggled to find herself. She was bullied by other students at school because they thought she was a freak. It took her a long time to accept herself. Therefore, when she started her singing career, ❶she always promotes the idea that "nobody can define your beauty except yourselves." At the same time, she named her second album, *Born This Way*, which is also the motto she often uses to encourage self-acceptance. ❷Many who attended her show were inspired by her quote: "Be yourself and love who you are. And be proud because you were born this way."

　　她既有天分又有名氣。她已經環遊世界在幾百萬粉絲前表演。在聚光燈下，她的服裝總是達到令人目瞪口呆的效果。現在，你應該猜得到，我說的就是在歌唱和填詞作曲都引人矚目的焦點——女神卡卡。

　　在她成名前，女神卡卡很努力的找尋自己。她曾在學校被其他學生霸凌，因為他們覺得她是個怪咖。她花了很多時間來接受自己。因此，當她開始她的歌唱事業時，她總是提倡「除了你自己，沒有人可以定義你的美」的這個觀念。同時，她也把自己的第二張專輯命名為「天生完美」，這也是她自己的座右銘，常用來發揚「接受自我」的這個想法。許多參加過她演唱會的人也受她的一句格言所鼓舞，那就是：「做你自己，愛你自己的樣子。然後為自己感到驕傲，因為你天生完美。」

- costume [ˋkɑstjum] **n** 服裝　　• sensation [sɛnˋseʃən] **n** 轟動的人或事
- bully [ˋbʊlɪ] **v** 霸凌　　• promote [prəˋmot] **v** 宣揚

Sentence Show

❶ She always promotes the idea that nobody can define your beauty except yourselves.

「她總是提倡除了你自己，沒有人可以定義你的美的這個觀念。」句中的「沒有人」明顯是一個不確定的人物，故使用了不定代名詞 "Nobody"。此外，"Nobody" 在 that 子句中，是作為主詞的功用。

❷ Many who attended her show were inspired by her quote.

不定代名詞 Many 為句子主詞。「許多參加過她演唱會的人也受她的一句格言所鼓舞。」句中的「許多人」參加過她演唱會，但沒有一個明確的數目，故視 "Many" 為不定代名詞。

 **Practice Time**

Q1：每個人都受到女神卡卡的啟發。

_____.

Q2：有人說女神卡卡很有才華，但其他人覺得她是一個怪咖。

_____.

Q1 Ans：Everyone is inspired by Lady Gaga.

Q2 Ans：Some say Lady Gaga is talented, but others think she is a freak.

Unit 11
冠詞

❝ Love may not make the world go round, but I must
❶admit that it makes the **❷ride** **❸worthwhile.** ❞
── Sean Connery 史恩‧康納来

（愛不一定能讓世界轉動，但我必須承認它讓人生旅程變得值得。）

❶ admit [əd`mɪt] **Ⅴ** 承認　❷ ride [raɪd] **ⁿ** 旅行
❸ worthwhile [`wɝθ`hwaɪl] **adj** 值得做的

　　冠詞有"a/an"與"the"兩類，均放置於名詞之前。在這句名言中，可以看到兩個冠詞 "the"。第一個名詞 world（世界）之前使用冠詞"the"，是因為世界只有一個；而第二個名詞 ride（旅程）之前使用冠詞"the"，因為這裡的「旅程」是限定為人生旅程。

🎬 Grammar Show ★

　　冠詞（Articles）是指放在名詞前面，用來表示該名詞是「特定」（使用不定冠詞"a/an"）或「不特定」（使用定冠詞"the"）的詞彙。現在就讓我們來看更詳細的介紹吧！

❶ 不定冠詞"a/an"後面接不特定的單數可數名詞；當名詞的第一個字母為母音時，則要加 an

　　a, an 通常會被翻譯成「一個、一支、一張、一輛、一本」等等。我們也可以說它是扮演著中文裡「單位量詞」的角色。從以下用法，我們就可以了解如何正確的使用它。

---放在非特定的普通名詞前面。

例 Do you have **a** pen? 你有一支筆嗎?

例 The policeman is talking to **an** old man.

　　警察正在跟一個老人講話。

---放在 **there is/are** 後面的名詞，無論是單數或複數皆為不特定，需使用 **a/an**，不可使用 **the**。

例 There is **a** lady in the park. 公園裡有一名女士。

例 There is **an** orange on the table. 桌上有一顆柳丁。

2 而定冠詞**"the"**後面接有特定，或是之前有明確指出的名詞。中文的翻譯通常為「這、那、這些、那些」：

--當在一個句子中，聽話者與說話者都知道是指那一個特定的名詞通常使用 **the**，例如:

例 Where is **the** kitchen? 廚房在哪裡? (限定在特定屋內的廚房)

例 **The** direction is correct.

　　那個方向是正確的。

--大部分專有名詞前不須加冠詞，但是也有例外，例如：

國家 (有組合而成的意味)	the United States, the United Kingdom
機構/公司	the University of Hong Kong, the Franklin Institute
自然景物 (用地名/人名命名)	the Great Barrier Reef, the Seine

 **Life Story**

Up till now, Sean Connery is still considered as the best *"007"*, James Bond, by the fans of this famous movie series. Even now at the age of 84, there are many magazines which name him as the sexiest man in the world.

In fact, among the fifty-something movies he has participated in, the roles he played most were just extras or supporting roles. ❶A person once asked him why he was willing to play supporting roles when he was already an international superstar. "I don't understand why many American actors don't like to take supporting roles. ❷If I think a thing is worth doing, I will do the thing with pleasure without caring about other factors," the Scottish born actor replied. Connery always stands by his beliefs. For example, he has supported the independence of Scotland since he was a teenager. He has lived outside his Scottish hometown for a long time because he made a promise to himself that he will only come back to settle down when Scotland is independent.

直到現在，史恩‧康納萊還是被許多《007》間諜電影的影迷認為是詹姆斯‧龐德的最佳扮演者。即使在 84 歲的現在，仍有許多雜誌選他為世界上最性感的男人。

事實上，在他參與的 50 多部電影中，他的角色很多只是臨時演員或配角。有個人曾經問他，為何他已是國際巨星了，還願意接演配角的角色。這位蘇格蘭出生的演員回答道：「我不明白為什麼許多美國明星不願意飾演配角。如果我覺得一件事值得做，我會帶著愉悅的心去做這件事，而不會去考慮其他的因素。」康納萊總是堅守自己的信念，比方他在青少年時期就支持蘇格蘭獨立。他已離開家鄉蘇格蘭在外定居多年，因為他對自己許諾，要等到蘇格蘭獨立後才會回來定居。

- series [`siriz] **n** 系列
- extra [`ɛkstrə] **n** 臨時演員
- participate [pɑr`tɪsə͵pet] **v** 參與
- worth [wɝθ] **adj** 有…的價值

Sentence Show ★

❶ A person once asked him why he was willing to play supporting roles. ⋯ the Scottish born actor replied .

這個詢問史恩‧康納萊問題的人，因為是文章中第一次被提及，冠詞需使用 "a"（一個人）；之後說到史恩‧康納萊回答這個人問題時，因為前面已提過他，所以冠詞使用"the"（前面提到的那一個人）。

❷ If I think a thing is worth doing, I will do the thing with pleasure without caring about other factors.

「如果我覺得一件事值得做，我會帶著愉悅去做這件事，而不會去考慮其他的因素。」這件值得做的事情第一次被提及時，使用冠詞"a"；之後再提到這件事時，因為已經有限定是哪件事了，所以使用冠詞"the"。

 Practice Time ★

Q1：史恩‧康納萊是一位演員。

_____.

Q2：這個演員來自於蘇格蘭。

_____.

Q1 Ans：Sean Connery is an actor.

Q2 Ans：The actor is from Scotland.

Unit 12
形容詞

"Real life isn't a **①straightforward** **②comedy**. Bad things happen too and they're not funny. But when you're unhappy, you don't go an **③entire** time without laughing. It's just life."

—— Jennifer Lawrence 珍妮佛・勞倫斯

（真實生活並不是一齣簡單的喜劇。壞事也會發生，而且它們並不有趣。然而，即使你不開心，也不能一直繃著臉。這就是生活。）

① straightforward [ˌstret`fɔrwɚd] **adj** 簡單的；坦率的

② comedy [`kɑmədɪ] **n** 喜劇 **③** entire [ɪn`taɪr] **adj** 整個的

　　影后珍妮佛・勞倫斯在這段關於生活態度的名言中，使用了許多的形容詞，讀者們能找出一共有幾個嗎？答案是 5 個 (straightforward, bad, funny, unhappy, entire)。而從這 5 個形容詞的使用方式，我們也發現了形容詞可以放在名詞之前，也可以放在動詞之後的特性。

Grammar Show

　　形容詞 (Adjective) 是用來修飾名詞或代名詞的字詞，有加強修飾句子的功能。在一個句子中它是可有可無的角色，即使一個句子中沒有形容詞，其文法結構還是完整的，並不會因為省略了形容詞，就影響到句子的文法結構。一般而言，通常可以在句子的兩個地方發現形容詞的蹤影：

1 形容詞+普通名詞：

例 Emily usually makes coffee.

→ Emily usually makes **good** coffee.

Emily 常泡咖啡。→Emily 常泡好咖啡。

（原本的句子結構已經完整，但是加上形容詞 "good" 讓聽者知道艾蜜麗泡的咖啡是怎樣的。）

例 Jessica is a musician → Jessica is a **talented** musician.

Jessica 是一位音樂家。→Jessica 是一位有天份的音樂家。

（原本的句子結構已經完整，但加上形容詞"talented"讓聽者更加了解 Jessica 是怎樣的一位音樂家。）

例 There is some fruit on the table.

→ There is some fresh fruit on the table.

桌上有一些水果。→ 桌上有一些新鮮的水果。

（加上形容詞 "fresh"，說明水果的狀態）

2 特別名詞之後+形容詞：形容詞要放在這些特別的（代）名詞之後，如：

someone, something, nothing

例 One day, you will meet someone **special**.

總有一天，你會遇到特別的人。

例 There is really nothing **interesting** at the party.

這舞會真的一點有趣的事都沒有。

例 My sister just told me something very **funny** on her way back home.

我的姊姊剛才告訴我她在回家途中發生的趣事。

 **Life Story**

[1]As the breakout star of the popular movies, *The Hunger Games* and *X-Men: First Class,* Jennifer Lawrence is the name the whole world is talking about.

[2]The beginning of her story may be no different from other Hollywood stars. Lawrence earned her career by herself. She first decided to be an actress at the age of 14. In order to start her acting career sooner, she graduated from high school two years early even achieving GPA 3.9 (the full marks are 4). Even though she is no longer considered as a starlet, she still works hard every day. Once in an interview with Glamour magazine, she mentioned she has never understood why some people have to stop working when they become successful. She thinks these people should work harder when they become successful because others are expecting more from them. For her, success doesn't mean she is allowed to work less. It is actually the other way around.

在賣座電影《飢餓遊戲》及《X 戰警：第一戰》中展露頭角的珍妮佛‧勞倫斯，已成為一個全世界都在談論的名字。

她的故事的開始也許和其他好萊塢明星並沒有不同。勞倫斯自己爭取了她的事業。她在 14 歲時就決定成為演員。為了早點開始她的演藝事業，她以 GPA3.9 的成績（GPA 的滿分為 4 分），提早兩年從高中畢業。即使她現在已經不再被視為是初出茅廬的新人，她每天仍努力不懈。她在一次《Glamour 雜誌》的專訪中提到，她不瞭解為何有些人在成功之後便停止工作。她認為這些人應該在成功後更努力，因為別人會對他們有更多的期望。對她而言，成功並不代表她可以少努力一點，而是恰恰相反。

- recognize [ˈrɛkəɡˌnaɪz] **V** 認出
- well-known [ˈwɛlˈnon] **adj** 知名的
- brand [brænd] **n** 品牌
- unrealistic [ˌʌnrɪəˈlɪstɪk] **adj** 不切實際的
- mention [ˈmɛnʃən] **V** 提到

Sentence Show ★

❶ As the breakout star of the popular movies, *The Hunger Games* and *X-Men: First Class*, Jennifer Lawrence is the name the whole world is talking about.

這句話的兩個形容詞分別為"breakout"（突然竄紅的）和"popular"（受歡迎的），用來修飾"star"（明星）和"movies"（電影）。這裡也可以清楚看到形容詞可有可無的特性，即拿掉的兩個形容詞後"As the star of the movies"仍為一個合文法的句子。

❷ The beginning of her story may be no different from other Hollywood stars.

"nothing"（沒有）為這句話裡的特殊代名詞，所以它的形容詞"different"（不同的）在此處就要挪至"nothing"後方做修飾，中文翻譯為：「沒有什麼不同的」。

 Practice Time ★

Q1：珍妮佛・勞倫斯是個聰明的女孩。

_____.

Q2：珍妮佛・勞倫斯總是期望她能認識某個特別的人。

_____.

Q1 Ans：Jennifer Lawrence is a smart girl.

Q2 Ans：Jennifer Lawrence always hopes she can meet someone special.

Unit 13
副詞

"Girl power is about loving yourself and having ❶confidence and ❷strength within, so even if you're not wearing a sexy ❸outfit, you feel sexy."

—— Nicole Scherzinger 妮可・舒辛格

（女孩的魅力來自於愛自己，以及內在的自信與力量。所以即使你沒有穿上性感的外衣，你仍然覺得性感。）

❶ confidence [ˋkɑnfədəns] n 自信 ❷ strength [strɛŋθ] n 力量

❸ outfit [ˋaʊt͵fɪt] n 外衣

以性感著稱的妮可告訴我們，性感是愛自己並對自己有自信。本句中的"within"為副詞，可翻譯為「在內部、在心中」。相較於一般"-ly"結尾的副詞，這個副詞的形式相當不同，那麼它的用法和一般副詞有沒有不同呢？

Grammar Show

副詞 (Adverb) 與形容詞都具有修飾字詞或是語氣的功能，放在動詞後或句尾皆可。只不過形容詞是用來修飾名詞，而副詞是用來修飾動詞、副詞或是形容詞。即使副詞看似多功能，但因為它通常只用來修飾或是加強語氣，所以如果省略副詞，其句子的文法結構還是正確完整的。

❶ 一般副詞可以歸類為以下五大項：

情態副詞	quickly, slowly, reluctantly, happily
程度副詞	too, very, quite, definitely

頻率副詞	usually, often, rarely, always, sometimes
時間副詞	now, before, yesterday, tomorrow
地方副詞	here, there, up, down, outside, inside

雖然省略了副詞也不會影響到句子的結構，但有了副詞，便可以使表達更清楚貼切。

從以下的例句，我們就可以了解到副詞的重要性：

如何	怎樣彈？	Ann plays guitar **happily**. (Ann 快樂地彈奏吉他。)
程度	彈得如何？	Ann plays guitar very **fluently**. (Ann 很熟練地彈奏吉他。)
頻率	多久彈一次？	*Ann **often** plays guitar. (Ann 常常彈奏吉他。)
時間	何時彈？	Ann played guitar **yesterday**. (Ann 昨天彈奏吉他。)
地方	在哪彈？	Ann plays guitar **inside the house**. (Ann 在屋內彈奏吉他。)

＊ "often"亦可放在句末，例如"Ann plays guitar quite often."然而，其他頻率副詞（如：usually, always 等）僅可以放置於動詞之前或 be 動詞之後，而不可放於句末。

解釋完副詞的功能，接下來看看形容詞如何演變成副詞：

1 形容詞後加上"ly"，即可成為副詞：

形容詞	副詞
honest	honestly
loud	loudly

2 形容詞字尾是 "y"，而前面是子音 (子音+y)，副詞需去 y 加 "ily"：

形容詞	副詞
lazy	lazily
merry	merrily

3 形容詞與副詞皆無變化：

形容詞	副詞
fast	fast
early	early

4 形容詞與副詞完全不同：

形容詞	副詞
good	well

 **Life Story**

The former member of Pussycat Dolls and now a solo artist, Nicole Scherzinger, just finished an over-five-year relationship. She coped quite well even though the whole thing was not easy for her. Many people think Nicole must be lonely right now but ❶she is actually glad to have her family and friends around. She knows sometimes it is easy for a girl to lose herself in a relationship and it is important to come back to who she is. Therefore, she is trying her best to piece her life back together. It's just like the common saying, "What doesn't kill you makes you stronger." Nicole indeed has become braver after breaking up.

Moreover, even when Nicole was at her darkest moment, ❷she still worked hard and never thought of taking drugs. In fact, she would rather have a pizza and a scoop of peanut butter instead. For her, these comfort foods are a better therapy to relieve sorrow.

前女子組合「小野貓」成員妮可‧舒辛格，現在為單飛歌手，最近結束一段超過五年的感情。即使整件事對她來說並不容易，但她仍然處理的很好。很多人覺得她一定會很寂寞，但她其實很樂意有家人及朋友在身邊。她知道有時女孩子容易迷失在感情裡，所以能找回自己是很重要的。也因此，她現在努力地把自己再拼湊起來。就像俗話說：「殺不死你的東西，會讓你變得更強壯。」，妮可確實在分手後變得更有勇氣。

此外，即使在她最低落的時刻，她依然努力工作且沒有想過要嗑藥。事實上，她寧可吃披薩或是一匙花生醬。對她來說，這些食物是舒解憂傷的更好療傷法。

- cope [kop] Ⅴ 處理
- lonely [`lonlɪ] adj 寂寞的
- brave [brev] adj 勇敢的
- scoop [skup] ⑩ 一勺
- relieve [rɪ`liv] Ⅴ 緩解

Sentence Show ★

❶ She is actually glad to have her family and friends around.

這個句子裡有兩個副詞，第一個是有"-ly"結尾，明眼人一看就看出的 "actually"（事實上），強調動作的「真實性」：她「真的」是很高興。而本句的第二個副詞，則是副詞形式較"actually"不明顯的地方副詞"around"（附近），說明妮可的家人朋友都在她身邊。

❷ She still worked hard and never thought of taking drugs.

雖然"hard"「認真地」雖然沒有"-ly"結尾，但它是一個副詞，需放在動詞後表示做某事的狀態，如這裡"worked hard"表示「工作認真地」。此外，亦有"hardly"形式的副詞，一般放在動詞之前，表示「幾乎不」，如"I could hardly stand." 我幾乎站不直。

 Practice Time ★

Q1：妮可很高興地吃著一塊比薩。

_____.

Q2：當妮可對於自己是誰感到開心時，她便可以活得自在與快樂。

_____.

Q1 Ans：Nicole ate a piece of pizza happily.

Q2 Ans：Nicole can only live freely and happily when she is happy with who she is.

Unit 14
同級與倍數

Great ❶advice comes from people that have been around ❷at least ❸twice as long as you.

—— Zac Efron 柴克・艾弗隆

（好的建議來自於那些至少活的比你兩倍久的人。）

❶ advice [əd`vaɪs] n 勸告　❷ at least ph 至少　❸ twice [twaɪs] adv 兩倍

　　在上述柴克的名言我們可以看到 twice as long as 的用法，你知道這是什麼意思嗎？這是表示「倍數」的使用喔！

Grammar Show ★

　　比較級(Comparative)可用來比較兩個形容詞或兩個副詞，在程度或等級上的不同。而比較的程度，則又可分為同等或是倍數的比較。

❶ 表示倍數

　　在做倍數比較時，需要使用「倍數詞」來表示，而倍數詞除了「半倍」"half"和「兩倍」"twice"為不同拼寫法外，其他倍數都是以數字加上 times 所組成，例如：三倍= "three times"，四倍= "four times"，以此類推。以下我們就分別來介紹形容詞與副詞的比較級吧！

❷ 形容詞倍數比較：**"倍數詞 + as + 原級 Adj. + as"/"**

倍數詞+比較級形容詞+ than"

例 Ariel is **twice as nice as** Annie.

Ariel 比 Annie 好上兩倍。

例 My brother is **three times taller than** Bryan.

我哥哥比 Bryan 高上三倍。

❸ 形容詞同級比較：**" as + 形容詞+ as"**

例 Michael is **as kind as** Kevin.

Michael 跟 Kevin 一樣仁慈。

例 The ant is **as small as** the bean.

這隻螞蟻跟豆子一樣小。

❹ 副詞倍數比較：**"倍數詞+比較級副詞+ than"**

例 My sister is a professional athlete. She can run **four times**

faster than me.

我姐姐是個專業運動員。她可以跑的比我快四倍。

例 She walks **three times slower than** me.

她比我走路慢三倍。

❺ 副詞同級比較：**"as + 副詞+ as"**

例 He can type **as fast as** I can.

他打字打的跟我一樣快。

例 Lucy sings **as beautifully as** Olivia does.

Lucy 唱的跟 Olivia 一樣好。

Life Story

The first thing people, especially girls, notice about Zac Efron must be his deep blue eyes. What is more, ❶his figure is as buffed as a Greek statue. There is no doubt at all why he was named one of the sexiest men in Hollywood.

Beginning in 2006, the three-part *High School Musical* series brought him a lot of fame and female fans. However, Zac's beautiful face and six-pack body are nothing to do with his success. Although his character, Troy, showed amazing talents at singing and dancing in the movie, Zac admitted that he was terrible at both before shooting. ❷He knew he was not as professional as his other co-workers on the musical so he worked almost three times harder than them. He showed his ambition by training every day. Finally, all the hard work he had put in during training paid off as the movie turned him into a teen icon. Meanwhile, his effort has never left him short of movie roles ever since.

人們，尤其是女孩子，注意到柴克‧艾弗隆的第一件事一定是他的深藍色的雙眸。除此之外，還有他如希臘雕像一般健壯的體態。毫無疑問地，他被稱為是好萊塢最性感的男人之一。

從 2006 年開始，三部「歌舞青春」系列電影帶給了他許多的名氣與女粉絲。然而，柴克俊俏的臉龐及六塊肌的身材，與他的成功並無關聯。雖然他在戲中的角色特洛伊在唱歌及跳舞上展現了令人驚艷的才能，但柴克承認他其實在開拍前，對於兩項技能都不擅長。他知道自己並不像劇中其他的演員一樣專業，所以他比他們多付出三倍的努力。他以每天接受訓練來顯示自己的決心。最後，他在訓練中所付出的努力得到了回報，他因這部電影成為了青少年的偶像。同時，他在這部片之後便持續收到戲約。

● buffed [bʌft] **adj** 健壯的　● statue [ˋstætʃʊ] **n** 雕像　● doubt [daʊt] **v** 懷疑

Sentence Show ★

❶ His figure is as buffed as a Greek statue.

這裡"as…as"句型表現了前後兩個名詞的對等同級關係：柴克的體態(His fig-ure)是和希臘雕像(a Greek statue)一樣肌肉線條明顯的。

❷ He knew he was not as professional as his other co-workers on the musical so he worked almost three times harder than them.

這句話同時出現了本單元中的兩個文法要點：「比較級的同級」和「比較級的倍數」。前者出現在"…he was not 'as professional as' his other co-workers on the musical" 表示「柴克沒有像其他演員『一樣專業』」；後者則是"…he worked almost three times harder than them"，三倍(three times)放置於比較級 harder 之前，表示三倍的努力。

 Practice Time ★

Q1：柴克現在的工作量是他 17 歲時的五倍多。

_____

Q2：柴克新電影《惡鄰纏身》的評價和他的《歌舞青春》一樣好。

_____

Q1 Ans：Zac's workload now is five times more than he had at 17.

Q2 Ans：The critics acclaim for Zac's latest movie Bad Neighbor was as high as for *High School Musical*.

Unit 15
比較級與最高級

"The heart is stronger than you think. It's like it could [1]go through anything."

—— Beyoncé 碧昂絲

（你的心比你想的還要更強壯。它就像可以經歷任何事一樣。）

[1] go through **ph** 經歷

"stronger" 和 "strong" 均為形容詞，但前者為後者的比較級，意思為「更強壯的」。那麼，在「更強壯的」之後，是否還有更高的層級呢？如果有，又該如何表達呢？

Grammar Show

1 形容詞比較級

大部分的形容詞比較級形式，都是在該單音節形容詞後加上"-er"，如 "short- short-er"（矮的- 較矮的），"old- older"（老的- 較老的）；但倘若有一個形容詞的發音是兩個音節以上，這時候就不在它後面加上"-er"，而是使用"more+形容詞"的方式，如："beautiful- more beautiful"（漂亮的- 較漂亮的），"interesting- more interest-ing"（有趣的- 較有趣的）。最後，部分形容詞的比較級則呈現不規則的形式，如："good- better"（好的- 較好的）或"bad- worse"（差的- 較差的）等。為了更好的理解比較級的使用法，現在就來看看一些例句吧！

例 Our car is **smaller** than your car.　我們的車比你的車小。

★ NOT: Our car is smaller than you. 需要比較同性質的東西，out car 不能和 you 相比

例 Yesterday's television program was **more interesting**.

昨天的電視節目比較有趣。

例 Her condition is getting **better**.

她的情況變得比較好了。

2 形容詞最高級

形容詞最高級表現形式則多為單音節形容詞後加上"-est"，如"shortest"（最矮的），"oldest"（最老的）。而兩個音節以上的形容詞則需使用"the most+形容詞"的方式，如：beautiful- the most beautiful（漂亮的- 最漂亮的），"ineresting- the most interesting"（有趣的- 最有趣的）。而之前提到的不規則比較級形式，在最高級時，也是以不規則的形式出現，如："best"（最好的）及"worst"（最差的）等。

例 John is **the tallest** boy in his school.

John 是學校裡最高的男孩。

例 This is **the most expensive** dress I have ever bought.

這是我買過最貴的衣服。

例 Her answer was **the furthest** from the correct one.

她的答案是和正確答案相差最遠的。

3 副詞比較級

例 The cat runs fast but the mouse runs **faster**.

貓跑得快，但是老鼠跑得更快。

例 Mary drives **more carefully** than John does.

Mary 開車比John更小心。

4 副詞最高級

例 Steve works **the hardest**.　　Steve 工作最認真。

例 Steve gets to work **the earliest** of all.　　Steve 上班最早到。

 **Life Story**

Nowadays, many people see Beyoncé as a flawless goddess. She has perfect skin, beautiful caramel hair and clear almond eyes. It seems that you could not possibly find anything wrong with her. In fact, what people think about Beyoncé is what really bothers her. She admits she is not satisfied with her appearance as ❶she wishes her ears were smaller. She also thinks she is just like everybody else. She gets insecure and sad sometimes and has to work for everything that she gets.

What may even surprise more people is that Beyoncé actually has only had two boyfriends: a childhood sweetheart and the rapper, Jay-Z, who she married in April 2008. When asked whether she ever wishes she had dated more, she replied she might have said yes to this question when she was younger. However, ❷she thinks she is at the greatest place at the moment. She believes she has found the right person and wouldn't trade her life for anything.

現今很多人視碧昂絲為無暇的女神。她有完美的皮膚、美麗的焦糖色頭髮以及清澈的杏仁狀眼睛；似乎很難在她身上發現毛病。事實上，碧昂絲對於人們這樣看待她，感到相當苦惱。她承認不滿意自己的外表，並希望自己的耳朵能小一點。她也認為自己就像一般人一樣，她會有不安全感，有時覺得悲傷，並且需要靠工作來獲得自己所得到的每樣東西。

而讓更多人感到驚訝的是，碧昂絲只交往過兩個男朋友：一個是她的青梅竹馬，另一個則是與她於 2008 年四月結婚的饒舌歌手 Jay-Z。當被問到她是否曾希望能與更多人約會時，她回答如果她在更年輕一點時被問到這個問題的話，她也許會說是的。然而，她現在覺得自己處於最好的狀態。她相信自己已經找到了對的人，並且不會用任何事物來和她的生活做交換。

● flawless [`flɔlɪs] **adj** 完美無瑕的 ● caramel [`kærəml] **n** 焦糖色

Sentence Show ⭐

❶ She wishes her ears were smaller.

碧昂絲提到，她希望她的耳朵「更小一點」。這裡其實涵蓋了一個「比較」的概念；她並不是希望擁有小耳朵 (not wish for small ears)，而只是希望「比現在的耳朵更小一點」。故此句使用"small"（小）比較級"smaller"（較小的）。

❷ She thinks she is at the greatest place at the moment.

最高級"greatest"說明碧昂斯覺得她現在的狀態「不止是好」("not just at a great place")，或是「比較好」("better")而已，而是與以前任何一個時期相比，都是「最好的」("is at the greatest place at the moment")；即程度上的比較為：great<greater<greatest。

 Practice Time ⭐

Q1：碧昂絲現在也許賺比較少錢，但她絕對是比較快樂的。

_____.

Q2：碧昂絲有最美麗的眼睛。

_____.

Q1 Ans：Beyoncé may earn less now but she is definitely happier.

Q2 Ans：Beyoncé has the most beautiful eyes.

Unit 16
介系詞與介系詞片語

" Everything has to be ❶earned through work, ❷persistence and ❸honesty. "

—— Grace Kelly 葛麗絲‧凱莉

（每件事皆必須透過努力、持久和誠實而賺得。）

❶ earn [ɝn] Ⓥ 賺得　❷ persistence [pɚˋsɪstəns] Ⓝ 持續　❸ honesty [ˋɑnɪstɪ] Ⓝ 誠實

　　介系詞的作用為表示其後的受詞與句中其他字句的關係。句中介系詞 "through"（透過），即表示後方各個受詞 (work, persistence and honesty) 和 "Everything has to be earned" 的關係。

🎬 Grammar Show ★

　　介系詞 (Preposition) 是用來表達句中動詞與受詞的之間的位置、方向、時間等關係；介系詞後通常接名詞，且不能單獨使用。常用的介系詞: "on, onto, off, toward, behind, beyond, by, beside, under, underneath, in, near, nearby"等。

例 The cat walked **on** the roof.

　　這隻貓走在屋頂上。（說明動詞「走」和受詞「屋頂」的「位置」關係）

例 He is running **behind** me.

　　他正跑在我後面。（說明動詞「跑」和受詞「我」的「方向」關係）

例 Could you please get **in** the car now?

　　可否請你現在馬上上車？（說明動詞「進入」和受詞「車」的「時間」關係）

　　介系詞並不限於一個單字，也有兩個或三個單字所組成的介系詞，如 "due to"（因為），"according to"（根據），"in front of"（在..前面），"in spite of"（儘管）等。

　　介系詞片語 (Prepositional Phrases) 是指由介系詞起頭，後接名詞或代名詞，而形成的片語形式 ，即 "介系詞+名詞/代名詞=介系詞片語"，例如 "in the car" 或 "till midnight" 等。介系詞片語在句子中有以下三大功能:

1 形容詞：放在名詞之後，用來修飾名詞或可做為補語

例 The student **in front of the classroom** is my friend.

教室前的那位學生是我的朋友。

2 名詞：可在句中作為主詞或補語

例 You will be **in trouble** if you don't pass this exam.

如果你沒有通過這個考試，你將會有麻煩。

3 副詞：放在動詞之後，用來修飾動詞或形容詞

例 Clark's parcel arrived just **after his birthday.**

Clark 的包裹就在他過完生日後送達。

註：補語是指任何字、片語、或子句用以補充說明句子的主詞或受詞，使其成為完整的句子。

Life Story

With the release of the movie *Grace of Monaco* in 2014, people are reminded of the elegant and beautiful Princess of Monaco, Grace Kelly, once again.

[1]In fact, apart from being the wife of Prince Rainier III, she was also a famous American actress in her day. She was nominated for both a Golden Globe Award and an Academy Awardin 1954, and then secured her status by winning the Academy Award for Best Actress in the same year. It seems Grace always knew what she wanted to do. [2]After graduating from high school, she decided to pursue her acting dreams in spite of the dismay of her parents. Later, to people's surprise, she retired from her rising acting career at the age of 26 to marry the Prince of Monaco and enter upon her duties in that country. She and the prince had three children. Unfortunately, she died in a car accident while driving with her youngest daughter, Princess Stéphanie who survived, in 1982.

隨著 2014 年電影《為愛璀璨：永遠的葛麗絲》的上映，人們又再次記起了這位優雅美麗的摩納哥王妃葛麗絲・凱利。

事實上，她除了是雷尼埃三世王子的妻子外，她還是那個時代有名的美國電影明星。她在 1954 年，同時獲得金球獎及奧斯卡獎的提名，並在其後贏得了奧斯卡最佳女主角。葛麗絲似乎總是知道自己要什麼。高中畢業後，儘管她父母不樂意，她仍然決定要追求演戲的夢想。之後，讓大家驚訝的是，她在 26 歲時從她如日中天的演藝工作退休，嫁給摩納哥王子並至該國履行王妃的義務。她和王子一共生了三個孩子。她在 1982 年時和她最小的女兒史蒂芬妮公主同車發生車禍，史蒂芬妮公主被救活了，但她不幸身亡。

- remind [rɪ`maɪnd] Ⓥ 提醒
- elegant [`ɛləgənt] adj 優雅的
- secure [sɪ`kjʊr] Ⓥ 保證
- in spite of ph 不管
- enter upon ph 著手進行

Sentence Show ★

❶ In fact, apart from being the wife of Prince Price Rainier III, she was also a famous American actress in her day.

這個句子中出現了一個介系詞及一個介系詞片語。在句子開頭，首先看到的是的介系詞片語"apart from"（除⋯之外），接下來則是在句末用來表示時間「在⋯（的時候）」的介系詞"in"。

❷ After graduating from high school, she decided to pursue her acting dreams in spite of the dismay of her parents.

介系詞的運用之廣，亦可以從這個含有三個介系詞的句子中看出。在句子前半部，分別出現了表示時間「在⋯之後」與位置「從⋯（地點）」的介系詞"after"和"from"；其後的主要子句裡則有介系詞片語"in spite of"「儘管」。

 Practice Time ★

Q1：葛麗絲・凱利住在摩納哥。

_____.

Q2：根據官方記載，葛麗絲有兩個女兒一個兒子。

_____.

Q1 Ans：Grace Kelly lived in Monaco.

Q2 Ans：According to official records, Grace had two daughters and one son.

Unit 17
對等連接詞

> I am not a big fan of women that have to be the ❶victim and need to be saved at all times. I don't ❷necessarily think that's how it is in real life, and I don't think that's how it should be in films.

—— Mila Kunis 蜜拉•庫妮絲

（對於那種女性是受害者，隨時需要被拯救的片子，我並不是很有興趣。我想真實生活不一定是這樣，然後我也不覺得這應該出現在電影上。）

❶ victim [`vɪktɪm] **n** 受害者　❷ necessarily [`nɛsəsɛrɪlɪ] **adv** 必定地

　　這裡對等連接詞"and"出現兩次，分別是"… have to be the victim and need to be saved at all times."和" I don't necessarily think that's how it is in real life, and I don't think that's how it should be in films."。前一句的 "and" 連接兩個子句，說明是怎麼樣的女性角色；後一句則連接兩個句子。因此，大家可以大致猜到"and"為何稱為「對等連接詞」嗎？

Grammar Show ★

　　對等連接詞(Coordinating Conjunctions)的功能是用來連接單字，片語或是子句。用對等連接詞所相連的單字，片語或子句皆具有相同的時態或詞性。

❶ **and**：「和、而且」

例 Mother bought fruit **and** vegetable in the market at a very decent price.

媽媽在市場用很合理的價格買了水果和蔬菜。（"and"連接 "fruit"和 "vegetable" 兩個單字）

②　but：「但是、可是」

例 John tried hard in the contest, **but** he failed.

約翰在比賽中努力嘗試，但失敗了。（"but"連接兩個句子）

②　or：「或」

例 Would you like some coffee **or** tea?

你要點咖啡或茶嗎？（"or"連接"coffee"和"tea"兩個單字）

③　nor：「兩者皆非」；用來表示否定，需搭配否定的句子

例 Julia could not speak, **nor** could she understand anything they said.

Julia 不能說話，也不能了解他們在說什麼。（nor連接的子句需要倒裝，故助動詞could在主詞she之前）

④　for：用來表示「理由」

例 He didn't go home last night, **for** there was no bus.

他昨晚沒有回家，因為沒有公車了。（"there was no bus"為理由）

⑤　so：用來表示「因果」

例 It was sunny yesterday, **so** we went to the beach.

昨天艷陽高照，所以我們去了海灘。（"It was sunny"為「因」，"we went to the beach"為「果」）

⑥　yet：意思和功能與 "but" 相同，皆可解釋為「但是、可是」

例 The car is good, **yet** it can be better.

這輛車不錯，但可以更好。

註：這七個對等連接詞，用諧音法背起來。*FANBOYS* (粉絲男孩)。

★ 對等連接詞連接子句時，兩邊的子句皆為主要子句。都是有主詞+動詞，且有完整句意的句子，都視為獨立的句子看待。

 *Life Story* ★

Mila Kunis confesses that ❶she was a "tomboy" who grew up climbing trees and playing sports with her brother. She started acting by accident. She was originally from Ukraine and moved to Los Angeles with her family at the age of seven. In order to help her learn English, her parents enrolled her in after-school acting classes. She then showed her determination to speak English as well as native speakers by only taking one year.

Another thing Kunis worked with determination on was losing about 9 kilograms transforming her body into the ultimate figure. Back in 2011, slim and fit, ❷she consumed 1,200 calories a day and took seven months of punishing ballet training, so she could play the ballet dancer, Lily, in the movie Black Swan. She said, "I believed I could do anything. I never for one moment thought that I couldn't do it. I believe in hard work. In self-drive and self-worth. Our body can do everything and anything; we just have to want to do it."

蜜拉‧庫妮絲承認她是個男孩子氣的女孩，她在成長期間都與她的哥哥一起爬樹及從事球類運動。她會開始演戲完全是個意外。來自於烏克蘭，在七歲時和家人搬到洛杉磯。為了幫助她學習英語，她的父母為她報名了課後的戲劇課程。之後，她展現出她的決心，以僅僅一年的時間將英語說得和當地人一樣好。

另外一件庫妮絲以決心辦到的事是她減去了 9 公斤的體重，將身形轉化為更終極的曲線。即使身材已經纖細又結實，在 2011 年時，為了可以演出電影《黑天鵝》中的芭蕾舞者莉莉一角，她每天只攝取 1200 卡路里，並且接受為期七個月嚴苛的芭蕾舞訓練。她說：「我相信我可以做任何事。我從沒有一刻覺得我辦不到。我相信努力工作。自我鞭策以及自我價值。只要我們願意，我們的身體可以做每件事和任何事。」

- confess [kən`fɛsn] Ⅴ 坦白
- determination [dɪˌtɝˈmɪˈneʃən] ⋒ 決心
- enroll [ɪn`rol] Ⅴ 參加
- transform [trænsˈfɔrm] Ⅴ 改造

Sentence Show ★

❶ She was a "tomboy" who grew up climbing trees and playing sports with her brother.

連接詞"and"連接兩個對等的動詞片語："… climbing trees"（爬樹）和 "playing with her brother"（和她的哥哥一起從事球類運動），分別說明庫妮絲成長期間所做的事。

❷ She consumed 1,200 calories a day and took seven months of punishing ballet training, so she could play the ballet dancer, Lily, in the movie Black Swan.

這句話裡有兩個對等連接詞，第一個是"and"，連接兩個類似的語義："…consumed 1,200 calories a day "（一天 1200 卡的飲食）和 "took seven months of punishing ballet training…"（七個月的嚴苛芭蕾舞訓練）；第二個是"so"，表示因果關係，因為有"so"之前的動作，所以庫妮絲才能演出《黑天鵝》中 Lily 的角色。

 Practice Time ★

Q1：節食和運動是蜜拉‧庫妮絲減重的方法。

_____.

Q2：英語不是蜜拉的母語，但她現在可以說的和當地人一樣好。

_____.

Q1 Ans： Going on a diet and doing exercise are the ways that Mila Kunis lost weight.

Q2 Ans： English is not Mila's native language, but she can speak as well as native speakers now.

Unit 18
從屬連接詞

My **❶definition** of stupid is wasting your **❷opportunity** to be yourself, because I think everybody has a **❸uniqueness** and everybody's good at something.

—— Pink 紅粉佳人

（我對「愚笨」的定義是：浪費你的機會去做你自己，因為我覺得每個人都有其獨特性和精通的事。）

❶ definition [ˌdɛfəˈnɪʃən] **n** 定義　　**❷** opportunity [ˌɑpəˈtjunətɪ] **n** 機會

❸ uniqueness [juˈniknɪs] **n** 獨特性

　　此句中出現了兩個連接詞，一個是上個單元的對等連接詞 "and"，其連接了 "everybody has a uniqueness" 和 "everybody's good at something" 兩個對等的句子；而本單元要介紹的從屬連接詞 "because"（因為）則是連接了從屬子句和主要子句，你知道這兩種的區別嗎？

 **Grammar Show**

　　從屬連接詞（Subordinating Conjunctions）用來連接兩個句子，即主要子句與從屬子句（具有修飾主要子句的功能，附屬於主要子句）。依照從屬連接詞的使用方法及情況，可大致分為以下：

❶ 時間：**after**（之後），**before**（之前），**as soon as**（一⋯就），**while / when / as**（當）

這些從屬連接詞所構成的子句，通常用來表示與主要子句的時間關係。此外，主要子句與從屬子句可互換前後位置，但如果從屬子句放在前面，需在主要子句前加上逗號。

例 My brother studied very hard **before** he took the examination.

= **Before** my brother took the examination, he studied very hard.

我弟弟在考試前很認真讀書。

例 It started to rain **as soon as** we left the office.

= **As soon as** we left the office, it started to rain.

我們一離開辦公室就開始下雨。

❷ 原因：**because/as/since**（因為），用來表示主要字句與從屬子句之間的因果關係

例 Mary couldn't join the party **because** she has broken her legs.

Mary 不能來參加派對，因為她的腿骨折了。

例 I don't really like this food **as** it smells too fishy.

我真的不喜歡這個食物，因為聞起來魚腥味太重了。

例 Please help Jason with his homework **since** he has skipped several classes.

請幫忙 Jason 做作業，因為他曠太多課了。

❸ 其他：**although/even though/though**（即使），通常有退一步的意味

例 He is still upset about the result **although** we have tried to cheer him up.

即使我們試著逗他開心，但他還是對結果很不高興。

例 The restaurant food is not great **even though** the price is very high.

餐廳的食物不好吃，即便如此，價格還很高。

Life Story

Pink (stylized as P!nk), whose real name is Alecia Beth Moore, was born in 1979. With "adventurous" hairstyles and tons of tattoos, she has become known for her unique style. She has admitted that she sees herself as eccentric and tomboy-like. However, **❶she has also said it is her thing even though she is not sure whether people considered it to be a good thing or not.**

Perhaps she is not as famous as Katy Perry, Britney Spears or Lady Gaga but she is definitely entitled to be regarded as the "most trailblazing and fearless pop artist" of her generation. She has powerful vocals and her lyrics often express what is on people's minds. **❷It is said that she has changed the field of pop music as she stood up for her music, broke the music industry's mold and even took on George W. Bush by writing the song *Dear Mr. President*.** Up till now, she has sold millions of albums worldwide and landed countless Billboard hits.

　　紅粉佳人 Pink（呈現形式為 P!nk）的真實姓名為艾蕾莎・貝絲・摩兒，出生於 1978 年。因為髮型「大膽」及身上無數的刺青，她因此因其獨特的造型而出名。她承認自己不拘一格也像個男孩子，但她也說，她覺得這是她自己的事，即使她不確定人們是否會認為這是一件好事。

　　也許她不如凱蒂・珮芮、小甜甜布蘭妮或女神卡卡這麼出名，但她絕對有資格被認定是她同期中「最前衛和最無懼的流行樂歌手」。她的嗓音有很大的感染力，而她的歌詞經常說出了大家的心聲。因為她捍衛自己的音樂、打破樂界模式，甚至於將對布希總統的憤怒寫在她的歌《親愛的總統》裡，評論家們說她已經改變了流行樂的領域。直到現在，她已經在全球銷售了數百萬張唱片，並且有著無數的告示牌熱門單曲。

- adventurous [əd`vɛntʃərəs] **adj** 大膽的
- tattoo [tæ`tu] **n** 刺青
- trailblazing [`treɪlbleɪzɪŋ] **adj** 前鋒的
- speak out **ph** 不顧忌地說出

Sentence Show ★

❶ She has also said it is her thing even though she is not sure whether people considered it to be a good thing or not.

在文法中，含有「無論」、「不管」、「儘管」等義的詞均為有表「讓步」之意。此句中的 "even though"（即使）即為其一，即含有「讓步」意涵的從屬連接詞。

❷ It is said that she has changed the field of pop music as she stood up for her music, broke the music industry's mold and even took on George W. Bush by writing the song Dear Mr. President.

"as" 在這裡做為表「原因」的從屬連接詞，說明為何人們覺得紅粉佳人改變了流行樂的原因（捍衛自己的音樂、打破樂界模式，將對布希總統的憤怒寫在她歌裡。）

 Practice Time ★

Q1：在紅粉佳人 10 歲前，她的父母已經離婚。

_____.

Q2：評論家尊崇紅粉佳人因為她是流行樂的先鋒。

_____.

Q1 Ans：Before Pink was ten, her parents had divorced.

Q2 Ans：Critics respect Pink because she is a pioneer of pop music.

Unit 19
轉折語

"I believe in love. However, I don't ❶sit around waiting for it. I buy houses."

—— Renée Zellweger 芮妮·琪薇格

（我相信愛情。然而，我不會只是坐著乾等。我買房子。）

❶ sit around ph 閒坐著

　　芮妮·琪薇格這句話看似不是什麼人生大哲理，但其實是告訴人們，不管愛情或是任何事情，都不要坐著等待它的發生。句中使用了轉折語"however"（但是），含有「補充說明」的概念，說明雖然「相信愛情」但補充說明她不會只是坐著等待愛情來臨。

Grammar Show

　　轉折詞 (Transitional Expressions) 的功能是用來連接、串連兩個句子，讓兩個句子的關係與邏輯更明顯清楚的表達出來。特別注意轉折詞為「副詞」，不可當連接詞用。根據不同的意思，常用到的轉折詞可分為以下:

❶ **補充說明：furthermore, moreover, also, in the second place, again, in addition, even more, next, further, besides...**

例 **In addition to** his great skill at cooking, he is also good at crafting.

他除了廚藝很好之外，手工藝也非常優秀。（補充說明除了廚藝好之外的另一項技能）

例 It is getting dark. **Besides**, the road is nearly impassable.

天漸漸黑了。此外，這條路簡直無法通行。

2 舉例說明：**to illustrate, to demonstrate, specifically, for instance, as an illustration, for example, first, second, lastly, finally...**

例 My cousin plays lots of sports, **for example**, tennis, basketball and volleyball.

我的表妹從事多項運動；比如，網球、籃球跟排球。（舉例表妹從事的運動項目）

3 比較/類比：**similarly, likewise, yet, nevertheless, nonetheless, after all, however, otherwise, on the contrary, in contrast, at the same time, on the other hand...**

例 Green makes your skin brighter; **on the other hand,** orange makes it darker.

綠色讓你的皮膚看起來更亮；相反地，橘色讓你的皮膚看起來很暗。

（比較兩個顏色的效果）

4 因果：**therefore, accordingly, as a result, thus, consequently, ...**

例 The road is under construction; and **therefore,** we have to take another road.

這條路正在施工中；所以，我們必須走別條路。

（因這條路不能走，所以要走別條路）

5 肯定/斷定：**in fact, of course, surely, indeed, truly, certainly, naturally, undoubtedly...**

例 **Of course,** hygiene is the priority for a restaurant.

當然，衛生對餐廳來說為首當要務。

 **Life Story**

You can refer 45-year-old Renée Zellweger to the modern definition of glamor. ❶She possesses all the elements of a high-glamor life: the designer clothes, the red-carpet poise and so on. However, these are not the only things Zellweger has. This Texas-born actress also has great talent for language. She played the role of Beatrix Potter, the British children's author and illustrator, in the movie *Miss Potter* in 2006. Judging by her accent in the movie, many people are convinced she was born and bred in England.

❷In another blockbuster *Bridget Jones's Diary*, she played the character of Bridget Jones, a girl who finally finds her Mr. Right after coming a long way.In contrast with her movie character, Zellweger is currently single and enjoys her status right now. Regardless of social expectation, she doesn't think being single means being unhappy. Alternatively, it's a lifestyle that enables her to make her own decisions and indulge herself.

　　你可以說 45 歲的芮妮・琪薇格等同於「魅力」這個詞在現今社會的定義。她擁有所有高檔生活的元素：設計師服裝、紅地毯亮相等等。然而，這些不是琪薇格唯一持有的東西。這個出生於德克薩斯州的女演員還擁有語言天賦。她在 2006 年電影《波特小姐》中扮演英國的兒童作家及插畫家碧兒翠斯波特。從她在電影裡的口語音判斷，很多人覺得她是在英國土生土長的。

　　在她的另一部賣座電影《BJ 單身日記》中，她飾演一個經歷重重困難最終找到真愛的女孩子。與電影角色不同的是，琪薇格現在單身，並且很享受這種狀態。不管社會的價值觀是如何，她不覺得單身就是不快樂。相反的是，這是一種她可以自己做決定，並且寵愛自己的生活方式。

- glamor [ˋglæmɚ] **n** 魅力
- possess [pəˋzɛs] **v** 擁有
- element [ˋɛləmənt] **n** 元素
- accent [ˋæksɛnt] **n** 口音
- indulge [ɪnˋdʌldʒ] **v** 享受，寵愛

Sentence Show ★

❶ She possesses all the elements of a high-glamor life: the designer clothes, the red-carpet poise and so on. However, these are not the only things Zellweger has.

轉折語"however"（然而）在這裡含有「比較」之意。句子首先說明芮妮琪薇格擁有各種上流生活的物質元素，但與這些「相比之下」，她還有擁有其他的東西。

❷ In another blockbuster *Bridget Jones's Diary*, she played the character of Bridget Jones, a girl who finally finds her Mr. Right after coming a long way. In contrast with her movie character, Zellweger is currently single and enjoys her status right now.

此句使用"In contrast"（與…形成對比）這個轉折語。和上句相同，這個轉折語也是帶有「比較」之意。將芮妮・琪薇格在電影上扮演的角色和她真實形象對比。

 Practice Time ★

Q1：芮妮・琪薇格拍過很多有名的電影，例如，《波特小姐》和《BJ 單身日記》。

_____.

Q2：芮妮・琪薇格是美國人；然而，她有很好的英國口音。

_____.

Q1 Ans：Renée Zellweger has shot many famous movies, for example, *Miss Potter* and *Bridget Jones's Diary*.

Q2 Ans：Reneé Zellweger is American; however, she has a very good British accent.

Part 2

時態、助動詞、動狀詞

Unit 01
簡單現在式

❝❶Drugs? Everyone has a choice and I choose not to do drugs.❞

—— Leonardo DiCaprio 李奧納多・狄卡皮歐

（毒品？每個人都有選擇的機會，而我選擇不吸毒。）

❶ drug [drʌg] ⓝ 毒品

　　明星濫用毒品的新聞時有所聞，李奧納多的這番話讓人刮目相看。他在這句話使用的時態為「簡單現在式」；第一個動詞 "has" 表示他認為 "everyone has a choice" 是「普遍認知的事實」；第二個句子 "I choose not to do drugs"，動詞 "choose" 表示選擇不吸毒是他的「習慣動作」。

Grammar Show ★

　　簡單現在式 Simple Present Tense 依主詞的不同，在動詞的表達形式上也會有所不同。以下為現在簡單式的各個主詞和動詞搭配的文法型式。

主詞	動詞型式	示例
I, you, we, they	be 動詞原型動詞	I am; you / we / they are I / you / we / they come
he, she, it, Mary, his friend 等	be 動詞第三人稱單數動詞	He / she / it / Mary / his friend is He / she / it / Mary / his friend comes

　　由上方表格可以看出，除第三人稱（1）單數動詞需視動詞在其後加 s 或 es（如："comes", "goes", "plays"或 "washes"等），（2）否定的形式為"does not (doesn't) +原型動詞"外，其他人稱則使用原型動詞，而否定形式則為"do not (don't) +原型動詞"。此外，簡單現在式也有不同的使用時機：

❶ 說明習慣或規律的行為

例 My father **watches** the news every day.

我的父親每天看新聞。

例 I don't **clean** my room.

我不打掃房間。

❷ 說明狀況或事實

例 Taipei **is** the capital of Taiwan.

台北是台灣的首都。

例 The sun **rises** in the east.

太陽從東邊升起。

❸ 說明想法或感覺

例 I **think** she is Japanese.

我想她是日本人。

例 She **likes** her dog.

她喜歡她的狗。

★ 簡單現在式的疑問句視人稱不同使用"do"或"does"做為句子開頭

例 **Do** they live in New York?

他們住在紐約嗎？（"They"為第三人稱複數）

例 **Does** she love her job?

她熱愛她的工作嗎？（"She"為第三人稱單數）

★ 簡單現在式可與頻率副詞"always"（總是），"often"（時常），"sometimes"
（有時），"never"（從不）等合用，表示做某動作的頻率

例 I **always take** a shower at seven o'clock.

我總是在七點淋浴。

例 Iris **never drinks** coffee.　　Iris 從不喝咖啡。

 **Life Story**

❶Is there anyone who has not seen or heard about the movie *Titanic?* It achieved huge success when it first showed on the big screen in 1997. Much of the female audience could not stop crying at the end of the movie scene in which Jack Dawson, played by Leonardo DiCaprio, sank into the sea. It is said that this movie transformed DiCaprio into a commercial movie superstar and made him popular among teenage girls and young women.

With wide fame, a large fortune and beautiful girlfriends, it is hard to believe that DiCaprio was actually not born with a sliver spoon in his mouth. His parents divorced when he was one year old. He lived mostly with his mother who worked several jobs to support both of them. Therefore, ❷after becoming one of the highest highest-paid actors in Hollywood, he often makes donation to people in need. While thinking about how good-looking and kind-hearted DiCaprio is, how can we ever take our eyes off him?

是否有人沒看過或聽說過電影《鐵達尼號》呢？這部電影在 1997 年首次於大螢幕上映時，便獲得極大的成功。許多女性觀眾在影片最後看到由李奧納多·狄卡皮歐扮演的傑克·道森沉入水底時，都無法停止哭泣。據說這部片讓狄卡皮歐成為了商業電影的巨星，並且也讓他受到年輕女子們的歡迎。

狄卡皮歐有名聲、財富以及美麗的女朋友們，因此很難想像他其實並不是含著金湯匙出生的。他的父母在他一歲時離婚，他大部分的時間是和母親一起生活的。他的母親必須同時做很多份工作來維持兩人的生活。因此，在成為好萊塢片酬最高的男星之一後，他常常捐款給需要幫助的人。想到狄卡皮歐是如此的英俊及有善心，我們又怎麼可能將目光從他身上移開呢？

- audience [`ɔdɪəns] **n** 觀眾
- commercial [kə`mɝ·ʃəl] **adj** 商業的
- sank [sæŋk] **v** 下沉（sink 的過去式）
- fortune [`fɔrtʃən] **n** 財富

Sentence Show ⭐

❶ Is there anyone who has not seen or heard about the movie Titanic?

這個疑問句使用「簡單現在式」"is"做為問句開頭，表示問話者在詢問是否有「有人沒有看過或聽過電影《鐵達尼號》的這個「狀況」。

❷ After becoming one of the highest highest-paid actors in Hollywood, he often makes donation to people in need.

主要子句的動詞為「簡單現在式」"makes"，此處表示捐款 "makes donation"是狄卡皮歐在成為好萊塢高片酬男星後的一個「習慣動作」。頻率副詞如 "often"（時常）, "always"（總是）, "never"（從未）等則常與此類簡單現在式動詞合用，說明某習慣動作發生的頻率。

 Practice Time ⭐

Q1：李奧納多・狄卡皮歐是位美國男演員。

_____.

Q2：李奧納多・狄卡皮歐總是和名模約會。

_____.

Q1 Ans：Leonardo DiCaprio is an American actor.

Q2 Ans：Leonardo DiCaprio always dates supermodels .

Unit 02
現在進行式

66 I am **❶fighting for** the girls who never thought they could win. 99

—— Nicki Minaj 妮琪•米娜

（我正在為那些覺得自己永遠沒有勝算的女孩而戰。）

❶ fight for `ph` 為……而戰

　　即使在兩性關係日趨平等的今天，仍然有很多的女孩對自己沒有自信，覺得自己不管做什麼都沒有勝算。妮琪•米娜以自身的成功例子展示給這些女孩，並使用了「現在進行式」（I am fighting for...）表示她現在「正在為」這些女孩們奮戰下去。

Grammar Show ★

　　現在進行式 Present Continuous Tense 通常是用來指「某個動作正在發生」；其肯定句的文法型式為"be+ Ving"，否定句形式為"be+ not+ Ving"。現在進行式的使用方式與句例如下。

❶ 說話的當下動作正在進行或發生

　　例 The bus **is coming**.　巴士來了。

　　例 I can't talk to you now. I **am doing** my homework.

　　　　我現在不能跟你說話。我正在做功課。

2 動作現在正在進行，但並不一定是在說話的當下發生

例 Rose **is learning** English at the moment.

Rose 目前正在學英文。（Rose 這陣子在學英文，但說話的當下，Rose 可能在做其他的事，並不一定是在學習英文）

例 "What is **Paul doing** these days?" "He **is writing** his book."

「Paul 這幾天在做什麼?」「他正在寫他的書。」（Paul 這陣子在寫書，但說話的當下 Paul 可能在做其他的事，並不一定是拿著筆在寫書。）

★ 表達意見時不可使用現在進行式

例 I **like** pop music. (*NOT* ~~I am liking pop music.~~)

我喜歡流行樂。

例 She **believes** he is right. (*NOT* ~~She is believing he is right.~~)

她相信他是對的。

★ 「簡單現在式」vs.「現在進行式」

--簡單現在式可說明重複的動作；現在進行式說明正在進行的動作

例 Stacy **goes** to the gym three times a week.

Stacy 一週去健身房三次。

例 Stacy **is going to** the gym now.

Stacy 正前往健身房。

--簡單現在式可說明某個情況或例行工作是永久的；現在進行式說明某個情況或例行工作是短暫進行的

例 I **work** at a restaurant.

我在一間餐廳工作。

例 I **am working** at a restaurant for three months.

我在一間餐廳工作三個月。

Life Story

The public knows Onika Tanya Maraj by her stage name Nicki Minaj. She was born in 1982 and is of mixed Indian and Afro-Trinidadian ancestry. Nicki didn't have a sweet childhood as her parents were frequently fighting during this time. Meanwhile, her father suffered from alcohol and drug addictions, and once even set their house on fire in an attempt to kill Nicki's mother. Perhaps this was the reason that Minaj lived her life through characters she created as a way of escape. She recalls that she had different identities such as "Barbie", "Rosa" and "Roman Zalanski".

❶When on TV, Nicki is usually wearing outlandish costumes, cosmetics, and, wigs. She wants people, especially girls, to know that in life nothing is going to be based on sex appeal. She also suggests women treat themselves like bosses and not allow people to run anything for them without their knowledge. It is said that Minaj's biography is going to be published soon. ❷The whole world is now looking forward to reading this book and eager to know more about this singer and her words of wisdom.

對於歐妮卡‧譚雅‧馬拉，大眾較為熟知的是她的藝名妮琪‧米娜。她在 1982 年出生，是印度人與非洲裔特里尼達人後代。妮琪並沒有一個愉快的童年，因為她的父母時常爭吵。同時，她的父親不僅酗酒，吸毒，並且曾經試圖縱火殺死她的母親。也許這就是為何妮琪當時創造出多重人格來做為逃避生活的方式。她回憶她所創造的人格有「芭比」、「羅莎」和「羅曼‧左倫斯基」。

妮琪上電視時，大部分的時間都穿著古怪的服裝、畫著古怪的妝及戴著古怪的假髮。她想讓人們，尤其是女孩們知道，人生沒有一件事是需要靠著性別的吸引力的。她也建議女性們要當自己的主人，不能讓別人在自己不知情的情況下為自己做決定。據說妮琪的自傳即將要出版了。全世界都正在期待這本書，迫切的想知道更多關於這位歌手的事以及她智慧的言語。

● ancestry [ˈænsɛstrɪ] **n** 血統　● wig [wɪg] **n** 假髮

Sentence Show ★

❶ When on TV, Nicki is usually wearing outlandish costumes, cosmetics, and wigs.

這裡使用「現在進行式」(is wearing) 而不用「簡單現在式」(wears) 是因為妮琪只有在電視上露面的時候打扮古怪,是一個暫時的現象而非永久的情況。

❷ The whole world is now looking forward to reading this book and eager to know more about this singer and her words of wisdom.

妮琪的自傳目前尚未出版,故期待能讀到這本書的這件事目前「正在發生」,所以這裡使用「現在進行式」(is looking forward to) 來表示這件事是全世界現在「正在期待」的事。

 **Practice Time** ★

Q1:米娜目前正住在紐約。

_____.

Q2:看!狗仔們正在拍妮琪・米娜的照片!

_____.

Q1 Ans:At the moment, Nicki Minaj is living in New York.

Q2 Ans:Look! Paparazzi are taking photos of Nicki Minaj!

Unit 03
現在完成式

"I have never been ❶afraid to ask for help."
—— Naomi Campbell 娜歐蜜・坎貝爾

（我從來不怕開口請求協助。）

❶ afraid [ə`fred] **adj** 害怕的

在這個短短的句子中，娜歐蜜・坎貝爾使用的是現在完成式 ("have never been afraid") 的時態，表達的是她「人生中曾有的經驗」。除了這個用法外，其他現在完成式的使用時機，請看下一個部分的說明和例句。

 **Grammar Show** ★

現在完成式 (Present Perfect Tense) 的肯定句形式為"主詞 + have /has + 過去分詞"，否定句形式為"主詞 + have / has not+ 過去分詞"。使用的時機和句例如下。

❶ 過去的某個動作到現在已經完成

例 I **have finished** my lunch.

我已經吃完我的午餐了。（吃午餐的動作從過去開始做，到現在已完成了）

❷ 人生中曾有的經驗

例 I **have seen** pandas in China.

我曾在中國看過熊貓。

例 He has not done any interesting things in his life.

在他一生從未做過任何有趣的事。

3 從過去累積到現在的經驗

例 My sister **has lived** aboard for many years.

我的妹妹已經在國外住了很多年了。

★ 現在完成式的疑問句型 "Have / Has + 主詞 (ever) + 過去分詞…?" 常用來詢問人是否有過某一種經驗

例 **Have you ever met** a famous person?

你有見過名人嗎？

★ "just", "already"和"yet"常與現在完成式一起使用

例 I **have just remembered** today is his birthday.

我剛想起來今天是他的生日。

例 Her boyfriend **has already left** her.

她的男友已經離開她了。

例 **Has** Jimmy **contacted** you **yet**?

Jimmy 聯絡你了嗎？

★ 表示時間的"for+一段時間"和"since+時間點"也常和現在完成式一起使用

例 Mother **has not had** a vacation **for quite a while**.

母親已經有好一陣子沒有去度假了。

例 I **have not seen** my uncle **since last month**.

我從上個月就沒看見我叔叔。

★ have / has gone to vs. have / has been to

例 Kevin **has gone to** London. He is having a great holiday.

Kevin 已經去了倫敦。他正在享受假期。（Kevin 仍在倫敦）

例 Kevin **has been to** London. He went there last winter.

Kevin 去過倫敦。他是去年冬天去的。（Kevin 有去過倫敦，但現在人並不在倫敦）

Life Story

Technically speaking, Naomi Campbell is not the first person that comes to mind when you are asked to name a celebrity. She is a model-turned-humanitarian reality TV star and mogul.

Although she is renowned for her bad temper, she is actually a very kind and generous person. For many years, she has been committed to the charity work of "Fashion For Relief," which to date has raised over five million pounds. Moreover, she stands up for what she believes in. Only few people know that ❶she has been offered jobs, by companies that supported apartheid, many times during her 25-year-plus modeling career. However, ❷she has never taken one of them because she is not going to work against her people. Instead of the word "irritable", she prefers to be called "bossy". This is because she doesn't like to lose. She likes to be sure that everything is under control. If she is told "no", she will always find another way to get her "yes".

嚴格來說,當你被要求說出一個名人的名字時,娜歐蜜‧坎貝爾不會是第一個你會想到的人。她從模特兒轉為慈善家及實境秀明星的大人物。

雖然她以壞脾氣著稱,但她其實是個既善良又慷慨的人。多年來,她已經由「流行為了慰藉」進行她的慈善工作,至今已募款超過五百萬英鎊。此外,她也是個支持自己信念的人。僅有少數人知道,在她 25 年多的職業生涯裡,她有多次被支持種族隔離政策的公司提供工作機會。然而,她從未接受過任何一個工作邀約,因為她不願意做不利於同胞的事。比起「易怒的」這個詞,她更喜歡被說是「愛發號施令的」。這是因為她不喜歡輸,她喜歡確保每件事都在掌握之中。如果有人對她說「不」,她總是會找到其他的方法得到正面的答案。

- celebrity [sɪˋlɛbrətɪ] **n** 名人 • humanitarian [hjuˏmænəˋtɛrɪən] **n** 慈善家
- charity [ˋtʃærətɪ] **n** 慈善 • apartheid [əˋpɑrtˏhet] **n** 種族隔離政策
- irritable [ˋɪrətəb!] **adj** 易怒的

Sentence Show ★

❶ She has been offered jobs, by companies that supported apartheid, many times during her 25- year-plus modeling career.

此處的現在完成式"She has been offered jobs, by companies that supported apartheid, …"表示的是一個「從過去到現在的經驗」，即娜歐蜜‧坎貝爾「從開始當模特兒到現在 25 年多的期間」一直有被支持種族隔離政策的公司邀約工作。

❷ She has never taken one of them because she is not going to work against her people.

現在完成式"she has never taken one of them…"表示了「過去到現在的經驗並且還有可能會繼續下去」。娜歐蜜從以前就被上述公司提供工作機會，但她「從過去到現在一直都沒有接受，而未來也可能不會接受」。

 Practice Time ★

Q1：娜歐蜜已經當了 25 年的模特兒。

_____.

Q2：娜歐蜜的慈善工作已經做多久了？

_____.

Q1 Ans：Naomi has been a model for 25 years.

Q2 Ans：How long has Naomi done her charity work?

Unit 04
現在完成進行式

❝ People are under the ❶illusion that every woman who has been successful must have been being controlled by a man. But I am the boss. ❞

—— Lily Allen 莉莉‧艾倫

（人們仍然有這種錯覺，就是每個已成功的女人背後一定有個一直控制她的男人。但我才是主人。）

❶ illusion [ɪˈljuʒən] n 錯覺

　　此句中的現在完成進行式"...have been being controlled..."表示一個從過去到現在還持續進行的動作；依照句中的意思，則是指「被男人控制」的這個動作還在持續進行中（但莉莉‧艾倫覺得這只是人們的錯覺）。

Grammar Show ★

　　現在完成進行式 (Present Perfect Progressive Tense) 用來表示「一個動作或是事件從過去的一個時間點開始，一直持續到現在，並且還在進行中」，其用法和句例如下：

❶ 肯定句：**"主詞 + have /has been+Ving+ (受詞)"**

　例 She **has been waiting** here for one hour.

　　她已經在這裡等了一小時了。

　　（從她開始等待的時間點開始，她已經等了一小時，並且還持續在等待）

Unit 04 現在完成進行式

例 The fire alarm **has been ringing** since ten o'clock this morning.

火災警報器從今早十點就一直在響。

例 The workers **have been digging** the garden.

工人們一直在花園挖掘。

2 否定句：**"主詞 + have / has not + been +Ving+ (受詞)"**

例 I **have not been doing** anything since this morning.

我從早上到現在就一直無所事事。

（無所事事的狀態從早上的時間點開始持續到現在，並且還在進行）

例 Mark **has not been working** for many years.

Mark 已經很多年沒有工作了。

例 Ellen **has not been taking** medicine for the last few days.

Ellen 從過去幾天開始就沒在服藥了。

3 疑問句：**"Have / Has +主詞+ been +Ving+ (受詞) ?"**

例 **Have you been taking** care of the garden since you moved to this house?

你從搬進這個房子就一直在整理這個花園嗎？

（整理花園的動作是否從搬進花園的時間點持續到現在呢？）

例 **Have you been waiting** for me since 5:00?

妳從五點開始就在等我了嗎？

例 **Has Tony been working** hard recently?

Tony 最近有認真工作嗎？

105

Life Story

In May 2014, 29-year-old Lily Allen released her latest album *She-ezus* and officially made a comeback to the music industry. Four years after she "retired" and "disappeared" into family life with her husband and two children. It is said that pop culture has changed. More specifically, in Lily's own words, ❶"Over these years, it has been becoming duller and more brutally judgmental than ever."

❷Although music publishing has been expecting Lily's new work for a long time, the feedback from the public was not so positive. She tried to awake women to their self-awareness by writing lyrics like "You'll find me in the studio and not in the kitchen" in her single *Hard Out Here*. However, people, mostly women, criticized the video for racism. Moreover, her other singles were also deemed "pop rubbish". Of course, Lily felt sad about this, especially being hit back down by her own sex, but she just left these unpleasant comments behind. "People have got their own agendas these days," she decided, "but the radio stations won't play the better stuff anyway."

2014 年 5 月，29 歲的莉莉‧艾倫發行了她最新的專輯「怪怪女教主」，同時正式回歸音樂界。在她「退休」與丈夫及兩個孩子相處的四年裡，流行文化被認為已經有了改變。更確切一點的用莉莉自己的話說：「是這些年它已經較以往變得更無趣也更殘忍嚴苛了。」

雖然樂界出版商已經等待莉莉的新作許久，但之後來自於大眾的回饋並不理想。莉莉在「生存之道」這首歌中寫下歌詞如：「你會發現我在錄音室裡，而不在廚房裡」，試圖喚醒女性的自我意識。然而，人們，大多數為女性，卻批評這首歌的 MV 帶有種族主義色彩；此外，她的其他單曲也被視為「流行垃圾」。莉莉當然對這些評價很傷心，尤其是還被同性背棄。但她將這些不快置之腦後，並說：「現在人們都有自己的意見，但不管怎樣，電台也沒有播出過比我更好的作品。」

● comeback [ˋkʌmˌbæk] **n** 重整旗鼓　● dull [dʌl] **adj** 乏味的

Sentence Show ★

❶ Over these years, it has been becoming duller and more brutally judgmental than ever.

此句中的主詞"it"代指的是上文中的"pop culture"（流行文化）。本句使用現在完成進行式說明流行文化從莉莉·艾倫宣佈「退休」的時間點開始變得比以前無趣與嚴苛，而這個情況一直持續到現在都還是這樣。

❷ Although music publishing has been expecting Lily's new work for a long time, the feedback from the public was not so positive

現在完成進行式"has been waiting"表達出從莉莉「退休」的時間點開始，唱片出版業已經持續進行這個「期待」的動作一陣子；"for a long time"（一段時間）即說明這個等待的時間。

 Practice Time ★

Q1：莉莉從青少年時期就一直在寫歌。

_____.

Q2：莉莉最近一直覺得不大舒服。

_____.

Q1 Ans：Lily has been writing songs since she was a teenager.

Q2 Ans：Lily hasn't been feeling very well recently.

Unit 05
簡單過去式

" I ❶worked my butt off to ❷prove to any ❸doubters that I was the man for the job. "
—— Sam Claflin 山姆・克拉弗林

（我很努力地向每一個懷疑我的人證明，我就是這個工作的不二人選。）

❶ work sb's butt off **ph** 很努力地（做一件事）　　❷ prove [pruv] **v** 證明
❸ doubter [`dɑʊtɚ] **n** 保持懷疑態度的人

　　有時候坐而言不如起而行。山姆・克拉弗林這句話中使用了「過去式」"I worked my butt off "，表示「努力工作（誇飾用法，屁股都磨光了）」的這個動作在當時已經完成了，所以之後他可以以此向懷疑他的人證明，他確實有接演這部電影的實力。

Grammar Show

　　簡單過去式 (Simple Past Tense) 用來表示「一個動作或是事件發生在過去，並且現在已經結束了」。使用方式和句例如下。

❶ 肯定句："主詞 + 動詞過去式 + (受詞)"

　　例 The organizer **cancelled** the event last Sunday because of the bad weather.

　　主辦單位上星期日因為天候不佳，取消這個活動。（取消的動作已在上週日完成）

例 I **reminded** you about this term when you booked the ticket.

當你在訂票時，我已經跟你提醒過這個注意事項了。

2 否定句：**"主詞 + did not + 原型動詞 + (受詞)"**

例 The bus **didn't come** until 10:00 this morning.

巴士直到今早 10 點才抵達。（在早上 10 點前抵達的動作並沒有完成）

例 Amanda **didn't cook** last night.

Amanda 昨晚沒有煮飯。

3 疑問句：**"Did+主詞+ 原型動詞+ (受詞) ?"**

例 **Did you clean** the room last weekend?

妳上週末有整理房間嗎？

例 **Did they order** pizza last Saturday while watching the football game?

他們上星期六看足球時有訂 pizza 吃嗎？

★ 「現在完成式」vs. 「簡單過去式」

--「現在完成式」說明過去和現在的情況；而「簡單過去式」只說明過去情況，不會知道現在的情況。

例 Linda **has packed** her suitcase.

Linda 已經整理好她的行李。（行李現在已經整理好了）

例 Linda **packed** her suitcase last night.

Linda 昨晚整理了她的行李。（行李昨晚整理好了，但現在不知道是不是還是整齊）

--「現在完成式」不可與時間點（如：yesterday, last month ）搭配使用。

(X) They **have bought** the house **last year**.

(O) They **bought** the house **last year**.

他們去年買了房子。

Life Story

Although he had appeared as the missionary, Phillip Swift, in the 2011 Hollywood blockbuster *Pirates of the Caribbean: On Stranger Tides*, ❶things did not go well when he was cast as Finnick Odair from the second installment of *the Hunger Games* film series, *The Hunger Games: Catching Fire*. There were many people who doubted whether he would be a suitable candidate for this part. Since these negative comments were everywhere, Claflin himself couldn't help but come across them at the time. ❷Instead of sitting there and being upset by those unpleasant words, he stood up to prove himself. The glowing reviews afterwards showed he was certainly the right man for the job.

Apart from being a hard-working, young actor, he is also a romantic husband who sees marriage as his greatest achievement and his wife as his muse. He often says he falls harder and deeper in love with his wife every second he looks at her. He is such a handsome, charming and talented man. It is no wonder that many women always complain why all the good men are taken.

雖然他曾在 2011 年賣座電影《加勒比海盜 神鬼奇航：幽靈海》中扮演傳教士菲利普・斯威夫特，但當他被選為擔綱《飢餓遊戲》第二集《飢餓遊戲：星火燎原》中的芬尼克・歐戴爾一角時，事情並沒有因此很順利。很多人質疑他是否是這個角色的合適人選。因為這些負面的評論鋪天蓋地，克拉弗林自己也無法漠視。但他沒有坐在那為這些不開心的言語神傷，而是站起來證明自己。隨後贊揚的影評也表示他的確是這個角色的正確人選。

除了是位努力的年輕演員外，他也是個浪漫的丈夫；他總是視婚姻為他最偉大的成就，而妻子則是他的繆斯女神。他常說，每一秒鐘看到他的妻子，都感覺對她的愛越多越深。他是一個如此英俊、迷人且有才華的男人；也難怪許多女人常抱怨為什麼所有的好男人都有另一半了。

● missionary [`mɪʃən‚ɛrɪ] n 傳教士　● installment [ɪn`stɔlmənt] n 連載

Sentence Show ★

❶ Things did not go well when he was cast as Finnick Odair from the second installment of *the Hunger Games* film series, *The Hunger Games: Catching Fire.*

在原文中，這句話描述的是過去發生的事，但有些人可能會疑惑：「為什麼動詞 go 並沒有改成過去式 went？」這是因為這裡使用的是否定句型；而簡單過去式的否定為："did not + 原型動詞"，故此處使用"go"而不使用"went"。

❷ Instead of sitting there and being upset by those unpleasant words, he stood up to prove himself.

"stand up"為一個片語，有「脫穎而出」的意思。依上下文此處應該使用過去式，故將原型動詞"stand"改為過去式"stood"。

 Practice Time ★

Q1：山姆不在乎那些負面評論。

_____.

Q2：山姆原本想當足球員

_____.

Q1 Ans：Sam didn't care about those negative comments.

Q2 Ans：Sam wanted to be a footballer before.

Unit 06
過去進行式

"I was watching Up In The Air and I thought, "Jesus, who's the old **❶**gray-haired guy?" And it was me. However, I am **❷**kind of comfortable with getting older because it's better than the other option, which is being dead."

—— George Clooney 喬治・庫隆尼

（當我某天正在看《型男飛行日誌》時，我想著：「天啊！那個灰頭髮的老傢伙是誰？」結果那是我自己。然而，我還是有點喜歡變老的，因為這比死亡這個選項更好一些。）

❶ gray [gre] adj 灰色的　**❷** kind of ph 有一點

　　曾經是黃金單身漢的喬治庫隆尼以幽默的方式說出了對「年紀增長」的見解，而我們確實也看到他至今仍是保持一頭灰 。第一句裡出現的「過去進行式」 "was watching" 表示看影片的這個動作在當時是一個「正在進行的動作」。

Grammar Show

　　過去進行式 (Past Progressive Tense)，用來表示「在過去某個時間點正在發生的動作或事情」。過去進行式常和表示過去時間的片語或子句合用。

❶ 肯定句: **"主詞 + 過去式 be 動詞 + Ving+ (受詞)"**

例 He **was making** coffee when the postman rang the doorbell.

當郵差按門鈴時,他正在煮咖啡。(在門鈴響的時間點,煮咖啡的動作正在進行。)

*注意在表示時間點的子句中,動詞需使用簡單過去式

例 The owner **was closing** the shop when we arrived there.

我們抵達時,老闆正在關門。(抵達的時間點,關門的動作正在進行)

❷ 否定句: **"主詞 + wasn't/weren't + Ving+ (受詞)"**

例 She **was not telling** the truth when her mother asked her what happened yesterday.

當她媽媽問她昨天發生什麼事時,她並沒有說實話。

例 We **were not doing** our homework in the living room when Father came back.

昨天當爸爸回來時,我們並沒有在客廳寫作業。

❸ 疑問句: **"Was/Were +主詞+Ving+ (受詞) ?"**

例 **Were you cooking** when I called you last night?

我昨晚打電話給你時,你正在煮飯嗎?

例 **Were they playing** baseball when the storm started yesterday?

昨天暴風雨開始時,他們正在打棒球嗎?

★ 「簡單過去式」vs.「過去進行式」

例 I **ate** an apple.

我吃了一個蘋果。(吃蘋果的這個動作已經結束完成了)

例 I **was eating** an apple.

我當時正在吃一個蘋果。(吃蘋果的動作在當時還在進行,尚未完成)

Life Story

Many people first recognize George Clooney from the long-running medical drama ER, for which he played Dr. Doug Ross and received two-Emmy Award nominations. Moreover, he is one of three people that has been given the title of "Sexiest Man Alive" twice by *People* Magazine. Ever since he divorced the actress Talia Balsam in 1993, he has been seen as a playboy. ❶While the public was still wondering whether he would ever be married again, he announced his engagement to the British-Lebanese human rights lawyer Amal Alamuddin on April 28, 2014.

In fact, Clooney is not just a pretty face. He is also noted for his political activism. ❷He opposed the Iraq war while the United States was leading an occupation force in Iraq between 2003 and 2011. According to him, people shouldn't beat their enemy through wars; instead they only create an entire generation of people seeking revenge. Furthermore, he is also a supporter of gay rights. Perhaps these explain why Clooney was named one of *Time* magazine's "100 Most Influential People in the World" three times.

很多人第一次知道喬治・庫隆尼這個演員，是經由長青劇《急診室的春天》裡道格羅斯醫生的這個角色；同時他也憑藉著這個角色獲得兩次艾美獎提名。此外，他也是曾經兩度獲得《人物》雜誌「現今最性感的男人」頭銜的三個人之一。自從他在 1993 年與女演員塔莉亞・芭珊離婚後，他就被視為是個花花公子。正當許多人猜測他是否還會再婚時，他在 2014 年 4 月 28 日宣佈了與英籍黎巴嫩人，同時也是人權律師的艾默・阿拉穆丁訂婚的消息。

事實上，庫隆尼並不單只是長得帥而已。他同時也因對政治積極參與的態度而著名。當美國在 2003 至 2011 年對伊拉克發動侵略性武力攻擊時，他對此表示反對。他認為人們不應該透過戰爭來打擊敵人，因為這只會讓整個民族的下一代產生報復心理。此外，他也是同志人權的擁護者。也許就是這些原因，讓他登上《時代》雜誌「世界上最有影響力的 100 個人」排行榜 3 次的原因。

Sentence Show ★

❶ While the public was still wondering whether he would ever be married again, he announced his engagement to the British-Lebanese human rights lawyer Amal Alamuddin on April 28, 2014.

這裡 "While the public was still wondering... he announced his engagement ..."說明了在他「宣佈訂婚」的這個時刻，大眾的猜疑這件事正在發生。而使用過去進行式表達了「猜疑」這個動作的持續。

❷ He opposed the Iraq war while the United States was leading an occupation force in Iraq between 2003 and 2011.

這裡過去進行式說明美國在 2003 年至 2011 年間，「正對伊拉克使用侵略性的武力攻擊」（而對此正在進行的事件，庫隆尼是表達反對的）。

 Practice Time ★

Q1：庫隆尼在 2003 年正在做什麼？

_____.

Q2：當某些人正在說些對同志不利的事時，庫隆尼卻募款支持同志權利運動。

_____.

Q1 Ans： What was Clooney doing in 2003?

Q2 Ans： While some people were saying things against gays, Clooney raised money to support the gay rights movement.

Unit 07
過去完成式

"I think it is important to have closure in any relationship that ends — from a romance to a friendship. You should always have a sense of ❶clarity at the end and know why it began and why it ended. You need that in your life to move cleanly into your next phase. Finally, I realized I had possessed this sense all my life."

—— Jennifer Aniston 珍妮佛‧安妮斯頓

（我覺得無論是愛情或友情，當一段關係結束時，有一個終止的動作是很重要的。你應該很清楚地知道一段關係如何開始和如何結束。你的人生中需要有這種體悟，讓你能乾脆地向前邁進下一個階段。最後，我領悟到，我在生活中已經有這份體認。）

❶ clarity [ˋklærətɪ] n（思想）清晰

　　這句名言的最後一句中，「過去完成式」"had possessed this sense all my life"這個動作（有這份體認）在珍妮佛‧安妮斯頓敘述她「領悟到」（過去式動詞 "realized"）她有這份體認前就已經發生。

 *Grammar Show* ★

1 **過去完成式 (Past Perfect Tense)**

可用來表示「在過去某個時間已經完成的動作或經驗」，其肯定形式為"had +過去分詞"，否定形式為 "had+ not +過去分詞"。過去完成式通常會與過去式搭配，用來表達在過去發生的兩件事情的先後順序；先發生的事情用「過去完成式」，後發生的事情則用「過去簡單式」表達。一般而言，使用過去完成式的機會較小，以下由一段敘述說明過去完成式的使用例句。

例 When Luke left home this morning, he wasn't feeling very awake. He **hadn't slept** very well. He **had walked** about a mile when he realized he **had forgotten** his mobile. **Had** he **left** it in the office the day before, or **had** he **left** it at home?

當 Luke 今早離開家時，他還不是很清醒。他沒有睡好。在他走了一哩路後，他才發現他的手機沒在身上。他是前一天把手機留在辦公室了呢？還是留在家裡了？

2 「現在完成式」vs.「過去完成式」

現在完成式說明持續現在的情況；過去完成式說明在過去某個時間點之前的情況。

例 The match is over. Newcastle **has won.**

比賽結束了。Newcastle 已經贏了。（比賽「現在」結束，Newcastle 到「現在」的這個時間點是贏的）

例 The match was over. Newcastle **had won.**

比賽已經結束了。Newcastle 已經贏了。（比賽在「過去」某個時間點結束，而 Newcastle 在「過去」的那個時間點是贏的。）

3 「簡單過去式」vs.「過去完成式」

例 When we arrived, they all **left.**

當我們到達時，他們走了。（我們到了，他們走了）

例 When we arrived, they **had** all **left.**

當我們到達時，他們已經走了。（他們在我們到達前就走了）

Life Story

Jennifer Aniston gained worldwide recognition for the character Rachel Green in the television soap *Friends* between 1994 and 2004. **❶By the time the program ended, she had already won several awards, such as Emmy and Golden Globe playing this role.** Fans are fascinated with her lovely smile, great personality and effortlessly beautiful hairstyle. She has frequently appeared on *People's annual list* of The Most Beautiful and once was voted by *Men's Health* as the "Sexiest Woman of All Time".

Aniston married Brad Pitt in 2000. The marriage was considered as the rare Hollywood success for a few years. Therefore, it was hard for people to believe when the marriage ended in divorce in 2005. **❷During this period, there was intense speculation in the media that Pitt had been unfaithful to Aniston with his *Mr. & Mrs. Smith* co-star, Angelina Jolie.** No matter what the real reason for the divorce was, Aniston never said anything behind Pitt's back. In addition, she always says she never regrets the relationship with Pitt because she thinks it was "seven very intense years together" and that "it was a beautiful, complicated relationship."

珍妮佛・安妮斯頓因演出 1994 年到 2004 年的肥皂劇《六人行》，而為人熟知。在這個節目結束的時候，她已經因為演出這個角色而獲得了許多獎項，如：艾美獎及金球獎等。粉絲們對她甜美的笑容、美好的個性以及不費力的美麗髮型感到著迷。她經常出現在《人物》雜誌年度「最美麗的人」排行榜上，某次還被《男性健康》雜誌票選為「從以前到現在最性感的女性」。

她在 2000 年嫁給布萊德・彼特。在幾年的時間裡，這段婚姻被認為是好萊塢裡罕見的成功。因此，當這段婚姻在 2005 年以離婚告結時，很多人都覺得無法相信。當時，媒體們強烈懷疑彼特背著安妮斯頓跟合演《史密斯夫婦》的安潔莉娜・裘莉秘密交往。不管離婚的真實原因是什麼，安妮斯頓從未在背後說過彼特的壞話。此外，她總是說她對這段感情並不後悔，因為這是「7 年情感濃烈的時光」，是「一段美好且複雜的關係」。

Sentence Show ★

❶ By the time the program ended, she had already won several awards, such as Emmy and Golden Globe playing this role.

前一句描述了《六人行》影集在 1994 年至 2004 年間播出，而，「贏得許多獎項」的動作在影集結束前發生了，故使用過去完成式"had won"。

❷ During this period, there was intense speculation in the media that Pitt had been unfaithful to Aniston with his Mr. & Mrs. Smith co-star, Angelina Jolie.

從「簡單過去式」("there was intense speculation in the media") 和「過去完成式」("Pitt had been unfaithful to Aniston") 的時態使用推測，在媒體們強烈懷疑之前，彼特不忠的事就已經發生了。

 **Practice Time** ★

Q1：珍妮佛·安妮斯早在飛機起飛之前，就抵達機場了。

_____.

Q2：珍妮佛·安妮斯頓很晚才到派對。所有的賓客早就都回家了。

_____.

Q1 Ans： Jennifer Aniston had arrived at the airport before the flight left.

Q2 Ans： Jennifer Aniston arrived very late at the party. All guests had already gone home.

Unit 08
過去完成進行式

> That's the way I used to look at things — if you had been focusing on the worst [1]scenario before it took place, you would have lived twice when it really happened. It sounds like [2]Polly-anna-ish [3]tripe but I'm telling you — it works for me.
>
> —— Michael J. Fox 米高・福克斯

（這是我過去經常看事情的方法：如果你在最壞的情況發生前就一直想著這件事，那麼當它真的發生時，你就等同於經歷了兩次。這聽起來有點像盲目的樂觀主義者的廢話，但我告訴你，這招對我很管用。）

❶ scenario [sɪˋnɛrɪˏo] 🔘 局面　❷ Pollyanna [ˏpɑlɪˋænə] 🔘 盲目樂觀之人
❸ tripe [traɪp] 🔘 廢話

　　"if you had been focusing on the worst scenario before it took place…" 過去完成進行式had been focusing 說明focus的這個動作在the worst scenario發生時已持續一段時間。

Grammar Show

　　過去完成進行式 (Past Perfect Progressive Tense) 指的是「一個動作在過去某事件發生前，已經持續了一段時間了，而該動作在此事件的當下仍持續進行中」。故過去完成進行式通常用來表示在過去發生的兩件事情的先後順序，較早發生的動作用「過去完成進行式」，後發生的事件則用「過去簡單式」表達。詳細說明及例句如下：

1 肯定句：**"主詞 + had been+ Ving+ (受詞)"**

例 I **had been working** on this project before he joined us.

當他加入我們團隊時，我已經負責這個計劃了。（「負責計劃」的動作先發生，之後他加入團隊）

例 My sister **had been living** in New York when 911 happened.

我的姊姊在 911 事件發生之前，已經住在紐約。（「住在紐約」的動作先發生，之後 911 事件發生）

2 否定句：**"主詞 + had been+ not + Ving+ (受詞)"**

例 Kate got a job yesterday. She **had not been doing** anything since she graduated from high school.

Kate 昨天找到工作了。她自從高中畢業後就沒有在工作。

例 I **had not been waiting** long.

我沒有等太久。

3 疑問句：**"had+主+ been+ Ving + (受詞)?"**

例 **Had you been cleaning the house** most of the morning?

你早上大部分的時間都在打掃家裡嗎？

例 The floor was wet. **Had it been raining**?

地上是濕的。有下過雨嗎？

 **Life Story**

Sometimes you may find an old movie called *Back to the Future* on a cable channel. The adorable leading actor of the movie, Michael J. Fox, is now fifty-three years old. ❶He was diagnosed with Parkinson's disease in 1991 but had been keeping his illness secret before he finally disclosed it to the public in 1998.

Parkinson's disease is a degenerative disorder of the central nervous system. The symptoms include shaking, slowness of movement and difficulty with walking. Fox started to show these symptoms before being properly diagnosed later. After his diagnosis, he refused to accept the result at first. ❷He had been drinking heavily because he was upset. Thankfully, he sought help and stopped drinking altogether. He even built a foundation to help advance any promising research, which is related to a possible way of curing Parkinson's disease. "In fact, Parkinson's has made me a better person. A better husband, father and overall human being," he said.

　　有時候你也許會在有線電視頻道上看到一齣名為《回到未來》的電影。劇中可愛的男主角米高‧福克斯現在已經 53 歲了。他在 1991 年時被診斷出帕金森氏症，但一直隱瞞這個消息，直到 1998 年才向大眾公開。

　　帕金森氏症是一種中樞神經退化及不協調的疾病。其症狀包含：抖動、動作緩慢和行走困難。福克斯在完全確診之前，就已經出現了這些症狀。在得知診斷結果後，他一開始拒絕接受這個結果。因為情緒的低落，他一直嚴重酗酒。幸好，他尋求了幫助，也同時戒了酒。他甚至創立了基金會，幫助促進任何可能治癒帕金森氏症的研究。他說：「事實上，帕金森氏症讓我變成了一個更好的人。更好的丈夫、父親以及更完整的人。」

- adorable [ə`dorəbl] **adj** 可愛的
- diagnose [`daɪəgnoz] **V** 診斷
- degenerative [dɪ`dʒɛnəˌretɪv] **adj** 退化的
- symptom [`sɪmptəm] **n** 症狀

Sentence Show ★

❶ He was diagnosed with Parkinson's disease in 1991 but had been keeping his illness secret before he finally disclosed it to the public in 1998.

在這句話中，首先，米高・福克斯在 1991 年被診斷出帕金森氏症；之後，在 1998 年向大眾公開病症之前，他一直是隱瞞病情的。「過去完成進行式」 "had been keeping his illness secret" 表示這個隱瞞病情的動作在 1998 年之前，已經持續了一段時間。

❷ He had been drinking heavily because he was upset.

在之後米高・福克斯尋求幫助之前，他一直因為心情低落而酗酒。「過去完成進行式」"had been drinking heavily"表示嚴重酗酒的動作在當時持續的進行。

 Practice Time ★

Q1：米高・福克斯過去一直很努力工作。

_____.

Q2：你這個下午大部分的時間都在看米高・福克斯的電影嗎？

_____.

Q1 Ans： Michael J. Fox had been working very hard.

Q2 Ans： Had you been watching Michael J. Fox's films most of the afternoon?

Unit 09
簡單未來式

> I am going to do what I want to do. I am going to be who I really am. I am going to [1]figure out what that is.

—— Emma Watson 愛瑪・華森

（我將會做我想做的事。我將會成為我真正樣子的人。我將會弄清楚那是什麼。）

❶ figure out ph 想出

　　愛瑪・華森這幾句話裡使用的是「未來式」"be going to"的形式，說明這些事不是她現在要做的，而是她在「未來打算進行的計劃」。「未來式」的另一個表達形式為"will"，兩者的用法及異同請參看下個部分。

Grammar Show

　　簡單未來式 (Simple Future Tense) 有兩種表達形式："will"和"be going to"，但兩者在用法略有不同。"will"的文法形式為"will+原型動詞"，在使用上所代表的含義如下：

❶ 說明未來將發生或預言有可能發生的事

　　例 This time next month I **will** be in America.

　　　下個月的這個時候我會在美國。（這件事將發生）

例 Don't worry. You **will** pass the examination.

別煩惱。你會通過考試的。（「通過考試」這件事在未來有可能會發生）

2 在說話的當下決定做某事

例 It's noisy outside. I **will** shut the window. (*NOT* I̶ ̶s̶h̶u̶t̶ ̶t̶h̶e̶ ̶w̶i̶n̶-̶ ̶d̶o̶w̶.̶) 外面好吵。我要去關窗戶。

例 "Would you like some coffee or tea?" "I **will** have tea, please."

「你想喝點咖啡還是茶？」「麻煩你，我想要茶。」

"be going to" 的文法形式為"be going to+原型動詞"，在使用上亦有各不同含義：

1 預言可能發生的事

例 The sky is cloudy. It **is going** to rain.

天空烏雲密佈。快下雨了。

例 This is a good book. People **are going to** love it.

這是一本好書。人們將會愛它。

2 在說話的當下說明未來將進行的事

例 I **am going to** meet him after lunch.

我將在午餐後與他見面。

例 Peter **is going to** pay his rent tomorrow.

Peter 明天將付房租。

★ "will" vs. "be going to"

--"will"為預言「覺得將發生的事」；"be going to"為預言「根據現況覺得將發生的事」。

--當談論未來的安排或計劃時，一般不用"will"而用"be going to+原形動詞"或"be +Ving"的型式。

例 Stanley **is going to get/is getting** married next month.

(*NOT* S̶t̶a̶n̶l̶e̶y̶ ̶w̶i̶l̶l̶ ̶g̶e̶t̶ ̶m̶a̶r̶r̶i̶e̶d̶ ̶n̶e̶x̶t̶ ̶m̶o̶n̶t̶h̶.̶)

Stanley 下個月要結婚。

 **Life Story** ★

①The British actress Emma Watson will turn 25 years old next year. Beginning in 1999, fans all over the world have now watched her playing the character of Hermione Granger, the best friend of Harry Potter in the *Harry Potter* film series for almost a decade. Today, she is an award-winning actress, a fashion icon, and a successful model.

Now, you may like to know one or two things about this girl who was voted the Sexiest Female Movie Star by *Empire* magazine. First, she went to college even though she admitted that she is rich enough to retire. With a fortune over 10 million pounds, she actually could stay at home all day but she insisted on finishing her studies. Secondly, she likes doing art, especially painting people or faces. Thirdly, she keeps a diary every day. Lastly, **②her latest work, a thriller movie named *Regression,* is going to be released in 2015.**

英國演員愛瑪・華森明年將滿 25 歲。從 1999 年開始有將近 10 年的時間，全世界的影迷們都一路看著她在《哈利波特》系列電影中，扮演哈利・波特的好朋友妙麗・格蘭傑的角色。到今天，她已是一個獲獎的女演員、時尚的指標以及成功的模特兒。

現在，你也許會想知道關於這個被《帝國》雜誌票選為「最性感電影女星」的女孩的一兩件事。第一，即使她承認她的財富已夠她「退休」，她還是選擇上大學。有著超過 1 千萬英鎊的身價，她其實可以整天待在家，但她堅持要完成她的學業。第二，她喜歡做藝術相關活動，特別是畫人物及肖像。第三，她每天寫日記。最後，她最新的作品是一部驚悚電影《回歸》（暫譯），即將在 2015 年上映。

- decade [ˋdɛked] **n** 十年　　• icon [ˋaɪkɑn] **n** 偶像　　• insist [ɪnˋsɪst] **V** 堅持

- paint[pent] **V** 繪畫　　• diary [ˋdaɪərɪ] **n** 日記

Sentence Show ★

❶ The British actress Emma Watson will turn 25 years old next year.

此句中的「簡單現在式」"will"含有「未來將發生的事」之意，即愛瑪‧華森滿 25 歲是明年（未來）即將發生的事。

❷ Her latest work, a thriller movie named Regression, is going to be released in 2015.

逗號中間的"a thriller movie named *Regression*"只是全句的一個補充說明，說明愛瑪‧華森最新作品的內容。去掉這個補充說明的話，可以更清楚看出本句使用「簡單未來式」(Her latest work "is going to" be released in 2015) 表達「未來的安排和計劃」（2015 年她的最新作品即將被上映）。

 Practice Time ★

Q1：愛瑪‧華森下個月將會和導演碰面。

_____.

Q2：愛瑪‧華森在牛津時將會住在她母親家。

_____.

Q1 Ans：Emma Watson is going to meet the director next month.

Q2 Ans：Emma Watson will stay with her mother in Oxford.

Unit 10
未來進行式

❝ The day I can't be ❶daring in my work or the way I live my life, I will then not be living on this ❷planet. ❞

—— Madonna 瑪丹娜

（當我不能再放膽工作或自在生活的那天我將不會再活在這個星球上。）

❶ dare [dɛr] **V** 膽敢　❷ planet [`plænɪt] **n** 行星

　　瑪丹娜這句話也許稍顯極端，但重要的是告訴我們，我們應該更勇於表達自己。「未來進行式」用於表達「某事在未來某時刻仍持續進行」，這裡 "will not be living" 表示居住的動作在未來不會再持續進行。

Grammar Show

　　未來進行式 (Future Progressive Tense)，表達形式為 "will be +Ving"，通常其後會接一個表未來的時間副詞，使整句話意思更完整。用法及句例如下：

❶ 表示「一個在未來持續進行的動作」，即在未來的某刻，這個動作是在進行中的

　例 They **will be playing** volleyball at 6:00 pm today.

　　他們今天下午六點將會打排球。（在下午六點（未來）會持續打排球的動作）

　例 I guess it **will not be raining** soon.

　　我猜很快就不會再下雨了。（很快（未來）就不會有下雨這個持續動作了）

★ 「簡單未來式」vs.「未來進行式」

例 The band **will play** when the singer enters.

（歌手將入場，然後樂隊將會演奏）

例 The band **will be playing** when the singer enters.

（樂隊演奏的動作在歌星入場前便持續在進行）

2 表達一個例行公事或規律性的動作

例 My mother **will be cleaning** the house tomorrow. She always does it on Sunday.

我媽媽將會在明天打掃房子。她總是在週日打掃。

例 I **will be passing** your company this afternoon. It's on my way home from work.

我今天下午將會經過你的公司。這就在我下班回家的路上。

★ 「現在進行式」vs.「未來進行式」

例 He **is seeing** Emily tomorrow. They have arranged to meet.

（此處現在進行式表示「安排」）

他明天要見 Emily。他們有安排要見面。

例 He **will be seeing** Emily tomorrow. They live in the same neighborhood.（此處未來進行式表示「例行工作」）

他明天會去看 Emily。他們住在附近。

3 疑問句詢問某人的計劃是否符合我們的預期安排

例 **Will** you **be making** dinner if I visit you around 8:00 pm today?

如果我今晚 8:00 去你家拜訪，你會正在煮飯嗎？

 **Life Story**

Madonna has always been a controversial figure, whether it's her personal life or her music career. As a student, she was known for both her high grade point average and unconventional behavior. She often did cartwheels or handstands in the hallways, and sometimes even pulled up her skirt for boys to see her underwear. When she performed her Billboard hit *Like a Virgin* at the MTV Video Music Awardsin 1984, she appeared on stage wearing a wedding dress and white gloves, which offended many religionists.

❶"Will she be continuing to do what she likes to do when the day comes that critics disapprove of her attempts?" The answer would be positive. Apart from being a singer, Madonna has also taken jobs as an actress, a fashion designer and a child-book writer. She received both praise and harsh feedback for doing them. However, she knows exactly what she wants and is not afraid to say what she wants. ❷No matter what Madonna's next move is, we are sure she will definitely be living life in her way.

不管是她的私人生活或是音樂事業，瑪丹娜一直是一個有爭議性的人物。在學生時代，她以優異的成績和不符校規的行為而出名；她常在走廊表演翻跟斗和倒立，有時甚至拉高她的裙子，好讓男孩們可以看見她的底褲。而當她在 1984 年的 MTV 音樂錄音帶大獎上表演她告示牌熱門曲目《宛如處女》時，她穿著婚紗戴著戴著潔白的手套的裝扮惹惱了很多的宗教人士。

「當評論家們都反對她所做的嘗試時，她是將會繼續做她想做的事呢？」答案應該是肯定的。除了歌手的身份外，瑪丹娜也嘗試了演員、服裝設計師和童書作者的工作。在這些工作中，她同時獲得了讚美和嚴苛的批評。然而，她確切地知道自己想要什麼，也不害怕說出自己想要什麼。不管瑪丹娜的下一步是什麼，我們相信她將會以她想要的方式生活。

● controversial [ˌkɑntrəˋvɝˏʃəl] adj 受爭論的　● harsh [ˏharʃ] adj 嚴厲的

Sentence Show ★

❶ "Will she be continuing to do what she likes to do when the day comes that critics disapprove of her attempts?"

此處將「未來進行式」"will be + Ving"的形式以問句呈現。句中詢問，在「評論家們不支持她的嘗試的那天（未來的某一刻）」，她是否「將會繼續做她喜歡做的事（持續進行的動作）」。

❷ No matter what Madonna's next move is, we are sure she will definitely be living life in her way.

"will be living"為「未來進行式」，此處表示在瑪丹娜「有下一步的規劃時（未來的某個時刻）」，她「將以自己的方式生活」的這個動作將會進行著。

 **Practice Time** ★

Q1：你今晚將會聽瑪丹娜的歌嗎？

_____.

Q2：下週的這個時間，瑪丹娜將會在倫敦表演。

_____.

Q1 Ans：Will you be listening to Madonna's songs tonight?

Q2 Ans：This time next week Madonna will be performing in London.

Unit 11
未來完成式

You shouldn't have to ❶give things up for someone. If this person loves you, he or she should love you for everything you do. I love acting and will have acted for more than ten years next month. I wouldn't give it up for anything, and I don't know anyone in my life who would ask me to give up.

—— Lindsay Lohan 琳賽‧羅涵

（你不應該為了某人放棄某事。如果這個人愛你，他或她應該會愛你所做的每件事。我熱愛演戲，我將在下個月演戲超過十年。我不會為了任何事放棄演戲，而且我的生命裡沒認識任何人，會要求我放棄演戲。）

❶ give something up 【ph】放棄某事

　　琳賽‧羅涵這句落落長的名言是要提醒大家，真正愛你的人，是不會強迫你放棄你喜歡的事的。而句中的 "(I) will have acted for more than ten years next month." 為「未來完成式」的用法。表示她「演戲超過十年」的這個動作，將在未來下一個月 (next month) 的這個時間點之前完成。

 **Grammar Show** ★

　　未來完成式 (Future Perfect Tense)，可用來表示「某動作在未來某個時刻前將完成」。此時態通常需要搭配另一個表示未來某刻的時間副詞片語或子句，使句子更為完整。另外，該時間片語或子句的動詞需為簡單現在式。

❶ 肯定句： "主詞 **+ will have +** 過去分詞**+ (**受詞**)"**

例 Mary **will have worked** here for three years by the end of this year.

到今年年底時，Mary 即將在這裡工作滿三年。（到今年年底，工作滿三年的這個動作將完成。（之後有可能繼續也有可能不會繼續））

例 The programmers **will have completed** this special software by 2020.

在 2020 時，工程師將會完成這個特別的軟體。（2020 年時，研發這個軟體的動作將完成）

❷ 否定句： "主詞 **+ will+ not have +** 過去分詞**+ (**受詞**)"**

例 Nancy **will not have improved** her Chinese by the time she comes back from China.

Nancy 從中國回來的時候，她的中文將不會有進步。（中文進步的動作在回國的這個時刻還是不會完成，即中文到那時還是不會有進步）

例 I **will not have done** cleaning when Father arrives home.

當爸爸回到家時，我將不會打掃完成。（打掃的動作在未來（爸爸到家時）還是不會完成）

❸ 疑問句： "**Will +** 主詞 **have +** 過去分詞 **+ (**受詞**) ?"**

例 **Will** Mike **have learned** enough skills by the time he graduates from the school?

當 Mike 從學校畢業時，他將學會足夠的技術嗎？（學會足夠技術這件事，在未來（畢業時）會完成嗎？）

 **Life Story** ★

❶By the end of 2014, Lindsay Lonhan will have been in entertainment industry for twenty-five years. She made her on-screen debut in *The Parent Trap*, in which she played dual roles of twins separated in infancy. She then became audiences'favorite for about fifteen years. There was a time that we could find her cast in a number of Hollywood blockbusters, including *Freaky Friday*, *Mean Girls* and *Herbie*. Lonhan became a household name and a frequent focus of the press at the time.

Compared with the last two years, we now rarely see her on screen these days. Instead, we are more likely to read negative news about her in the press. She has been referred to as a "party girl" since 2006. Her night partying behavior has even caused her to havev various late arrivals and absences from sets. Moreover, she has been arrested several times because of her drinking and drug problems. Lonhan once said everyone has highs and lows to learn from. ❷Let's hope by the next time we see her, she will have learned her lesson and become the girl we used to love.

2014 年底時，琳賽・羅涵的演藝生涯將滿二十五年。她的銀幕處女作為《天生一對》，她在其中一人分飾兩角，演出一對在襁褓中即被分離的雙胞胎。之後的十五年，她成為了觀眾的最愛。有段時間我們能在各個好萊塢賣座電影，如：《辣媽辣妹》、《辣妹過招》和《瘋狂金龜車》裡看到她的身影。琳賽羅涵在當時成為了家喻戶曉的名字，也是媒體時常關注的對象。

相較於過去兩年，我們現在很少看到她出現在銀幕上。取而代之的是，更常讀到有關她的負面報導。從 2006 年開始，她就被視為是「夜店咖」。她夜夜笙歌的行為也導致她經常從拍攝現場遲到早退。此外，她也因為酗酒和嗑藥的問題被拘留很多次。她曾經說過，每個人都必須從自己高潮和低潮的時刻去學習。讓我們期望下次見到她時，她將能學到教訓並再次成為我們曾經喜愛的那個女孩。

● infancy [`ɪnfənsɪ] **n** 嬰兒時期　● household [`haʊsˌhold] **adj** 為人所熟知的

Sentence Show ★

❶ By the end of 2014, Lindsay Lonhan will have been in entertainment industry for twenty-five years.

「未來完成式」"will have acted"表示琳賽・羅涵在「2014 年底」這個「未來」的時刻時,她「在演藝圈超過二十五年」這件事將被完成。

❷ Let's hope by the next time we see her, she will have learned her lesson and become the girl we used to love.

此句中的「未來完成式」為"will have learned her lesson and become the girl we used to love";本句說明影迷們希望在「下次見到琳賽・羅涵」這個「未來」的時刻時,她「學到教訓和再次成為我們曾經喜愛的那個女孩」這件事將被完成。

 Practice Time ★

Q1:我將會在晚餐時間前看完琳賽・羅涵的這部電影。

_____.

Q2:琳賽・羅涵希望在她三十歲時將會贏得許多獎項。

_____.

Q1 Ans:I will have watched this Lindsay Lonhan film by dinner time.

Q2 Ans:Lindsay Lonhan hopes she will have won lots of prizes when she is thirty.

Unit 12
未來完成進行式

> China's cinema will have been ❶rising for ten years by the end of this year. It has had more ❷exposure, so my chances of becoming internationally known are better. But the first thing I have to do is to learn English. If I can ❸grasp the language, then perhaps I can think about the U.S.

—— Ziyi Zhang 章子怡

（中國的電影到今年已經運動發展了 10 年。曝光率更高，我被國際認識的機會也就更多了。但首先我要做的是學習英語。如果我可以理解這門語言，那麼也許我就可以考慮到美國發展的事。）

❶ rising [`raɪzɪŋ] adj 上升的　　❷ exposure [ɪk`spoʒɚ] n 暴露
❸ grasp [græsp] v 理解

　　這是章子怡在十幾年前所說的話，而如今她已成為國際知名的電影明星。除了中國電影崛起的因素外，對英語的勤奮學習也是她成功的要素之一。未來完成進行式」("will have been rising")，表示崛起的動作「從以前持續到現在，並將延伸到未來某一時刻」。

Grammar Show

　　未來完成進行式 (Future Perfect Progressive Tense)，可用來表示「在過去發生的事情或動作持續到現在，並延伸到未來」。與未來完成式一樣，一般需搭配一個未來時間的副詞片語或子句，句子才會完整，且此副詞片語或副詞子句的動詞需使用現在式。句型用法和句例如下：

1 肯定句：**"主詞 + will have been+ 現在分詞+ (受詞)"**

例 I **will have been waiting** for him for 30 minutes by the time he gets here.

當他到這裡時，我將已經等了他 30 分鐘了。（等他的動作在他到達時已進行了 30 分鐘，並且還會繼續下去）

例 He **will have been learning** guitar for 3 years by the end of this month.

到這個月底之前，他將整整學吉他學了三年了。

2 否定句：**"主詞 + will not have been + 現在分詞+ (受詞)"**

例 Julie **will not have been waiting** for Bill when he gets here.

當 Bill 抵達這裡時，Julie 將不會再繼續等他了。（在 Bill 到的時候，Julie 已經不會再持續這個等待的動作了）

例 He **will not have been working** on this project by this time next year.

明年的這個時刻，他將不會再進行這個計畫了。

3 疑問句：**Will + 主詞 have been+ 現在分詞 + (受詞)?**

例 **Will Daisy have been waiting** on tables when we arrive at her restaurant?

當我們抵達 Daisy 的餐廳時，她將會正在服務客人嗎?

★ 「未來完成式」vs.「未來完成進行式」

- I **will have learned** five languages by 2015.

（到 2015 年，將完成學五國語言的動作，但會不會繼續學不知道）

- I **will have been learning** five languages by 2015.

（到 2015 年，將完成學五國語言的動作，並且還會持續學習）

 **Life Story**

Graduating from the Central Academy of Drama, Ziyi Zhang made her on-screen debut in *The Road Home,* directed by Yimou Zhang, in 1999. One year later, she landed a leading role in Ang Lee's smash hit *Crouching Tiger, Hidden Dragon.* The movie transformed her into an internationally known movie star overnight. ❶By the end of 2014, she will have been concentrating on her acting career for exactly fifteen years.

❷Moreover, Zhang will have been working in Hollywood for ten years next month. Her good looks and excellent performance brought her to the attention of the western media. She was on the cover of *Time* magazine in 2005- the first Chinese woman to achieve this honor. Apart from having a pretty face, she is intelligent in every single sense. Once in an interview, she said, "People who trust me will never have been swayed by what has been said about me, and for people who don't, no amount of good reports will persuade them. I think that all I should do is to be who I am and do what I should."

畢業於中央戲劇學院，章子怡在 1999 年演出了銀幕處女作《我的父親母親》。一年之後，她又在李安轟動一時的熱門作品《臥虎藏龍》中擔任女主角。這部電影讓她一夜之間成為國際知名的電影明星。到 2014 年底，她整整致力於從事演藝工作 15 年。

章子怡的美貌和優秀的演技吸引了西方媒體的目光。她在 2005 年榮登《時代》雜誌特別版封面，而她同時也是第一個獲此殊榮的中國女性。除了美麗的臉孔，她的智慧也顯現在任何一個角度上。她某次在一個訪問中說道：「認同我的人從不會因為外界怎麼批評我而改變；而對於不認同我的人，任何的正面評價也不會說服他們。我想我只能做我自己，做我應該做的。」

- smash [smæʃ] **adj** 轟動一時的
- excellent [ˋɛkslənt] **adj** 傑出的
- intelligent [ɪnˋtɛlədʒənt] **adj** 聰明的
- sway [swe] **v** 動搖

Sentence Show

❶ By the end of 2014, she will have been concentrating on her acting career for exactly fifteen years.

此句用「未來完成進行式」（"will have been concentrating on"），表示章子怡的演藝事業是從她一出道開始到現在已整整 15 年，而未來她還是會繼續從事演藝工作。

❷ Moreover, Zhang will have been working in Hollywood for ten years next month.

章子怡的這句話使用了「未來完成進行式」（"will have been working"）。表示她到下個月時，她將在好萊塢工作了 10 年，並且未來還是會持續下去。

 Practice Time

Q1：到今年 10 月，章子怡在北京住了 20 年。

_____.

Q2：到六點時，我已看了 3 個小時章子怡的電影了。

_____.

Q1 Ans： Ziyi Zhang will have been living in Beijing for twenty years this October.

Q2 Ans： I will have been watching Ziyi Zhang's movies for three hours by six o'clock.

Unit 13
Can, Could

"You can't ❶control how other people see you or think of you. But you have to be ❷comfortable with that."

—— Helen Mirren 海倫・米勒

（你不能控制其他人怎麼看你或揣測你。但你必須對此感到自在。）

❶ control [kən`trol] **V** 控制　❷ comfortable [`kʌmfə‧təbl] **adj** 舒適的

　　我們常常會很在意別人對我們的看法，但嘴長在他們臉上，我們無法阻止其他人的言論，所以不要讓自己太在意了。句中的 "you can't control..."表示「你不能控制」，"can"在這裡為表示「能」之意。

Grammar Show

　　"can"是助動詞，中文通常解釋為「會、能」，"can"後方的動詞需使用原型動詞。"can"的否定形式為"cannot/can't"，其使用方式和句例如下：

❶　表達某人有能力或機會去做某事

　例 Bob **can** cook curry very well.

　　　Bob 可以把咖哩煮的很好。

　例 It's sunny outside. We **can** take a walk later.

　　　外面陽光和煦。我們待會可以出去走走。

2 與「許可、同意」有關的動作.

例 **Can** I use your toilet?

我可以借用你的洗手間嗎？（詢問許可）

例 You **can't** go to Mila's party tonight.

你今晚不能去蜜拉的派對。（拒絕許可）

例 Each passenger **can** only take one bag onto the plane.

每位乘客都只能帶一個包包上飛機。（談論許可）

3 表達提議

例 I **can** give you a ride if you like.

如果你想要，我可以載你一程。

"could"，也是助動詞，中文解釋亦為「會、能」，其後亦接原型動詞。否定形式為"could not/couldn't"，用法及例子如下：

1 做為**"can"的過去式**，用來表示在過去有能力或可以做某事

例 I **could** play the piano when I was six.

當我六歲時，我會彈鋼琴。

2 詢問許可及討論許可

例 **Could** I borrow your iPad, please?

我可以借用你的 iPad 嗎？（詢問許可：使用"could"提出請求會比用"can"更為禮貌）

例 Three years ago, we **could** still park our cars anywhere.

三年前我們仍然可以將車停在任何一個地方。（討論許可）

★ 注意"could"不可做為「同意或拒絕請求」之用。

(*NOT* ~~You could buy this cake.~~)

Life Story

By the beginning of 2014, the outstanding and forever-glamorous 68-year-old Helen Mirren had won an Oscar, two Golden Globes and most recently the Bafta Academy Fellowship award. ❶Considering her age and the honors she has received, most people may say she could retire and enjoy the sunshine of LA, where her family live. Contrary to these assumptions, she loves what she is doing and constantly thinks about who she wishes to work with. It seems she is far from done.

Mirren knows reputation doesn't come easy. "Everyone wants to be a movie star or a model, to be in the papers, but few realize just what hard work it is, getting up early, and so on," she admits. Therefore, she works hard but never spends hard. ❷She once said that she could wear a jacket from a thrift store without having any uncomfortable feelings while walking down the street. She is best known for her portrayal of Her Majesty the Queen but she is in fact more like a grandmother living next door.

直到 2014 年初始，68 歲、優秀且充滿魅力的海倫‧米勒，已經獲得了一座奧斯卡獎、兩座金球獎，以及最近獲頒英國電影學院終身成就獎。考慮到她的年紀及已經獲得的榮耀，許多人也許會說她可以退休並在她家人所在的洛杉磯享受陽光了。與這些猜想正好相反，她喜歡她現在所做的事，也時常想著她想和誰合作。看來她離退休還很遠。

米勒知道名聲來之不易。她承認道：「每個人都想當電影明星、模特兒，或是出現在報紙上，但只有少數人知道這其中包含了多少辛苦，比如要早起等等。」因此她努力工作，但不亂花錢。她曾經說，她可以穿著二手商店買來的夾克走在路上而不會覺得丟臉。她最有名的作品是飾演女王伊麗莎白二世，但她實際上更像住在我們隔壁的鄰家老奶奶。

- contrary [ˋkɑntrɛrɪ] **adj** 相反的
- constantly [ˋkɑnstəntlɪ] **adv** 時常地
- reputation [ˏrɛpjəˋteʃən] **n** 名譽
- thrift shop **ph** 慈善二手商店

Sentence Show ★

❶ Considering her age and the honors she has received, most people may say she could retire and enjoy the sunshine of LA, where her family live.

這句話裡說的是一般大家對海倫・米勒的猜想,所以主要子句動詞 "say"和子句裡的助動詞"can"均是使用簡單現在式。此處"can"有表達「有機會做某事」之意,其後所接動詞需為原型動詞。

❷ She once said that she could wear a jacket from a thrift store without having any uncomfortable feelings while walking down the street.

一開始的"she once said"(她曾經說)說明這個句子使用的是過去式;故後面 said 子句裡「她可以穿二手商店買來的衣服」中的「可以」需使用"can"的過去式"could"。

 Practice Time ★

Q1:米勒現在可以退休但她不願意。

_____.

Q2:米勒曾說她無法停止工作。

_____.

Q1 Ans:Mirren can retire now, but she doesn't want to.

Q2 Ans:Mirren once said she couldn't stop working.

Unit 14
Will, Would

"The older you get, the more ❶fragile you understand life to be.I think this will be good ❷motivation for getting out of bed joyfully each day."

—— Julia Roberts 茱莉亞‧羅勃茲

（當你年紀越大，你就越了解生命有多脆弱。我想這會是每天帶著愉悅心情起床的好動力。）

❶ fragile [`frædʒəl] adj 易碎的　❷ motivation [ˌmotə`veʃən] n 動力

　　句中的"will"並不做「簡單未來式」（如：I will visit my aunt tomorrow. 我明天將會去拜訪我阿姨。）使用，而是做為「預測」之意。即茱莉亞‧羅勃茲認為如果人們能了解到「生命脆弱」，這件事就「可能」成為他們愉快起床的動力。

Grammar Show

　　"will"是助動詞，可翻譯為「即將/將來會」，其後需接原型動詞；否定形式可寫為"will not"或"won't"。"will"的各個使用法及例句如下：

❶ 用在未來式

例 He **will leave** for Boston next Sunday.

他將會在下週日離開這裡前往波士頓。

例 She **will not stay** long. 她不會久留。

2 說明決定、企圖或提議

例 It's hot. I **will turn** on the air conditioner.

太熱了。我要開冷氣了。（決定）

例 I **will send** the letter for you.　我會幫你寄信。（提議）

3 說明預測

例 One day people **will travel** to Mars.

總有一天人類可以到火星旅行。

"would"也是助動詞，句型使用方式與"will"相同，均是於其後加上原型動詞。"would"的用法和例句如下:

1 對過去或可能發生的情況表示推測

例 If Alice cleaned the house all day, she **would sleep** well that night.

假如 Alice 一整天打掃房子，她當晚會睡得很好。（假設推測的情況）

例 It **would be** a good idea to make a complaint by email.

寫電子郵件去抗議可能是個好主意。（可能的情況）

2 使用"**would like**"表達要做某事，但語氣較"**want**" 委婉，可翻譯為「想要」

例 I'**d (would) like** to talk to Elsa, please.

我想要跟 Elsa 說話，麻煩你。

3 疑問句形式為"**Would you+原型動詞…?**"有表達客氣的請求或詢問之意

例 **Would you explain** the situation to me, please?

可以請你解釋這個情況給我聽嗎？（客氣的請求）

例 **Would you like** some more coffee?

你想要一些咖啡嗎？（詢問）

★ 亦可使用"Would you mind+ Ving…?"做為更客氣的請求

例 **Would you mind explaining** the situation to me?

你介意解釋這個情況給我聽嗎？

★ Life Story ★

According to box-office records, Julia Roberts is one of the highest-paid actresses in Hollywood. Moreover, she has been named one of *People* magazine's "50 Most Beautiful People in the World" eleven times. Therefore, ❶it will not be exaggerating to say that anyone in the world who likes to see movies must know who Julia Roberts is.

❷When Julia was young, she never dreamed she would become the most famous actress in America. As a child, she originally wanted to be a veterinarian because of her love for animals. However, she chose to study journalism and tried acting later instead. She had her first break in 1988 and received her biggest success in *Pretty Woman*, the signature movie of 1990. As the most popular actress of romantic comedies, she has a lot of amazing quotes about love, such as "you know it's love when all you want is that person to be happy, even if you're not part of their happiness."

根據票房記錄，茱莉亞・羅勃茲現在是好萊塢片酬最高的女星之一。此外，她也被《人物》雜誌評為「50 個世界上最美的人」11 次。因此，也許說這個世界上喜歡看電影的人都知道誰是茱莉亞・羅勃茲，並不誇張。

當茱莉亞年輕的時候，她從沒想過自己會成為美國最知名的女星。在她還是個小孩時，因為喜愛動物，她原本想當一名獸醫。但她之後選擇讀新聞系並嘗試演戲。她在 1988 年獲得首次出演機會，並因 1999 年的知名電影《麻雀變鳳凰》獲得巨大的成功。身為最受歡迎的浪漫喜劇女演員，她有很多與愛情有關的名言，例如：「你知道這是愛情，當你全心全意的希望那人快樂，即使他的快樂不是因為你。」

- exaggerated [ɪgˋzædʒəˌretɪd] **adj** 誇張的
- originally [əˋrɪdʒənlɪ] **adv** 起初
- veterinarian [ˌvɛtərəˋnɛrɪən] **n** 獸醫
- journalism [ˋdʒɝnḷˌɪzm] **n** 新聞業
- signature [ˋsɪgnətʃɚ] **n** 特色

Sentence Show ★

❶ It will not be exaggerating to say that anyone in the world who likes to see movies must know who Julia Roberts is.

此處"will"含有「預測」之意。由於在本句之前已提到茱莉亞‧羅勃茲的事蹟（片酬很高及多次獲得雜誌票選），故這裡推測如果說「世界上喜歡看電影的人都知道茱莉亞‧羅勃茲」，聽起來並不會很誇張。

❷ When Julia was young, she never dreamed she would become the most famous actress in America.

"would"在這裡的用法是做為「預測可能發生的情況」使用。對於「成為美國最受有名的明星」這個可能發生的情況，茱莉亞年輕的時候從沒有想過。

Practice Time ★

Q1：他們說原本茱莉亞‧羅勃茲會有 2 部電影在 2006 年上映。

_____ .

Q2：總有一天茱莉亞‧羅勃茲會造訪台灣。

_____ .

Q1 Ans：They said Julia Roberts would have two films released in 2006.

Q2 Ans：One day Julia Roberts will visit Taiwan.

Unit 15
May, Might

❝ Life may open up ❶opportunities to you one day, and you either take them or you stay ❷afraid of taking them. ❞

—— Jim Carrey 金・凱瑞

（人生也許某天開啟機會給你；你不是接受這些機會，就是持續害怕接受他們。）

❶ opportunity [ˌɑpɚ`tjunəti] **n** 機會　❷ afraid [ə`fred] **adj** 害怕的

　　"Life may open up opportunities to you one day"，句中出現助動詞"may"表示「生活有天給你機會」這件事並不是一個肯定會發生的事實，它只是一個「可能性」，有可能會出現這個機會，也有可能不會有這個機會。

Grammar Show

　　may 和 might 均為助動詞，兩者之後均需接原型動詞，使用的情況如下：

❶ **may 和 might 均可用於表達「猜測、可能」，且兩者可替換使用**

　例 John **may/might leave** his bag on the bus.

　　John 可能把他的包包留在公車上了。

　例 You **may/might not want** to know the truth.

　　你可能不會想知道真相。

★ 某些文法書上規定了 may 和 might 的使用方式:

「可能性較大的情況用"may";可能性較低的情況用"might"」;

「現在可能發生的情況用"may";過去可能發生情況用"might"」

但在現代英文中,對此兩字的用法已沒有這樣嚴格的區分;只要是表達「可能性」時,兩者皆可使用。

❷ 在談論過去,或是在說話的當下情況仍未明朗,只能猜測,此時可使用 may have 或 might have

例 I **may/might have** been walking my dog when you called.

你打電話來的時候,我可能去遛狗了。(談論過去情況)

例 The candidate doesn't think that his campaign advertisement **may/might have** offended some people.

那個候選人沒有想到他的競選廣告可能會冒犯了很多人。(在做廣告的當下沒有預測到這個情況)

★ "might have"亦常用於談論「可能發生而未發生」的情況

例 If I had earned enough money, I **might have** gone to school instead of starting work .

如果我有賺足夠的錢,我可能會上學,而不是開始工作。

❸ may 可做為疑問句開頭,表示「禮貌性請求、允許」;而 might 一般不做疑問句使用

例 **May** I sit here?

我可以坐這裡嗎?

❹ may 和 might 均可用做「禮貌性建議」

例 You **may/might** consider talking to your boss.

你也許可以考慮和你的老闆談談。

Life Story

The legendary comedian Jim Carrey's father was a saxophone player but became an accountant to pay the bills. Unfortunately, he lost his job at age 51 and this incident changed everything for the family. In Carrey's own words, the whole family was "experiencing poverty at that point." When he turned 16, he had to drop out of school to work. Later, in an interview with Correspondent Steve Kroft, he admitted he was angry at the world for what happened to his father.

❶While other people face the same situation as Carrey had, they may keep complaining about the world. Instead, Carrey turned his anger and anxiety into a source for his comedy. He sees depression as a necessary ingredient to learn and create things. He even claimed an interesting person should be desperate sometimes. Moreover, he cited his father's example to encourage young people to pursue their dreams. "❷I learned many great lessons from my father, not the least of which was that you could fail at what you don't love, so you might as well take a chance on doing what you love."

著名喜劇演員金・凱瑞的父親曾是個薩克斯風演奏家，但為了家計成為了一名會計師。不幸的是，他在 51 歲時被裁員，而這件事也影響了整個家庭。以金・凱瑞自己的說法，就是整個家庭「在當時歷經貧困」。當他 16 歲時，他必須輟學工作。在之後和記者史蒂芬・卡夫特的訪談上，他承認曾因當時發生在他父親身上的事而對這個世界感到生氣。

當其他人面對和金・凱瑞一樣的情況時，他們可能會繼續抱怨這個世界。但金・凱瑞將他的怒氣和焦慮轉為他喜劇的素材。他認為憂傷是學習和創作的來源。他甚至認為，一個有趣的人應該有某種程度的憂傷。此外，他也用他父親的例子來鼓勵年輕人追求夢想。他說：「我從我父親身上學到很多寶貴的經驗；然而最重要的是若選擇做你不喜歡的事，你可能會失敗，倒不如冒險去做自己熱愛的事情。」

● anxiety [æŋˋzaɪətɪ] 🄝 焦慮　　● depression [dɪˋprɛʃən] 🄝 沮喪

Sentence Show ★

❶ While other people face the same situation as Carrey had, they may keep complaining about the world.

"may"表示某事發生的可能性，此處表示其他人在遭遇金・凱利的情況時，「他們『可能』會持續抱怨這個世界」（= ...perhaps they keep complaining about the world）。

❷ I learned many great lessons from my father, not the least of which was that you could fail at what you don't love, so you might as well take a chance on doing what you love.

在舉了父親的例子後，金・凱瑞覺得年輕人「做自己熱愛的事『也許』才是最好的」（=...so perhaps you as well take a chance on doing what you do.）

 Practice Time ★

Q1：金・凱瑞現在可能可以處理任何情況。

_____.

Q2：身為好萊塢最賣座的影星之一，金・凱瑞可能沒有財務的問題

_____.

Q1 Ans：Jim Carrey may be able to deal with any situation now.

Q2 Ans：As one of Hollywood's most bankable stars, Jim Carrey might not have any financial problem.

Unit 16
Must, Have to

"You have to just **❶accept** your body. You may not love it all the way, but you just have to be **❷comfortable** with it, comfortable with knowing that that's your body.**"**

—— Rihanna 蕾哈娜

（你必須接受你自己的身體。也許你完全不喜歡它，但你必須對它感到自在；也就是知道這是你自己的身體,並感到自在。）

❶ accept [ək`sɛpt] **V** 接受　**❷** comfortable [`kʌmfə·təbl] **adj** 舒服的

　　在整形風潮盛行的今天，蕾哈娜以這句名言鼓勵大家接受原本的自己。句中的"have to"加上"accept your body"及"be comfortable with it"，表示蕾哈娜覺得「接受你的身體」和「對它（自己的身體）感到自在」都是「必要」的事。

🎬 Grammar Show

　　"must"是助動詞，中文翻譯為「必須」，用來表示說話者認為「某事或某行為是重要的或是必須做的」；肯定句型"must+原型動詞"，否定句型"mustn't +原型動詞"。用法和例句如下：

❶ **此事或此行為是責任或義務**

　　例 Every citizen **must pay** taxes.

　　　每個公民都必須納稅。

② **此事或此行為很重要**

例 I **must finish** my report before the deadline.

我必須在最後期限前完成我的報告。

③ **根據合理的推測或說話者的認知，此事或此行為是很有把握的猜測**

例 It **must have been** raining a few minutes ago as the ground is wet.

由於地板是濕的，幾分鐘前一定下過雨。

④ **說話者強烈建議某事**

例 If you go to China, you **must see** the Great Wall .

如果你到中國，你一定要去看長城。

"have to"也是「必須」的意思，通常表示某事「因為規則或某個情況的關係，不得不去達成」。其肯定句型為"have to+原型動詞"，否定句型為"don't/doesn't+ have to"：

例 All the applicants **have to do** the health check.

所有的申請者都必須做健康檢查。（這是一個規則）

例 I **have to go** to bed before 10 o'clock tonight; otherwise, I will be so tired tomorrow morning.

我必須在 10 點之前上床，不然我明早會很累。（因為會有很累的狀況，所以不得不早點上床）

★ "must" 和"have to" 常常可以交互使用，因為某些事既是「說話者認為是重要的」同時也是一個「規則」

例 May **must/has to** pass the exam or she will not be accepted by the university.

May 必須通過考試，否則她將不能被大學錄取。（通過考試很重要，而且也是一個升學的規則）

 **Life Story** ★

As the most-viewed artist on YouTube and the most-liked person on Facebook, Rihanna was definitely a big hit and the "Queen of Social Media" in the summer of 2013. Therefore, it's hard to believe a popular girl like her actually got teased at school. Back in her school days in Barbados, where she grew up, she was bullied by her classmates because her skin color was lighter than theirs. Instead of being upset, she felt grateful. She thought these experiences were the arrangement of God, which would prepare her for the future.

Even today, she still gets misunderstood a lot. Some people judge her just by a couple of pictures and a few crazy headlines they read on the Internet. ❶Under these circumstances, she has to put 100% effort into her music as this is the best way for people to understand the real Rihanna. For this reason, ❷she always says she must know who she is first before telling her story in music.

身為 YouTube 上最多人點閱及 Facebook 上獲得最多讚的歌手，蕾哈娜絕對是 2013 年夏天最熱門的人物以及「社群網站皇后」。因此我們很難相信，像她這樣受歡迎的女孩事實上在學校時常受到嘲笑。回溯至她在家鄉巴貝多的學校生活，她當時因為皮膚顏色較同學們來的淺，受到霸凌，但她以感激的心情取代了氣憤。她覺得這些經驗都是上帝的安排，是為了她日後做準備。

即使在今天，她仍然受到許多誤解。有些人由網路上看到的幾張照片及讀到的幾則誇大的頭條來評判她。在這種情況下，她必須盡 100％的努力在音樂上，因為這是讓人們認識真正蕾哈娜的最好方法。因為這個原因，蕾哈娜總是說她必須在用音樂訴說自己的故事前，先認識自己。

- definitely [ˋdɛfənɪtlɪ] adv 明確地
- grateful [ˋgretfəl] adj 感激的
- headline [ˋhɛd͵laɪn] n 標題
- tease [tiz] V 取笑
- judge [dʒʌdʒ] V 評定

Sentence Show ★

❶ Under these circumstances, she has to put 100% effort into her music as this is the best way for people to understand the real Rihanna.

"She has to put 100% effort into her music"，表示「她必須盡全力在她的音樂上」，因為「在大家都誤解她的情況下」，這是一個最好的方法。

❷ She always says she must know who she is first before telling her story in music.

這裡用"she must know..."（她必須認識……），表示蕾哈娜（說話者）認為「先認識自己」這件事是很重要，且必須要做的。

 Practice Time ★

Q1：你一定要看看蕾哈娜的 Instagrams @badgalriri。他們非常有趣！

_____.

Q2：蕾哈娜認為人們必須知道生活中重要的是什麼。

_____.

Q1 Ans：You must check out Rihanna's Instagrams @badgalriri. They're very interesting!

Q2 Ans：Rihanna thinks people have to know what's important in life.

Unit 17
Should, Ought to

❝In a relationship, each person should ❶support the other. They ought to ❷lift each other up.❞

—— Taylor Swift 泰勒‧史薇芙特

（在一段感情中，每個人都應該支持另一半。他們應該要互相扶持。）

❶ support [sə`port] **V** 支持　❷ lift up **ph** 扶持

　　泰勒‧史薇芙特這句話裡的"should"和"ought to"均可翻譯為「應該」。第一句話中的"should"帶有「說明這件事是正確可行的」之意；第二句話裡的"ought to"則有「提供意見」之意。關於兩者的更多用法說明，請看下個部分。

🎬 Grammar Show ★

　　"should" 是助動詞，中文可解釋為「應該、必須」；肯定句形式為"主詞+should+原型動詞+受詞"，否定句則改為"shouldn't+原型動詞"。"Should"的三種用法及例子如下：

❶ **談論我們認為正確或應該做之事，如：責任等**

　　例 Employers should provide their employees with a proper job description.

　　僱主應該提供適當的工作概述給他的員工。

2 給予建議

例 You **should see** a doctor if your back pain is not getting better.

如果你的背痛沒有改善，你應該要去看醫生。

3 根據所發生的現況，推測或期望某事的發生

例 The instructor **should explain** how to play this sport in advance.

教練應該會事先說明該如何進行這項運動。

★ should 還有另一種肯定句型為: "主詞+should+ have +過去完成式"，用來表示「過去應該要做，卻沒有做的事」，說話者通常有責備或懊悔的意味

例 You **should have told** me earlier that she will not join us.

你應該早點告訴我她不會來加入我們。

例 I **should have studied** harder, but I didn't know this exam was so important.

如果我知道這個考試這麼重要，我應該要更努力唸書。

"ought to"的語氣較 should 強烈，亦可解釋為「必須、應該」，句型用法與 should 相同，使用方式和例句則如下:

1 表達某事符合道德或某人的責任，是正確該做的事

例 The politicians **ought to** admit that they made a mistake.

政治家們應該承認他們犯了錯誤。

2 根據正常的情況而對某事做出推測

例 The weather in Taiwan **ought to** be hot in July.

台灣七月的天氣應該很熱。

3 提供建議

例 You **ought to** make a cake for her birthday.

你應該為她的生日做個蛋糕。

 *Life Story* ★

Since she is called country music's darling,[1] people tend to think Taylor Swift should have been the most popular kid at school. In fact, her school life wasn't always so sweet. Kids at her school thought she was weird because she liked country music and thus made fun of her. Swift tried to see the whole thing in a positive way as later in an interview she said, "If I hadn't come home from school miserable every day, maybe I wouldn't have been so motivated to write songs. I should probably thank them!"

Swift is known for narrative songs about her personal experiences. She herself also claims that listening to her albums is like reading her diary.[2] Some people like the way she writes her songs while others think she oughtn't to expose her personal relationships. Nevertheless, no matter which terms people use to define Swift, "stingy" will never be one of them. Her philanthropic efforts have been recognized by the Do Something Awards and the Tennessee Disaster Services. Furthermore, she even received The Big Help Award from Michelle Obama in 2012.

由於她被稱為「鄉村音樂甜心」，人們傾向於認為泰勒・史薇芙特應該是學校裡最受歡迎的孩子。事實上，她的學校生活並不是那麼甜蜜。學校裡的孩子覺得喜歡鄉村音樂的她很奇怪，也因此嘲笑她。史薇芙特則試著以積極的角度來看整件事，所以她在後來的訪問裡提到：「如果我不是每天從學校回來都很悲慘的話，也許我就沒有寫歌的動機了！我應該要謝謝他們！」

史薇芙特的歌曲以闡述自己的個人經驗出名。她自己也曾宣稱，聽她的專輯就如讀她的日記一般。有的人喜歡她這種寫歌的方式，有的人則認為她不該暴露自己的私人情感。然而，無論人們用哪個詞彙去定義史薇芙特，「吝嗇」絕對不會是其中一個。她的慈善行為已經被「做點事」獎項及「田納西災害服務」認可。此外，她更在 2012 年，從蜜雪兒・歐巴馬手中接獲「幫大忙」獎項。

● miserable [ˋmɪzərəbl] **adj** 痛苦的　　● motivated [ˋmotɪvetɪd] **adj** 有動機的

Sentence Show ⭐

❶ People tend to think Taylor Swift should have been the most popular kid at school.

這裡的"should"帶有「猜測、期望」之意；由於上一句提到了泰勒・史薇芙特被稱作鄉村音樂甜心，所以人們說她是學校裡最受歡迎的孩子時，是帶有一種猜測，而不是他們所見的真實情況。

❷ Some people like the way she writes her songs while others think she oughtn't to expose her personal relationships.

句中將"ought to"加上否定"not"形成"oughtn't to"，表示「某事不是正確可做之事」。此處指有些人認為泰勒・史薇芙特「不應該」將私人情感寫進歌裡，因為這「不是正確可做之事」。

 Practice Time ⭐

Q1：泰勒・史薇芙特的同學們應該向她道歉。

_____.

Q2：人們應該多關注泰勒・史薇芙特的音樂而不是八卦。

_____.

Q1 Ans： Taylor Swift's classmates should/ought to apologize to her.

Q2 Ans： People should/ought to pay more attention to Taylor Swift's music instead of her gossip.

Unit 18
Need, Dare

❝I don't need Prince ❶Charming to have my own happy ❷ending.❞

—— Katy Perry 凱蒂・珮芮

（我不需要白馬王子來給我快樂的結局。）

❶ charming [`tʃɑrmɪŋ] **adj** 迷人的　❷ ending [`ɛndɪŋ] **n** 結局

　　在女孩們期待白馬王子的到來時，有個性又有主見的凱蒂・珮芮提出了自己的想法，她說"I don't need Price Charming…"（我不需要一個白馬王子）。這裡"need"即為「需要」之意，用來表示對於某事的必須性。詳細的用法請參考下個部分的文法說明。

Grammar Show

　　"need"做為動詞時，中文可解譯為「應該、必須」，和"have to"的意思相同。用法及例句如下：

❶ 談論「應該做某事」時，我們使用"主詞+ need+ to +原型動詞+受詞"；而否定句則可使用"主詞+ don't/doesn't + need+ to +原型動詞+受詞"或"主詞+ needn't+原型動詞+受詞"

例 You **need to take** the medicine three times a day.
　　你必須一天吃三次藥。

例 Joe **doesn't need to go** to school/**needn't go** to school on weekends.

Joe 週末不需要上學。

2 談論「必須得到某物」時，使用"主詞+need+受詞（某人/物）"；否定句為 "主詞+don't/doesn't +need+受詞（某物）"但不可用"主詞+needn't+受詞（某物）"

例 Joan **needs** a new car.

Joan 必須得到一輛車。

例 She **doesn't need** a computer. (*NOT* ~~She needn't a computer.~~)

她不需要一台電腦。

★ 此外，"need"過去式為"needed"，否定用法為"didn't need/didn't need to"。

"dare"做為一般動詞時，中文可翻譯為「敢，竟然」。以下為"dare"的用法解釋：

1 肯定句："主詞+ dare + (to) +原型動詞+ 受詞"

例 You **dare (to) tell** a lie.

你竟敢說謊。

例 **Dare to be** yourself!

勇於做自己！

2 否定句："主詞+ don't / doesn't + dare + (to) +原型動詞+受詞

例 Bill **doesn't dare to challenge** his boss.

Bill 不敢挑戰他的老闆。

例 I **don't dare to say** what I thought.

我不敢說出我所想的事。

★ "dare"的過去式為"dared"，否定用法為"didn't dare (to)"。此外，需注意"dare to"一般不做為進行式時態 (be daring to) 使用。

 **Life Story** ★

From the anthem of summer 2008 *I Kissed A Girl* to the latest hit song *Dark Horse*, Katy Perry proved to us that she is far from being a one-hit wonder. With these chart-toppers, she has definitely cemented her place as pop's most beloved princess.

Katy is so gorgeous and loveable that it is difficult to imagine she has been divorced. She separated from her husband, the British comedian and actor, Russell Brand in 2012. Back at the time she decided to marry Russell, ❶many of her friends asked her how she dared to make this decision since her husband-to-be is a Casanova. ❷She said she believed Russell to be the love of her life and thus didn't need anyone's approval for her marriage. Therefore, one can well imagine how depressed she was after signing the divorce papers. While the public predicted the divorce might affect her career, she put on a brave face and completed her ongoing concert tour. "If you are presenting yourself with confidence, you can pull off pretty much anything," she said.

從 2008 年夏天的「國歌」：《我親吻了一個女孩》，到近期的熱門單曲《黑馬》，凱蒂‧佩芮已經向我們證明了她不是一片歌手。而她許多專輯均佔據排行榜上前幾名的事實，也鞏固了她成為最受喜愛的流行樂女教主的地位。

凱蒂是如此的出色和令人喜愛，以致於很難相信她已經離過一次婚。她和她的前夫，英國的喜劇演員羅素‧布蘭德於 2012 年分手。在她決定嫁給羅素時，她許多的朋友說他的未來老公是個花花公子，問她怎麼敢嫁給他。她說她相信羅素是她一生的摯愛，所以她不需要別人對她婚姻的許可。也因此，可以猜想在她簽下離婚協議書後，她的心情有多低沈。當大眾預估離婚可能會影響她的事業時，她還是努力堅強起來，完成她還沒完成的巡迴演唱會。她說：「如果你能顯得有自信，你就可以成功完成許多事。」

• anthem [ˈænθəm] **n** 國歌　　　　　• cement [sɪˈmɛnt] **v** 鞏固

Sentence Show ★

❶ Many of her friends asked her how she dared to make this decision since her husband-to-be is a Casanova.

本句使用"主詞+ dare + (to) +原型動詞+受詞"的句型："she dared to make this decision"），表示凱蒂‧珮芮「有勇氣去做這個決定」。此處原本的問句形式為："How dare she⋯?"（她怎麼敢⋯？）為一個"dare"的慣用疑問句型。

❷ She said she believed Russell to be the love of her life and thus didn't need anyone's approval for her marriage.

此處為否定句型，使用"主詞+didn't +need+受詞（某人/物）" 的形式，可翻譯為「不需要某事/某人」；此處 "didn't need anyone's approval"即「不需要任何人的認可」。

 Practice Time ★

Q1：凱蒂有勇氣說出她的想法。

_____.

Q2：凱蒂不需要其他人來告訴她該做什麼。

_____.

Q1 Ans：Katy dares to speak her mind. / Katy dares to say what she thinks.

Q2 Ans：Katy doesn't need other people to tell her what to do.

Unit 19
Used to

I used to think the worst thing in life was to [1]end up all [2]alone. It's not. The worst thing in life is to end up with people that make you feel all alone.
—— Robin Williams 羅賓・威廉斯

（我過去曾想，人生最糟的事是孤獨終老。但其實不是。人生最糟的事是，結果要與那些讓你感到孤單的人一同終老。）

1 end up ph 以…終結　**2** alone [əˋlon] adj 孤獨的

　　2014 年羅賓・威廉斯被研判因憂鬱症自殺身亡；對照他曾經說過的這句話，感覺特別耐人尋味。一開頭他說"I used to think…"表示他曾經的想法，但之後已不再這麼想（已不再覺得人生最糟的是孤獨的終老）。而此句之後的句子，則說明了他後來的新想法。

Grammar Show

　　"used to"有兩種常見的句型，皆和表示「習慣」有關：

1 **"主詞 + used to +原型動詞+ 受詞"**

　　這個句型是用來表示「過去的習慣或現象，但現在已經沒有了」。做否定句或問句時，需使用"didn't used to…"及"Did…use to…?"。

例 When I was a little girl, I **used to take** a walk in the forest.

　　當我還是小女孩時，我習慣在森林裡散步。(現在已沒有在森林散步的習慣)

例 My father **used to run** twice a week.

我的父親過去每週跑步兩次。(我的父親現在已經沒有每週跑步兩次的習慣)

例 Lisa didn't **use to drive** to work.

Lisa 過去不習慣開車去工作。(現在已經習慣開車上班了)

例 Did they **use to be** very good friend?

他們曾經是非常好的朋友嗎？(暗指現在已經不是非常好的朋友了)

2 "主詞 **+ be 動詞/get+ used to +** ⟨ Ving / 事物 ⟩"

這個句型是用來表示「也許一開始覺得某事或某動作很奇怪，但現在已成為一個習慣或一件習以為常的事情」。

例 I **am used to** this working schedule now.

我現在已經習慣這個工作行程了。(暗指過去可能不習慣此安排)

例 Bella got **used to taking** a shower in the evening.

Bella 習慣在晚上洗澡。(暗指過去可能不習慣在晚上洗澡)

例 I will never **get used to** the heat in Taiwan.

我永遠不會習慣臺灣的炎熱。(表示過去覺得不適應，持續到現在及未來都還是無法成為一個習慣)

 **Life Story**

Fans around the world were shocked by the news of Robin William's death. He was found dead after committing suicide by hanging at his home on August 11, 2014

William was a great actor and comedian who won the Academy Award for Best Supporting Actorfor his performance in *Good Will Hunting* and also received countless awards for acting. Even though ❶he got used to being called the "legendary comedian", he was actually a quiet boy when he was little. He did not overcome his shyness until he joined his high school drama department. As his interest in acting developed, he even became one of only 20 freshmen accepted by Juilliard School. During his early career, ❷he used to be addicted to drugs and alcohol. Fortunately, he got clean and said, "Being on stage is not exactly the place to go when you're paranoid. It was a short trip to hell." He made us laugh. He made us cry. Most importantly of all, his movie and immeasurable talent touched all our hearts deeply.

世界各地的影迷在知道羅賓・威廉斯的死訊後，都非常的震驚。他在 2014 年 8 月 11 日時被發現在自家中自縊身亡。

威廉斯是一個優秀的演員和喜劇家。他曾以《心靈捕手》贏得了奧斯卡最佳男配角獎，並獲得了無數的演藝相關的獎項。即使在他一生已經習慣了被稱為「傳奇性的喜劇演員」，其實他小時候是個安靜的男孩。他一直到加入了高中的戲劇社團才克服了他的害羞。在對戲劇的興趣漸漸增長後，他甚至成為朱莉亞音樂學院 20 名新生之一。在他早期生涯中，他曾經成癮於毒品及酒類。幸運的是，他最後戒掉了，並且說：「當你出現被害妄想時，你不應該站上舞台。這是一個通往地獄的捷徑。」他讓我們大笑，也讓我們大哭。最重要的是，他的電影及不可計量的才能深深地感動了我們的心。

● alcohol [ˈælkəˌhɔl] **V** 酒精　　　● paranoid [ˈpærənɔɪd] **adj** 有妄想症的

Sentence Show ★

❶ He got used to being called the "legendary comedian".

"got used to being called"（習慣被叫做）表示羅賓・威廉斯也許一開始覺得對這個稱呼很怪，但後來就習慣了。"be/get used to"後如有動詞，需改為 "V-ing"形式需加上原型動詞。

❷ He used to be addicted to drugs and alcohol.

"He is addicted to drugs and alcohol"（他對毒品和酒精上癮）表示這是過去的習慣，後來他就不再對這些東西上癮了。"used to"後需加上原型動詞，故原本的片語"is addicted to"（對...上癮）便改為" be addicted to"。

 **Practice Time** ★

Q1：羅賓・威廉斯已習慣在洛杉磯的生活。

_____.

Q2：羅賓・威廉斯曾經在加州做過單人相聲表演。

_____.

Q1 Ans：Robin Williams was used to life in LA.

Q2 Ans：Robin Williams used to do stand-up comedy showsin California.

Unit 20
表示推測的助動詞

I told my mom, 'I'm not buying another magazine until I can get past this thought of looking like the girl on the ❶cover. She said, "Miley, you are the girl on the cover,' and I was, like, 'I know, but I don't feel like that girl every day.' You can't always feel perfect.

—— Miley Cyrus 麥莉‧塞勒斯

（我告訴我的母親：「在我斷了『看起來像這個封面女郎』的念頭之前，我不會再買其他的雜誌了。」她說：「麥莉，可是這個封面女郎就是你啊！」而我說：「我知道。但我覺得我不是每天都像封面上這個女孩一樣美。」你不可能總是覺得自己很完美。）

❶ cover [ˋkʌvɚ] n 封面

　　此句中的助動詞否定形式"can't"用來表示「推測某事不可能發生」。例如此句中，麥莉塞勒斯的意思即為「總是完美這件事是不可能發生的」。

 Grammar Show

　　用來表示「推測」的助動詞，是從「情態助動詞」（Modal Auxiliary Verbs）中延伸出來的。顧名思義，它是用來幫助主要動詞把「推測」的意思表達更完整；常見的「推測助動詞」有 must, can / could, may / might 和 should：

❶ **must 表示「非常肯定」的推測：**

"must + be 動詞/動詞原型" → 對「現在」肯定的推測

例 They **must be** very happy about their victory.

他們一定對勝利感到非常快樂。

★ "must+原型動詞"亦常用來表示做某事的必要性

例 You **must study** hard. 你必須努力唸書。

"must + have p.p." → 對「過去」肯定的推測

例 I didn't see Annie at the party. She **must have gone** somewhere else.

我在舞會上沒有看到 Annie。她一定是去別的地方了。

"must + have + been + Ving" →表示對「現在或是未來」肯定的推測

例 John just fell asleep at his desk, he **must have been feeling** tired.

John 趴在桌上睡著了，他一定是一直都很累。

❷ **can/could, may/might** 則用來表示對某事「不是很肯定」的推測

"can/could, may/might + be 動詞/動詞原型" → 對「現在」的可能性推測

例 Lois **may go** to the cinema for relaxation as she just finished a big project.

Lois 有可能去看電影放鬆自己，因為她今天剛結束一個大計劃。

"can/could, may/might + have p.p." → 對「過去」的可能性推測

例 My sister **could have gone** to the concert when I arrived home.

當我到家時，我姊姊有可能已經去音樂會了。

❸ 「推測某事不可能發生」：

"can/could, may/might + not+ be 動詞/原型動詞" → 對「現在或未來」推測的否定

例 If Jimmy doesn't leave home now, he **can't be** at school on time.

如果 Jimmy 現在沒有離開家，他就不能準時到校。

"can/could, may/might + not+ have p.p." → 對「過去」推測的否定

例 My brother hasn't called me back, but he **may not have got** my message. 我弟弟還沒有回電給我，但他可能是還沒有收到我的留言。

★ "must not"多用來表示「禁止；一定不能」，較少用來表示「不可能」。

Life Story

[1]You may have watched a Disney Channel children's television series named Hannah Montana before. The leading role in the program was portrayed by Miley Cyrus, who played a schoolgirl with a secret double life as a teen pop star. Her lovely smile and cheerful personality made her a new American sweetheart soon after the program was aired. Therefore, [2]this could be the reason why most people find it hard to accept her controversial performance and clothing style at the 2014 MTV Video Music Awards .

As for Cyrus, she did not really care what people think of her new image. She believes only God can judge each person. What's more, if there is someone to love us, we can just forget those haters. Her philosophy is "don't be anything you don't want to be, always be yourself ". After playing a character as sweet as Hannah for several years, Cyrus now just wishes she could show the "real her" to the public.

　　你也許以前曾看過迪士尼兒童頻道的影集《孟漢娜》。該影集的主角由麥莉・塞勒斯擔任，她飾演一位有著學生和青少年偶像雙重身份的女孩。她甜美的笑容與令人愉悅的個性，讓她在影集播出後，很迅速地成為新一代的美國甜心。因此，這也許是很多人很難接受她在後來 2014 年 MTV 音樂錄影帶頒獎典禮上，那些受爭議的穿著與表演風格的原因。

　　對於塞勒斯來說，她並不是很在意人們對她新形象的想法。她相信只有上帝可以評判我們每一個人；此外，如果有一個愛我們的人，我們就可以忘掉那些恨我們的人。她的哲學是「不要成為任何你不想成為的人，堅持做你自己」。在扮演孟漢娜這樣甜美的女孩多年後，現在塞勒斯只想讓大眾看到真正的她。

- cheerful [`tʃɪrfəl] **adj** 使人感到愉快的
- afterwards [`æftɚwɚd] **adv** 之後
- philosophy [fə`lɑsəfɪ] **n** 哲學
- air [ɛr] **V** 播放
- judge [dʒʌdʒ] **V** 評判

Sentence Show ★

❶ You may have watched a Disney Channel children's television series named Hannah Montana before.

這裡"may have watched"的文法形式為"may + have +p.p."，即表示「對過去的可能猜測」。這裡是猜測讀者中有人也許以前曾經看過《孟漢娜》這個節目。

❷ This could be the reason why most people find it hard to accept her controversial performance and clothing style at the 2014 MTV Video Music Awards.

此處"This could be the reason⋯"中的"could + be 動詞"的形態用來表示「對某事不是很確定的推測」。此處表示作者對於人們不能接受麥莉‧塞勒斯新形象的原因只是一個猜測。

 Practice Time ★

Q1：麥莉‧塞勒斯一定對於她以前演出的甜美形象很厭倦了。

_____.

Q2：麥莉‧塞勒斯今年年底可能會出新專輯。

_____.

Q1 Ans：Miley Cyrus must be tired of the sweet character she used to play.

Q2 Ans：Miley Cyrus may release her new album at the end of this year.

Unit 21
不定詞

> I don't dislike any of my exes. If I took time to form a relationship, it's gonna hurt when we move on, but are you puttin' [1]White-Out over all that beautiful time together? That was real time in your life. It's [2]connected to where you are today.
>
> —— Matthew McConaughey 馬修‧麥康納

我不會討厭我任何一位前任。如果我花時間去建立一段感情，當再繼續下去時會帶來傷痛，這時你會用立可白把這些美好時光都塗掉嗎？這可是你人生中真正過去的時間。這跟你的今天是連在一起的。

❶ White-Out n 立可白　❷ connect v 連結

　　在麥康納的這席話，我們會看到兩個 "to"。一個是第二句的 to form，和最後一句 be connected to。差別在於，第一個是不定詞的元素之一，第二個是介系詞。不定詞是什麼？請看下面說明。

Grammar Show

　　不定詞也是動狀詞家族的一個成員。「to + 原型動詞」就是他的樣子。所以上面的名言 to form 就是一個不定詞。我們來看看他的用法。

1 當名詞

例 **To err** is human; **to forgive** is divine.

犯錯為凡人；原諒為聖人。（to err 還有 to forgive 為不定詞，名詞功能做主詞使用）

例 What do you plan **to do** after work?

你下班後安排做什麼？（to do 為不定詞，名詞功能做動詞 plan 的受詞使用）

2 當形容詞

例 Carol usually has a recipe **to look** while she is cooking.

Carol 通常煮飯時會有一本食譜來看。

（to check 為不定詞，形容詞功能修飾名詞 recipe）

3 當副詞

例 We go to a library **to borrow** books.

我們去圖書館為了借書。

（to borrow 為不定詞，副詞功能用來修飾動詞 go，表示原因）

例 Are you old enough **to drink** alcohol? 你年紀夠大喝酒嗎？

（to drink 為不定詞，副詞功能用來修飾形容詞 old）

例 We are glad **to hear** of your good news.　我們很高興知道你的好消息。

例 Holly is easy **to cry.**　Holly 很容易就哭。

例 He is dying **to see** his wife.　他非常想見他太太。

4 獨立用法，不定詞用來修飾整句話

to tell the truth 老實說, to speak frankly 老實說, to be honest 老實說, to be brief 簡單說, to begin with 首先, needless to say 不用說也知道, to be sure 確定地說…

例 **To tell the truth**, his boss is his wife.

老實說，他的老闆是他太太。

例 **To begin with**, I want to thank for your invitation.

首先，我想感謝您的邀請。

例 **Needless to say**, bad habits are damaging to our body.

不用說也知道，不好的生活習慣對我們的身體是有害的。

 **Life Story**

After Matthew McConaughey graduated from high school, he moved to Australia to do some odd jobs, such as scooping chicken dung. Later, he made up his mind to return to U.S. and entered university. Almost one step away from becoming a lawyer; however, he chose a different path of life. ❶He pursued his dream, a professional actor, in order to live life with no regrets. He once said: "You want to be a writer? Start writing. You want to be a filmmaker? Start shooting stuff on your phone right now."

In 2000-2005, with his good looks and down-home charm, he stared many click-flicks and usually flaunted his fab abs in and off the screen. ❷Unlike his characters in the movies; he was eager to have a family. He said "I always wanted to be a father and thought it would be great, but it just took the right woman and the right time to make it all happen." Luckily, his dream came true; he married his right woman in 2012 and has three adorable kids.

在馬修・麥康納從高中畢業後去過澳洲打工，他做過很多奇怪的工作，比如：挖雞糞。後來，他下定決心回美國念大學。只差臨門一腳就可以當上律師；然而，他選擇一個不一樣的道路。為了一個無憾的人生，他追尋他的夢想──成為一名專業的演員。他曾說：「你想當作家嗎？寫作吧。你想當到導演嗎？那就從用自己手機錄影開始。」

在 2000-2005 年，因為他的帥臉和南部鄉下溫暖的魅力，他主演很多浪漫喜劇也經常在片中或日常生活炫耀他完美的腹肌。不像他電影裡所飾演的角色，他一直渴望家庭。他說：「我一直想要當爸爸也覺得這會很棒，但這需要一個對的女人和對的時機讓這一切發生。」幸運地，他的夢想成真，他與他的真命天女在2012 年結婚並育有三名可愛的小孩。

- scoop [skup] **V** 挖、拾起
- down-home **adj** 具有美國南方熱情的
- flaunt [flɔnt] **V** 炫耀
- fab abs **ph** 超棒的腹肌

Sentence Show

❶ He pursued his dream, a professional actor, in order to live life with no regrets.

「in order to + 原型動詞」用來表示「為了…」常見用法可以記下來。本劇的意思為，他追求他的夢想，為了一個無憾的人生。

❷ Unlike his character in the movies; he was eager to have a family. He said "I always wanted to be a father and thought it would be great, but it just took the right woman and the right time to make it all happen."

eager to+ 原型動詞，為不定詞修飾形容詞 eagar 的用法。表示「很樂意去做…事」。I always wanted to be，to be 為不定詞，做動詞 want 的受詞。

最後一句，to make it all happen 的 to make 也是不定詞，形容詞用法修飾前面的名詞片語 right woman 和 right time。

 Practice Time

Q1：為了得到角色，馬修‧麥康納為試鏡準備很多。

_____.

Q2：老實說，他在《藥命俱樂部》的表現真是太好了！

_____.

Q1 Ans： In order to get a character, Matthew McConaughey prepared a lot for an audition.

Q2 Ans： To tell the truth, his performance in *Dallas Buyers Club* is just fabulous!

Unit 22
動名詞

I have a fear of being boring.
—— Christian Bale 克里斯汀・貝爾

我害怕覺得無聊。

曾演過《蝙蝠俠》系列電影的克里斯汀，是名常常挑戰自己的演員。他的名言中我們看到，being 是動名詞，boring 是現在分詞，你知道怎麼分嗎？

Grammar Show

現在分詞是「形容詞」；而動名詞是「名詞」。動名詞是由「動詞+ing」而成的，在句子中我們要把當作名詞來看。首先來介紹，動名詞的功用：

1 當主詞

例 **Reading** helps you learn English.

閱讀幫助你學英文。

例 **Singing** is fun.

唱歌很好玩。

2 當「特定某些動詞」的受詞

例 I like **shopping**.

我喜歡逛街買東西。

例 He enjoys **practicing** Chinese calligraphy.

他喜愛練習書法。

例 Keep on **working**!　繼續工作！

例 I began **learning** German.　我開始學德文。

例 I don't mind **helping** you.　我不介意幫你。

★　在 be 動詞後面加的 V-ing 有時是現在分詞。

例 I am **eating** an apple.

我正在吃蘋果。

3　當介系詞的受詞

例 How can I understand the words without **looking** up dictionary?

我要如何知道這些字而又不用查字典？（without 為介系詞）

4　當為補語使用

例 His favorite hobby is **cooking.**

他最喜歡的嗜好是烹飪。（此補充說明主詞 His favorite hobby）

5　動名詞 **vs.** 現在分詞

例 Since Alex was ten years old, **swimming** has been his passion.

Alex 從十歲開始，游泳一直是他的熱愛。→為動名詞，當主詞。

例 A jellyfish killed Alex's **swimming** coach.

水母害死了 Alex 的游泳教練。→當現在分詞，形容名詞 coach。

例 Alex is **swimming** now, and a shark is approaching him.

Alex 正在游泳，而一個鯊魚正在靠近他。→當現在分詞，表示「現在進行式」。

Life Story

Christian Bale, a British actor, is known by starring a role of Batman. Before he got attention, he starred in smaller projects from independent producers. Christian usually has a big body transformation for a new movie. For example, he lost 28 kg for "*The Machinist*" to have a skeletal appearance. ❶After that, he was tasked with achieving 45 kg in six months for fitting the look of bulky Batman. Bale recalled it as far from a simple accomplishment: "...when it actually came to building muscle, I was useless. I couldn't do one push up the first day. All of the muscles were gone, so I had a real tough time rebuilding all of that." With the help of his personal trainer, he succeeded and even became too strong; therefore, he had to lose 8 kg before the shooting.

He said, "I do like taking stuff seriously that a lot of people look at as nonsense. I enjoy the insanity of that. And I like the commitment that is needed for that." ❷Well, it is not a surprise that he denied acting Batman in serial 3, and chose to play others challenging characters!

以扮演蝙蝠俠聞名的英國籍演員克里斯汀‧貝爾。他在成名之前，大部分的作品為在獨立製作的小成本影片中擔綱演出。克里斯近來常因為角色劇情的需要而調整身材。例如，他為了演 The Machinist 這部戲而爆瘦 28 公斤成為骷髏人。下戲後，為了要符合蝙蝠俠精壯的身材，他必須在六個月之內增重 45 公斤，且必須練出健美肌肉。他回想起來時，還是覺得這一點都不是一個簡單的事。他說：「但是實際要鍛鍊肌肉時，我超沒用的。第一天時，我根本連一個伏地挺身都做不來。所有的肌肉都不見了，這真的很難重新練出肌肉。」但是在健身教練的幫助下，他成功了，且還太壯了，所以在開拍前還必須減 8 公斤。

他曾說:「我喜愛對一般人來說是瘋了的執著。我享受其中的瘋狂。且我熱衷於付出。」也可以理解，這名演員為什麼不再接演蝙蝠俠3，而選擇挑戰更多的角色！

● skeletal [ˋskɛlətəl] **adj** 骨瘦如柴的　● bulky [ˋbʌlkɪ] **adj** 健壯的

Sentence Show ★

❶ After that, he was tasked with achieving 45 kg in six months for fitting the look of bulky Batman.

這裡你可以看到兩個動名詞，achieving 和 fitting。都是因為分別在介系詞 with 和 for 的後面，所以用動名詞。其實，道理很簡單，就是介系詞後面加的是名詞，而動名詞也是名詞的一種。

❷ Well, it is not a surprise that he denied acting as Batman in serial 3, and chose to play others challenging characters.

看到兩個 V-ing 的形式，acting 與 challenging。acting 是動名詞，在 deny，動詞表示否認，後接動名詞。（在 Unit 24 單元會更一進步說明）。challenging 則不是動名詞，而是現在分詞，當形容詞用修飾名詞 characters 角色。

 Practice Time ★

Q1：減肥和增肥對克里斯汀·貝爾來說不難。

_____.

Q2：演戲是克里斯汀·貝爾的熱愛。

_____.

Q1 Ans：Losing and gaining weight is not difficult for Christian Bale.

Q2 Ans：Acting is Christian Bale's passion.

Unit 23
動詞後接不定詞

❝ Why should I care about what other people think of me? I am who I am, and who I want to be. ❞
—— *Avril Lavigne* 艾薇兒‧拉維尼

（為什麼我要在意別人怎麼想我？我就是我，做我想成為的人。）

　　大部分的動詞後面如果要再接一個動詞時，第二個動詞通常可以是「不定詞」("to V") 形式，也可以是「動名詞」("Ving") 形式，如："start to think"及"start thinking"。然而，像上句中的動詞"want"則是其後只可接不定詞的動詞。現在，讓我們來看看，還有哪些動詞是後面只能接不定詞的吧！

Grammar Show ★

　　若沒有適當的連接詞或標點符號，一個英文句子裡只能有一個動詞。故當一個動詞後面出現另一個動詞時，必須使用「動詞+ to+原型動詞」或是「動詞+Ving」形式。然而，有些動詞僅能擇一形式使用，亦即，有些動詞後只能接「to+原型動詞」，有些僅能接「動名詞」("Ving")。本單元將首先討論前者。

　　後面只能接不定詞的動詞，常用如下：advise, ask, beg, challenge, command, convince, forbid, invite, permit, remind, require, tell, warn, urge, encourage, help, teach, train, allow, cause, choose, force, get, hire, expect, want, refuse…

例 Mary **plans to take** a trip to the USA this summer after she finishes her degree.

Mary 計畫今年夏天在她完成她的學位之後，去美國旅遊。

例 This car is way too expensive for me. I cannot **afford to buy** it.

這台車子對我來說太貴了。我買不起它。

例 Father is so disappointed at his son's dishonesty that he **refused to forgive** him.

父親對他兒子的不誠實感到如此地失望，以致於拒絕原諒他。

例 Sophie **expected to finish** the work by December.

Sophie 預期在十二月底前完成這份工作。

例 He **decided to leave** here immediately after he received the letter from his parents.

他收到父母的信之後就決定立刻離開這裡。

例 Remind me **to buy** some milk today.

提醒我今天買點牛奶回來。

例 Jessica advised they **to hold** a birthday party.

Jessica 建議他們辦一場生日派對。

例 Mom encourages Wisdom **to play** piano.

媽媽鼓勵Wisdom彈鋼琴。

註：對於非母語的我們來說，像這種哪些動詞後面一定要接不定詞或是動名詞的規則，的確是一個會讓人頭昏腦脹的麻煩。最好的方法，就是每遇到一次就背它一次。久了就可以記起來囉！

Life Story

Even though she knows some people might not appreciate her tomboy fashion and thick eyeliner, Canadian pop singer **❶Avril Lavigne still chooses to ignore these negative comments**. Actually, she is quite comfortable with her look and doesn't think there is anything which needs to be changed. Besides, she is keener on putting her music ahead rather than her image. Her debut album *Let Go* made her the youngest female soloist to reach the UK number 1. Since the release of *Let Go*, she has sold more than 30 million albums worldwide.

Ever since she started her career, Avril has stuck to her principle: "always be true to yourself". Firstly, **❷she refused to be a bubble gum pop singer**. Secondly, she rejected some gorgeous publicity shots because she thought those images don't really look like her. Finally, she only wrote and sang the songs she liked. All in all, we may conclude that Avril is anything but boring and normal.

即使她知道有些人也許不會欣賞她男孩氣的裝扮和厚重的眼線，艾薇兒‧拉維尼仍然選擇忽略這些負面的評論。事實上，她對自己的樣貌感到很自在，也不認為有哪個部位是需要改變的。除此之外，比起外貌，她更喜歡把音樂放在第一位。她的首張專輯《展翅高飛》讓她成為獲得英國排行榜第一名中最年輕的女性獨唱歌手。自發行《展翅高飛》後，她的專輯已在全世界銷售超過三千萬張。

從艾薇兒開始當歌手，她就一直堅持自己的原則：「永遠做最真的自己」。第一，她不願意當一個只以青少年為主要聽眾的歌手；第二，她有時會拒絕拍一些好看的宣傳照，因為她覺得那些照片並不像她。最後，她只寫和唱她喜歡的歌曲。整體來說，我們可以總結艾薇兒一點也不無聊與平凡。

● appreciate [əˋpriʃɪˏet] **V** 欣賞　● ignore [ɪgˋnor] **V** 忽略　● be keen on **ph** 喜歡…
● bubble gum **ph** 泡泡糖此處指以青少年為主要聽眾的流行音樂（的）
● reject [rɪˋdʒɛkt] **V** 拒絕

Sentence Show ★

❶ Avril Lavigne still chooses to ignore these negative comments.

句中動詞"choose"（選擇）之後如果要再接另一個動詞，只能接不定詞；故另一個動作「忽視」使用"to ignore"形式。

❷ She refused to be a bubble gum pop singer.

和上句的動詞"choose"相同，此句中的動詞"refuse"（拒絕）亦只能在其後使用不定詞，不可使用動名詞形式。故後方另一個動詞為"to be"（當）為不定詞形式。

 Practice Time ★

Q1：艾薇兒立志成為一個獨特的流行樂歌手。

_____.

Q2：全世界的樂迷們都期望能參加艾薇兒的演唱會。

_____.

Q1 Ans：Avril aims to be a unique pop singer.

Q2 Ans：Fans all around the world expect to attend Avril's concert.

Unit 24
動詞後接動名詞

"You can't look back; you have to keep looking [1]forward."

—— Lucy Liu 劉玉玲

（你不能往回看，你必須持續向前看。）

❶ forward [`fɔrwəd] adv 向前

　　在前一個單元提到過，某些動詞後面只能接不定詞，即"動詞+to+原型動詞"，而此單元則是會討論哪些動詞後面只能接動名詞，即"動詞+Ving"。上方劉玉玲的名言裡所出現的"keep looking forward"中的動詞"keep"，即屬於本單元的動詞範圍之一。

Grammar Show

　　動名詞"Gerund"的表現形式為"動詞+ing" (Ving)；當一個動詞後面出現另一個動詞時，除了使用前一單元的「不定詞」 ("to V") 外，有時則僅能接「動名詞」。這樣說或許有點抽象，首先就讓我們來看看看哪些動詞後面只能接動名詞吧！

❶ 後面只能接動名詞的動詞，常用到的如下：**avoid , enjoy , finish, keep (on), deny, admit, acknowledge, appreciate, anticipate, consider, escape, fancy, forgive, miss, quit, feel like, recall, recommend, resent, prohibit, discuss, practice, mind, give up, recollect ...etc**。

例 Molly **enjoys spending** time with her family very much.

Molly 非常享受與家人共度的時光。

例 Uncle Henry **quit smoking** many years ago because his doctor said it is better for his health.

Henry 叔叔好幾年前就戒菸了，因為他的醫生說這樣對他的健康比較好。

例 Carol **considered going** to cooking class to learn some Chinese dishes.

Carol 在考慮去上烹飪課，學幾道中國菜。

2 有些特別的動詞，後面可接不定詞或動名詞，但是句子意義會不同

--"**stop**"後接不定詞，有「停下原本正在做的事，然後開始去做某事」之意；接動名詞時，則表示「停止現在正在做的事」。

例 Simon **stopped to clean** the dishes.

Simon 停下他手上的事，去洗碗盤。

例 Simon **stopped cleaning** dishes.

Simon 停止洗碗盤。

--"**forget**", "**remember**"後接不定詞時，表示「忘記/記得去做某事」；後接動名詞時，則有「忘記/記得已做過某事」之意。

例 He **forgot / remembered to lock** the door.

他忘了 / 記得鎖門。

例 He **forgot / remembered locking** the door.

他忘了 / 記得他已經鎖門了。

Life Story

Having experienced some ups and downs in her career, the multi-talented actress Lucy Liu is now one of the most successful Chinese-American actresses in Hollywood.

When asked to name a Chinese-American actress, most people will say Liu. She is well known for her roles in *Kill Bill*, *Charlie's Angels* and the recent soap opera *Elementary*. However, [1]she admitted being a typecast Hollywood actress is actually not very easy. She said, "I wish people wouldn't just see me as the Asian girl who beats everyone up, or the Asian girl with no emotion. People see Julia Roberts or Sandra Bullock in a romantic comedy, but not me." [2]Since she enjoys acting so much, she never thought about quitting. She is determined to be a pioneer and finally prove that she can be cast as more characters than just an action star or a Dragon Lady, which are the stereotypes of Chinese women in Hollywood movies.

在經歷了事業的起落後，多才多藝的劉玉玲現在已經是好萊塢最成功的美籍華裔女星之一。

當被要求說出一個華裔女星的名字時，許多人都會說出劉玉玲的名字。她以《追殺比爾》、《霹靂嬌娃》以及最近的影集《福爾摩斯與華生》中的角色而知名。然而，她承認做為一個擁有不同出身的女演員在好萊塢發展並不容易的。她說：「我希望人們不會將我看做是打倒每個人的亞洲女孩，或是沒有情緒的亞洲女孩。人們視茱莉亞・羅勃茲和珊卓・布拉克為浪漫喜劇女星，但他們不會覺得我是。」因為她非常享受演戲這件事，她從未想過放棄。她決心成為一個先鋒，並在最終證明自己可以演出更多不同的角色，而不是只能成為武打明星或母老虎那些好萊塢電影中典型的中國女性角色。

- accomplishment [ə`kɑmplɪʃmənt] n 成就
- motivator [`motɪvetɚ] n 動力
- colleague [kɑ`lig] n 同事
- perseverance [ˌpɝsə`vɪrəns] n 堅持不懈

Sentence Show ★

❶ She admitted being a typecast Hollywood actress is actually not very easy

動詞"admit"（承認）後面如果要加動詞，需使用動名詞形式，故此處動詞 "be"需改為"being"。

❷ Since she enjoys acting so much, she never thought about quitting

如同上句一樣，動詞"enjoy"（享受）後方的動詞亦需使用動名詞形式，故動詞 "act"需改為"acting"。此外，句首的"since"在這裡不做「自從」解釋，而是 「因為」的意思。

 Practice Time ★

Q1：劉玉玲心存感激能做為一個美籍華裔女星。

_____.

Q2：劉玉玲考慮演出不同的角色。

_____.

Q1 Ans：Lucy Liu appreciates being a Chinese-American actress.

Q2 Ans：Lucy Liu considers playing different roles.

Unit 25
現在分詞、過去分詞

❝ You are ❶amazing just the way you are. ❞
—— Bruno Mars 火星人布魯諾

（你現在的樣子就是最美的樣子。）

❶ amazing [ə`mezɪŋ] adj 驚為天人的

　　此句中的"amazing"（驚為天人的）為現在分詞，但並非做為進行式使用，而是做為一個修飾主詞的形容詞，也就是用來修飾 "you"（你），說明「你」是「讓人驚為天人的」。

Grammar Show ★

　　又多了一個術語「分詞」有沒有搞混呢？分詞是由「動詞」演變而來的，而分詞有兩種為「現在分詞」、「過去分詞」。「現在分詞」的形式為"Ving"；而「過去分詞」的形式則為"Ved/Ven"。

　　分詞扮演「形容詞」的角色。而分詞和不同的助動詞結合在一起就是我們之前所學到的諸多時態。例如，be動詞+現在分詞= 進行式；have / has + 過去分詞= 完成式。是不是理解了呢？請看下面句子囉！

❶ **動詞變成「現在分詞」的規→律如下：**
　　　直接在動詞之後加上"ing"，如: talk → talking
　　　當動詞字尾是 "e" 時，則要去 "e" 加 "ing"，如: make → making
　　　單字為單音節，而這個音節的母音又是短母音時，則需要重複字尾子音，再加
"ing"，如: sit → sitting

② 動詞變成「過去分詞」的規律如下:

直接在動詞之後加上"ed",如: talk → talked

當動詞字尾是"子音+ y" 時,則要去 "y" 加 "ied",如: study → studied

若字尾有不發音的 "e" 時,過去分詞可在後面直接加 "d",如: close →closed

動詞末兩個字母為「母音+子音」時,過去分詞則需重覆字尾+ed,如: plan → planned。

③ 「現在分詞」和「過去分詞」均可表達不同的時態,說明句中動作發生的時間。「現在分詞」用來表示動詞的「現在式」、「正在進行」的狀態;「過去分詞」則用來表示動詞的「被動」或是「已完成」的狀態。

★ 「現在分詞」和「過去分詞」做為「動詞時態」的使用,可參考本書 Part 2。而「過去分詞」做為「被動語態」的使用,則可參考 Part 4。

④ 「現在分詞」和「過去分詞」均為做「形容詞」使用;前者表示「某事是…的」;後者則表示「某人感到…的」。

例 This book is **interesting**.

這本書很有趣。

例 I am **interested** in this book.

我對這本書很感興趣。

例 He is **bored**.

他感到無聊。

例 He is a **boring** person.

他令人感到無聊。

	過去分詞	現在分詞
無聊、沒趣	bored (感到無趣的)	boring (令人無趣的)
有趣	interested (感到有趣的)	interesting (令人有趣的)
失意沮喪	frustrated (感到沮喪的)	frustrating (令人沮喪的)
興奮	excited (感到興奮的)	exciting (令人興奮的)
困惑	confused (感到困惑的)	confusing (令人困惑的)
受驚、害怕	frightened (感到害怕的)	frightening (令人害怕的)
氣惱	annoyed (感到氣惱的)	annoying (令人氣惱的)

Life Story

Bruno Mars was born in Hawaii. He was nicknamed "Bruno" by his father when he was a child, because his father thought he resembled the professional wrestler Bruno Sammartino. Later, he adopted his stage name from this nickname, adding "Mars" at the end because "a lot of girls say I'm out of this world, so I was like I guess I'm from Mars."

Shortly after moving to Los Angeles in 2004 to pursue his music career, he signed for a record company. However, ❶the result was quite disappointing. The deal went nowhere. ❷It seemed no one was interested in his music. Instead of choosing another career path, he stuck to his goal. Although he aimed to be a solo artist from the beginning, he was also willing to write, to produce and to do anything that it took to be recognized as an artist. All in all, it was the talent and persistence Bruno Mars showed that contributed in a big way to his success.

出生於夏威夷的火星人布魯諾 。當他還是孩子的時候，他的父親為他取了小名「布魯諾」，因為當時他和職業摔角手布魯諾·薩馬蒂諾很相像。之後，他使用了這個小名做為他的藝名，並加上了「火星人」在其後，因為「很多女孩都說我就像從外星球來的，所以或許我是來自火星的吧！」

在搬到洛杉磯追求他的音樂事業後，他很快地在 2004 年和一間唱片公司簽約。然而，結果很令人失望。唱片公司與他的合作並沒有任何的進展。似乎沒有人對他的音樂感興趣。他並沒有因此選擇其他的職業規劃，而是堅持他的目標。雖然他從一開始的目標就是做為一個獨唱歌手，他仍然願意為他人寫作並製作歌曲，並做一切可以被認定是一名歌手的事情。從各方面而言，火星人布魯諾的才能和堅持不懈是締造他的成功的一大部分。

- nickname [`nɪk͵nem] Ⅴ 給…起綽號
- resemble [rɪ`zɛmbl] Ⅴ 相像
- wrestler [`rɛslɚ] ｎ 摔跤選手
- adopt [ə`dɑpt] Ⅴ 採用

Sentence Show ⭐

❶ The result was quite disappointing.

現在分詞"disappointing"（令人失望的）做為被動的形容詞修飾主詞"the result"（結果），說明這個結果是「令人失望的」。此處不可使用過去分詞形式"disappointed"（感到失望的），因為只有「人」會「感到失望的」（主動形容詞），但「事情」不會。

❷ It seemed no one was interested in his music.

"interested"（感到有興趣的）為一個過去分詞形式的主動形容詞，說明子句中主詞"no one"（沒有人）是「不感興趣的」的。此外，對「某事感到興趣」需使用介系詞"in"加事物，即"be interested in+事物"。

 **Practice Time** ⭐

Q1：人們對火星人布魯諾的新歌感到很興奮。

_____.

Q2：火星人布魯諾的新歌很令人興奮。

_____.

Q1 Ans：People are excited about Bruno Mars' new songs.

Q2 Ans：Bruno Mars' new songs are very exciting.

Part 3

句型

Unit 01

單字、片語、子句

"I always ❶look for a challenge and something that's different."

── Tom Cruise 湯姆・克魯斯

（我總是尋求挑戰，並尋找特異的事物。）

❶ look for ph 尋找

讓我們由這個句子的各個部分來舉例說明本單元的重點。"I", "challenge", "something"等字都叫做「單字」，而"look for"則為「片語」。還有子句，你知道哪裡嗎？

 **Grammar Show** ★

❶ 單字"**Vocabulary**"，是所有句子組成的最小元素，依詞性和意思的不同，可排列出不同的句子。八大詞類為：

「名詞」→ "dog" (狗)，"city" (城市)，"uncle" (叔叔) 等。

「代名詞」→ "you" (你/妳)，"I" (我)，"he / she" (他/她) 等。

「動詞」→ "jump" (跳)，"walk" (走路)，"eat" (吃) 等。

「形容詞」→ "cute" (可愛的)，"terrible" (很糟的)，"young" (年輕的) 等。

「副詞」→ "slowly" (慢慢地)，"loudly" (大聲地)，"heavily" (重重地) 等。

「介系詞」"on" (在…上面)，"under" (在…下面)，"next" (在旁邊)

「連接詞」→ "and" (和 / 與)，"but" (但是)，"be cause" (因為)

「感嘆詞」→ "oh" (喔)，"whoa" (哇)，"Hmm" (嗯)

❷ 片語 **"Phrases"**，沒有主詞與動詞的單字組合是片語

例 The finger food **at the party** was delicious.

　舞會上的小吃很美味。（"at the party"是介系詞片語當形容詞用，用來形容前面的 "food"）

例 **Playing tennis** is fun.

　打網球是有趣的。（"playing tennis"是名詞片語，此處做為主詞使用）

❸ 子句和句子

--句子 (Sentence) 也是由一群字所組成，其中包含一個主要動詞，且句意完整。第一個字的字母要大寫。

例 She wants to be a teacher.

　她想當老師。

--子句 Clause 分為四類，**(1)** 主要子句；**(2)** 從屬子句（副詞子句）；**(3)** 關係子句（形容詞）**(4)** 名詞子句。在之後的單元，我們會在說明 **(2)**、**(3)**、**(4)**。

例 He fell doenstairs and broke his leg.

　他從樓梯上摔下來，而且還摔斷腿。（and 連接兩個主要子句）

例 **Before he went to work,** he ate a sandwich for breakfast.

　在他去上班之前，他吃了一個三明治當早餐。（在一個完整的句子中，我們看到底線標的從屬子句）（he ate a sandwich for breakfast為主要子句，可單獨存在）

例 This is the song **that I listened to last night.**

　這首歌是我昨晚聽的。（"that I listened to last night"是形容詞子句，用來形容前面的"song"）

例 **What she reads** is very interesting.

　她讀的東西非常有趣。（"what she read"是名詞子句，在句中做為主詞使用）

 **Life Story**

Tom Cruise was born in New York and grew up in near poverty. However, ❶money shortage may not have been the only problem Cruise faced when he was young. At the time, the family was dominated by his abusive father, who constantly beat and kicked young Cruise. He was unable to escape from his father's bullying until his mother finally left his father when he was twelve.

What happened in the past doesn't affect the way Cruise sees life. He is still passionate about life and his job. He always says he loves what he does and feels privileged to be able to do what he loves. ❷Although he is an international superstar, he has never even for one day been late to a set. When he works, he always works very hard. He once describes himself as an "all-or-nothing kind of person". He will never do things halfway. If he is going to do something, he goes all the way and gives 100%.

　　湯姆‧克魯斯在紐約出生，成長時期家境近乎貧窮。然而，金錢的匱乏不僅僅是克魯斯年輕時所要面對的問題。在當時，他的家中由兇暴的父親主導，而父親常常毆打及踢年幼的克魯斯。他直到 12 歲時，母親離開父親，才逃離父親的家暴。

　　過去所發生的事並沒有影響克魯斯看待生活的方式。他仍然對生活及工作有著熱情。他總是說，他喜歡他所做的事，也覺得很幸運能夠做喜歡做的事。雖然他是一個國際巨星，但他沒有一天晚到片場。當他工作時，他總是很努力工作。他有次形容自己是「要嘛就不做，要做就是做到最好的那種人」。他絕對不會做事做一半。如果他要做某事，他一定會堅持到最後並百分之百付出。

- poverty[ˋpɑvɚtɪ] **n** 貧困
- escape [əˋskep] **V** 逃跑
- privileged [ˋprɪvɪlɪdʒd] **adj** 幸運的
- shortage [ˋʃɔrtɪdʒ] **n** 缺少
- passionate[ˋpæʃənɪt] **adj** 熱情的

Sentence Show ★

❶ Money shortage may not have been the only problem Cruise faced when he was young.

人名亦可視為單字的一種，所以這句話裡一共由 14 個單字所組成。 "Money shortage"為名詞片語，亦為此句的主語；而"when he was young"在這裡則是一個表示「時間」的從屬子句，用來修飾主要子句"money shortage may not have been the only problem Cruise faced"。

❷ Although he is an international superstar, he has never even for one day been late to a set.

這是 16 個單字組成的句子。句中以逗號區分出前方的「從屬子句」和後方的「主要子句」。主要子句中則又可依序看出「名詞片語」"one day"和「形容詞片語」"late to a set"等。

Practice Time ★

Q1：湯姆・克魯斯是一個舉世聞名的演員。

_____

Q2：雖然湯姆・克魯斯和他妻子離婚了，他還是常和他可愛的女兒保持聯絡。

_____

Q1 Ans：Tom Cruise is a famous actor all over the world.

Q2 Ans：Although Tom Cruise divorced his wife, he still often keeps in touch with his lovely daughter.

Unit 02
直述句

❝ I have always felt that if you ❶back down from a fear, the ghost of that fear never goes away. It ❷diminishes people. ❞

—— Hugh Jackman 休‧傑克曼

（我總是覺得，如果你因為害怕而放棄，害怕的鬼魂就永遠不會離開。它會削弱人們。）

❶ back down 𝐩𝐡 打退堂鼓　❷ diminish [dəˋmɪnɪʃ] 𝐕 削弱

　　上述名言的第二個句子是「簡單句」，即基本的「主詞+動詞+受詞」句型。而此簡單句的形式，則屬於「陳述說話者意見」的「直述句」。

Grammar Show ★

　　直述句 "Declarative Sentence" 的基本句型為「簡單句」；使用直述句的目的通常是說話者「表達自己意見、陳述事件或事實」。常見的直述句句型，可依動詞形式分為下列幾種：

❶ be 動詞

例 I **am** a student. 我是個學生。

例 His uncle **is** cooking. 他的叔叔正在煮東西。

例 John **was** my classmate at school. John 是我以前學校的同學。

2 一般動詞

倘若此一般動詞為不及物動詞，即該動詞本身的意義很完整，則動詞後可不需加受詞，直述句句型可為「主詞+不及物動詞」：

例 Birds **fly**. 鳥會飛。

例 Mr. Brown **spoke** at the meeting yesterday.

　　Brown 先生昨天在會議上發言。

而使用及物動詞時，因為動詞的意義不夠完整，故需使用「主詞+及物動詞+受詞」的句型讓語意更加完整：

例 I **love** my mother.

　　我愛我的母親。（倘若只有"I love."則語義不明，到底我愛的是誰？或是什麼？）

例 She **saw** Peter this afternoon.

　　她今天下午有看到 Peter。（倘若只有"She saw"則不知道她到底看到了什麼。）

3 助動詞

例 She **can** sing "A Whole New World".

　　她會唱《*A Whole New World*》。

例 Lily **may** go to America next week.

　　Lily 可能下週會去美國。

4 完成式動詞

例 I **have never seen** this man before.

　　我以前從未看過這個男人。

例 Jason **has lived** in Taipei for ten years.

　　Jason 已經在台北住了 10 年了。

 **Life Story**

Hugh Jackman is an Australian actor. Although his long-running role as Wolverinein the *X-Men* film series has won him international recognition, Jackman is nothing like the character in real life. He is soft, polite and always sees his family as his priority.

By 2016, Jackman and his wife Deborra-Lee, who is 13 years older than him, will have been married for 20 years. ❶He loves and respects his wife. He once joked, "Your wife is always right, very simple. I think I am going to get it tattooed on my forehead." He and his wife adopted two children. He often says that he learns from parenting and raising his children. ❷Being with his kids always gives him a lot of surprise and inspiration. For example, he claims that he has possessed better time management skills since he had two kids. He has learned how to find a balance between his family life and his career. Let's hope he can manage to show us his new film soon.

休・傑克曼是一位澳洲的演員。雖然他在《X 戰警》系列電影中長期演出的金剛狼角色,為他贏得了國際的知名度,在現實生活中,傑克曼和這個角色一點也不相像。他很溫和、有禮貌,並且總是把他的家庭視為首要。

在 2016 年時,傑克曼將與大他 13 歲的妻子黛博拉李結婚 20 年。他愛他的妻子,並且也尊敬她。他曾開玩笑說:「你的妻子永遠是對的。就是這麼簡單。我想我將把這件事刺青在我的額頭上。」他和他的妻子領養了兩個孩子。他常說他從為人父母和養育孩子中學習。和他的孩子在一起,總是給他很多的靈感和啟發。比如說,他宣稱在有了兩個孩子後,他擁有更好的時間管理能力。他學會如何在家庭生活和事業中獲得平衡。讓我們期望他能很快地讓我們看到他的新片。

- recognition [ˌrɛkəgˋnɪʃən] **n** 識別 ● priority [praɪˋɔrətɪ] **n** 優先
- tattoo [tæˋtu] **v** 刺青 ● forehead [ˋfɔrˌhɛd] **n** 前額 ● possess [pəˋzɛs] **v** 擁有

Sentence Show ★

❶ He loves and respects his wife.

此句為使用一般動詞的直述句。"love"和"respect"均為及物動詞，故後面需要有受詞"his wife"，整個句子的語義才能完整（才知道休傑克曼愛著的和尊敬的人是誰。）

❷ Being with his kids always gives him a lot of surprise and inspiration.

這個句子看來複雜，但拆開來分析後就會發現也是一個使用一般動詞的直述句。"Being with his kids"為主詞，"gives"為及物動詞，而受詞"him"使整個句子的語義更加完整。

 Practice Time ★

Q1：休・傑克曼的家鄉在澳洲。

_____ .

Q2：休・傑克曼會演戲也會唱歌。

_____ .

Q1 Ans：Hugh Jackman's hometown is in Australia.

Q2 Ans：Hugh Jackman can act and sing.

Unit 03
否定句

I do think it's important for young women to know that ❶magazine ❷covers are ❸retouched. People don't really look like that. 🎙️

—— Kate Winslet 凱特•溫絲蕾

（我真的覺得讓年輕的女性們知道雜誌封面都是經過後製的這件事很重要。人實際看起來並不是那樣。）

❶magazine [ˏmægə`zin] ⓝ 雜誌　❷cover [`kʌvɚ] ⓝ 封面　❸retouch [rɪ`tʌtʃ] ⓥ 潤飾

🎬 Small Talks

　　"don't"為"do not"的縮寫，在這裡依句意可翻譯為「不是」。be 動詞"am, is, are"、助動詞"do, does"之後加上否定詞"not"可表示否定之意。

🎬 Grammar Show

　　"not"為否定詞，是用來表示否認，拒絕，或與事實相反。當句子中的 be 動詞"am, is, are"或助動詞"do, does"後面跟著否定詞"not"時，句子就會由原本的肯定語句變為否定語句。

例 I am a student.
　　我是學生。
　　I am **not** a student.
　　我不是學生。

例 They are from America.

他們是從美國來的。

They are **not** from America.

他們不是從美國來的。

例 I do like to go out with you.

我真的喜歡和你出去。（這邊的 do 為強調用法）

I do **not** like to go out with you.

我不喜歡和你出去。

例 He does love his wife.

他真的愛他的妻子。（這邊的 does 為強調用法）

He does **not** love his wife.

他不愛他的妻子。

★ "am, is, are"均為 be 動詞，從上述例子可看出，加上"not"後句子成為否定句。此外，"be 動詞+not"也可用縮寫方式表達："am not"= "ain't"（"am not"其實一般較少使用縮寫，ain't 是較為通俗的口語或俚語裡的用法，較不正式），is not=isn't，are not=aren't。

除了在 be 動詞或助動詞後加"not"形成否定句以外，有些單字其實本身已具備定否定意味，所以當句中有這些單字出現時，不可以再加"not"來形成否定句。例如: no+名詞 (nobody, nowhere, no one, nothing)，hardly, barely, seldom, never。

例 Mother always exercises in the morning.

媽媽永遠在早上運動。

Mother **never** exercises in the morning.

媽媽從不在早上運動。

例 Everyone enjoys listening to her singing.

每個人享受聽她的歌聲。

No one enjoys listening to her singing.

沒有人享受聽她的歌聲。

Life Story

Kate Winslet began her career when she was 16, and then achieved recognition for her leading role as Rose DeWitt Bukater in the movie *Titanic*, the highest-grossing film of all time.

While shooting *Titanic* at the age of 22, she was quite insecure about her chubby body image. However, now almost 40, the acclaimed actress and mother of three is confident of her appearance. She once admitted she has a crumble baby belly and breasts which are worse since her kids were born. "❶I don't look fantastic all the time," she said. "Nobody is perfect. I just don't believe in perfection." Perhaps this is the reason many people now see her as a role model though Kate doesn't think she is special at all. "❷My life is not the soap opera people would like it to be; in fact, it's not a soap opera at all. It's just a life," she concluded.

凱特‧溫斯蕾在 16 歲時開始她的演藝事業，之後在最賣座的電影《鐵達尼號》中飾演女主角蘿絲‧狄威特‧布克特，打開了知名度。

在拍攝《鐵達尼號》時，22 歲的她對於自己豐腴的身材感到很沒有安全感。然而，在將近 40 歲的現在，這位倍受讚揚的女演員、同時也是三個小孩的母親，對於自己的外表有了自信。她曾經承認她有突出的產後小腹，而胸部曲線也因生過孩子而不如以往。「我並非無時無刻都是完美的，」她說。「沒有人是完美的，我也不相信有人是完美的。」也許是這個原因，現在很多人視她為模範。但凱特卻不認為自己有何特別之處。「我的生活不是人們所期望的肥皂劇；事實上，它一點也不像一齣戲」，她說。

- recognition [ˌrɛkəgˈnɪʃən] **n** 知名度 ● acclaimed [əˈklem] **adj** 受到讚揚的
- belly [ˈbɛlɪ] **n** 肚子 ● soap opera **ph** 肥皂劇 ● conclude [kənˈklud] **v** 做結論

Sentence Show ★

❶ I don't look fantastic all the time.

這個句子的動詞是"look"，依照句子的意思要翻譯為「看起來」；而 "look"前面有否定詞 "don't"，否定了"look" 這個動作，表示「不是看起來」。此外，要注意句子的主詞是第一人稱 "I"（我），所以使用否定詞時，必須用 "don't"，而不是 "doesn't"。

❷ My life is not the soap opera people would like it to be.

我的生活 (my life) 屬於第三人稱，所以動詞使用 "is"，而不用 "am"或 "are"。否定詞 "not" 放在動詞之後，此類句子的表達形式為「A 不是 B」，在本句中亦即「我的生活不是人們所期望的肥皂劇」。

 Practice Time ★

Q1：凱特・溫斯蕾不是美國人。

_____ .

Q2：凱特・溫斯蕾並不在乎她的體重。

_____ .

Q1 Ans：Kate Winslet is not an American.

Q2 Ans：Kate Winslet doesn't care about her weight.

Unit 04
Yes / No 疑問句

Do we need distance to get close?
—— Sarah Jessica Parker 莎拉・傑西卡・派克

（我們需要距離來讓彼此靠近嗎？）

　　這是個助動詞"Do"開頭的問句，這類問句的答案通常會包含"yes"或"no"。本句還原為直述句是"We need distance to get close."。那麼直述句變問句的規則是什麼？又還有沒有其他包含"yes"或"no"回答的問句形式呢？

Grammar Show ★

　　疑問句 (Interrogative Sentence) 是用來提出問題的句子，句尾一定要加問號？來表示。疑問句可分兩大類: Yes/No 疑問句和 5W1H 疑問句，本單元將先說明所謂的「Yes/No 疑問句」，而 5W1H 疑問句則會在後面的 Unit 5 元解釋。

❶ Yes/No 疑問句

「Yes/No 疑問句」通常是問話人在尋求同意或是許可時所使用的疑問句。而回話人會在詳細回答前先給予 Yes/No 的回答。那麼，我們要如何從直述句變為「Yes/No 疑問句」呢？在回答這個問題前，我們先來看兩個直述句變為「Yes/No 疑問句」的例子：

例 直述句：He is from Taiwan. 他來自台灣。
　　疑問句：**Is he** from Taiwan? 他來自台灣嗎？

例 直述句：They go to school by bus. 他們搭公車上學。

疑問句：**Do they** go to school by bus? 他們搭公車上學嗎？

2 直述句變疑問句

從以上兩個例句組可看出，be 動詞的直述句變為疑問句時，僅需將 be 動詞置於句首，並依時態做變化；而一般動詞的直述句，則依主詞人稱與時態的不同，在句首加上"Do", "Does"或"Did"。另外還需注意的是，如果回答"Yes"，則後面要加「肯定句」；如果答"No"，則後面要接「否定句」

例 **Is your cousin** going to the ice cream shop now?

No, she is not.

你的表妹現在正要去冰淇淋店嗎？

不，她不是（正要去冰淇淋店）。

例 **Are they** in the same art class?

Yes, they are in the same art class.

他們上同一堂美術課嗎？

是的，他們上同一堂美術課。

例 **Did he** tell you about his adventures?

No, he didn't

他有告訴你他的冒險故事了嗎？

不，他沒說。

例 **Do you** usually play games with Chris?

Yes, I usually play games with Chris.

你經常會跟 Chris 玩遊戲嗎？

是的，我經常跟 Chris 玩遊戲

Life Story

[1]Do you know the American television romantic sitcom named *Sex and the City*? If the answer is positive, you should also know the leading role of Sarah Jessica Parker. The show follows the lives of four female friends and the most common topic they discuss in each episode is relationships.

"[2]Are single women less attractive?" While most people may still be thinking of the answer to this question, Parker has already given her answer: "No". Although she has been happily married for almost 20 years, she still has her own perspective on the idea of being single. Nowadays, the public tends to think people who choose to be single are less attractive. Parker points out these people are actually very sexy and smart. In her opinion, these people are just taking time to decide what they want in their lives and whom they want to spend it with.

你知道一齣叫做《慾望城市》的美國影集嗎？如果答案是肯定的，那麼你一定知道戲裡的女主角莎拉‧傑西卡‧派克。這齣戲是關於四個女性好友的生活，而男女關係則是每一集裡最常被談論的話題。

「單身女子都比較沒有吸引力嗎？」也許當很多人還在思考這個問題的答案時，派克已經給出了她的答案：「不會的。」即使她已經快樂地結婚近 20 年，她對於單身這件事仍有自己獨特的看法。當社會大眾認為選擇單身的人通常比較不出眾時，派克卻覺得這些人非常迷人和聰明。照她的說法，這些選擇單身的人，只是正在花時間決定他們要什麼樣的生活，以及和什麼樣的人一起生活。

- romantic [rə`mæntɪk] adj 浪漫的
- positive [`pɑzətɪv] adj 確定的
- attractive [ə`træktɪv] adj 有吸引力的
- perspecticve [pɚ`spɛktɪv] n 看法
- episode [`ɛpə͵sod] n （連續劇的）一集

Sentence Show ★

❶ Do you know the American television romantic sitcom named *Sex and the City*?

這句話的直述句原句是"I know the American romantic sitcom named *Sex and the City*."（我知道一個叫做《慾望城市》的美國影集）。因為本句動詞是一般動詞"know"、主詞是第一人稱單數"I"，所以改為疑問句時，需在句首使用"Do"，並把主詞改為"you"，即成為本句的問句形式。

❷ Are single women less attractive?

本句的直述句原句是"Single women are less attractive."（單身女子比較沒有魅力。）；因為句中主詞是複數 women，所以 be 動詞用"are"，所以改為疑問句時，需把"are"提到句首，成為本句的問句形式：「單身女子比較沒有魅力嗎？」

 Practice Time ★

Q1：莎拉・傑西卡・派克是學生嗎？

_____ .

Q2：莎拉・傑西卡・派克愛她的丈夫嗎？

_____ .

Q1 Ans：Is Sarah Jessica Parker a student?

Q2 Ans：Does Sarah Jessica Parker love her husband?

Unit 05

5W1H 疑問句

❝ When do I feel my best? When I haven't looked in a ❶mirror for days, and I'm doing things that make me happy. ❞

—— Anne Hathaway 安•海瑟薇

（我什麼時候會覺得自己最好？是在當我很多天沒有看鏡子時，以及做能讓我自己開心的事時。）

❶ mirror [`mɪrə] ❶ 鏡子

　　這裡是"5W1H"疑問句中以"when"（何時）開頭的疑問句。和 Yes / No 問句一樣，5W1H 也是問句的一種方式。差別在，回答 Yes / No 問句時我們會回答 Yes / No，而 5W1H 我們會就是說出單純答案。

 **Grammar Show** ★

　　「Yes/No 疑問句」已在 Unit 4 解釋過，這裡我們就來解釋「5W1H」的用法：

　　「5W1H」問句是指由 "What"（什麼），"When"（何時），"Where"（何地），"Who"（何人），"Why"（為什麼）和 "How"（如何）起首的疑問句。其基本句型結構為：「5W1H」+ be 動詞/助動詞+主詞+（受詞/補語）？

❶ **What**：問「什麼」，通常用來問一件物品，事件或是理由等等

例 **What** is your name?

　　妳的名字是什麼？

例 **What** does John do for a living?

John 的工作是什麼？

2 **When**：問「時間」

例 **When** is the last train?

最後一班火車是幾點？

例 **When** does the concert start?

音樂會何時開始？

3 **Where**：問「地點」

例 **Where** is the nearest parking lot?

最近的停車場在哪裡？

例 **Where** does Julia live?

Julia 住在哪裡？

4 **Who**：問「誰、人物」

例 **Who** didn't clean the closet?

誰沒有清空櫃子？

例 **Who** is going to sign up for the contest?

有誰要報名參加這比賽？

5 **Why**：問「原因」

例 **Why** are you laughing?

妳在笑什麼？

例 **Why** do you always arrive late for the meeting?

為什麼你每次開會都遲到？

6 **How**：問「方法、感覺」

例 **How** are you today?

你今天好嗎？

例 **How** do you usually go to work?

你平常怎麼去上班的？

Life Story

"①Who is Anne Hathaway?" After the release of *The Devil Wears Prada, One Day and Les Misérables,* this seems to be a silly question to ask. Perhaps the question we should ask is "②Why is she so popular? What does she do to make people love her so much?"

To start with, she quit her religious belief to show her support for her brother. She was raised Roman Catholic and announced she wanted to be a nun when she was a child. However, after realizing her brother Michael was gay, she decided not to attend Catholic Church anymore because she couldn't support a religion that was against her brother. Secondly, she is a big believer in equality. She thinks there is nothing she can't do because she is a girl. Just like the assistant she played in the movie *The Devil Wears Prada,* she always works with great perseverance, effort and in accordance with her beliefs. Probably these are the answers we seek for our original questions.

　　「誰是安・海瑟薇」在電影《穿著 Prada 的惡魔》、《真愛挑日子》、和《悲慘世界》上映後，這似乎是個傻問題。或許我們應該問的問題是：「為什麼她這麼受歡迎？她做了什麼讓人們這麼喜愛她？」

　　首先，她為了支持她的哥哥而放棄了她的宗教信仰。她在天主教家庭長大，並在小時候就宣告長大後要成為一名修女。然而，在知道她的哥哥麥克是同性戀者後，她決定再也不上天主教堂，因為她無法支持一個反對她兄長的宗教。第二，她很相信性別同等的概念。她認為，沒有一件事是因為她是女孩子所以就不能做的。就像她在《穿著 Prada 的惡魔》電影裡的助理一角，她總是帶著堅忍的毅力和努力，以及自己的信仰工作。也許這些就是我們所尋找的上方問題的答案了。

- silly [ˋsɪlɪ] **adj** 愚蠢的
- raise [rez] **v** 養育
- assistant [əˋsɪstənt] **n** 助理
- religious [rɪˋlɪdʒəs] **adj** 宗教的
- equality [iˋkwɑlətɪ] **n** 平等

Sentence Show ★

❶ Who is Anne Hathaway?

這句是以疑問詞"who"（誰）開頭的問句。一般這樣的問句，答案會是說明對方的身份或是和聽話者的關係等。這裡原本的回答可以是"she is an actress."（她是一位女演員。），但因為安海瑟薇已經很知名了，故文章中沒有做這樣的回答，而是說這是一個愚蠢的問題。

❷ Why is she so popular? What does she do to make people love her so much?

第一個"why"（為什麼）為句首的疑問句，問的是某事的原因，如此處問的是「安・海瑟薇受歡迎的原因」；而第二個問句以"what"（什麼）開頭，問的是「安・海瑟薇做了『什麼』使她受到人們喜愛」。

 Practice Time ★

Q1：安・海瑟薇是如何變成演員的？

_____.

Q2：安・海瑟薇是哪裡人？

_____.

Q1 Ans：How did Anne Hathaway become an actress?

Q2 Ans：Where is Anne Hathaway from?

Unit 06
祈使句

> Listen, smile, agree. And then do ❶whatever you were gonna do anyway.
>
> —— Robert Downey Jr. 小勞勃・道尼

（聆聽、微笑、同意。然後去做任何你本來要做的事。）

❶ whatever [hwɑtˋɛvɚ] **pron** 任何…的事

　　大家應該注意到上方這兩句話中均沒有主詞，這就是祈使句的一個重要特點。祈使句的主詞為「你」（you），故兩句話的原句應為"You listen, smile, and agree." 和" You do whatever you were gonna do anyway"。而句中的"gonna"則為"going to"的口語化寫法。

Grammar Show ★

　　祈使句"Imperative Sentence"是用來表示「命令、請求或禁止」的句子，通常主詞為「你/妳」，但在句中，主詞通常是被省略的，這是因為使用祈使句時，說話者與聽話者通常是在同一個語境下，說話者不需特別在句中提到"you"（你），聽話者也知道說話者說話的對象是自己，故可省略主詞。此外，祈使句的句尾通常以！結尾。例句如下：

❶ **祈使句的肯定句型：原型動詞+ (受詞)**

　　例 (You) Do the homework! 寫作業！(省略主詞"你")

例 (You) Go ahead! 就直接去做吧！(省略主詞"你")

例 (You) Keep off! 請勿靠近！(省略主詞"你")

2 祈使句的否定句型：**Don't+ 原型動詞+ (受詞)**

例 (You) Don't do the homework. 不要寫作業！(省略主詞"你")

例 (You) Don't go! 不要走！(省略主詞"你")

3 be 動詞的祈使句：**Be / Don't be+ 動詞原型+ (受詞)**

例 (You) Be yourself! 做你自己！(省略主詞"你")

例 (You) Don't be quiet! 請不要安靜！(省略主詞"你")

4 用使役動詞所構成的祈使句：**Let / make / have + 受詞+ 原型動詞**

例 (You) Let me go! 讓我走！(省略主詞"你")

例 (You) Make me a cup of tea! 給我泡一杯茶！(省略主詞"你")

例 (You) Have Emma come to my office! 讓 Emma 來我的辦公室！(省略主詞 "你")

5 請求語氣的祈使句：**Please+原型動詞**

例 Please be quiet! 請安靜！

例 Please don't waste food! 請不要浪費食物！

 **Life Story**

"❶Do not do drugs!" This may be the thing Robert Downey Jr. would say if he is asked to give advice to the youth.

From 1996 through 2000, Downey was arrested on charges of using drugs, including heroin, cocaine and marijuana, several times. He explained the reason he was addicted to drugs was because his father had been giving drugs to him since he was little. Although later he went through rehab programs numerous times following court orders, the treatments were never successful. It was not until 2001 that Downey was finally ready to work toward a full recovery from drugs. While talking about his past experiences of failing to control his addictive behavior on the *Oprah Winfrey Show*, he said to people who were suffering from drug addiction, "❷Please go reach out for help! It's not that difficult to overcome these seemingly ghastly problems... what's hard is to decide to do it!"

「不要吸毒！」如果小勞勃・道尼被要求給年輕人一些建議，這也許是他會想說的話。

從 1996 年到 2000 年，道尼因為使用包含海洛因、古柯鹼和大麻在內的毒品而被多次逮捕。他解釋他吸毒的原因是從小他的父親就一直給他毒品。雖然之後他遵從法院宣判進行康復治療計劃多次，治療卻從未成功。一直到 2001 年，道尼終於戒毒並準備好開始工作。當他在歐普拉脫口秀中談到自己過去戒毒失敗的經驗時，他對當時有毒品成癮之苦的人們說：「請去尋求協助！要克服這些看起來可怕的問題不難……難的是下決心去處理它！」

- arrest [əˋrɛst] **Ⅴ** 逮捕
- rehab [ˋrihæb] **ⁿ** 康復治療
- charge [tʃɑrdʒ] **ⁿ** 指控
- ghastly [ˋgæstlɪ] **adj** 可怕的

Sentence Show ★

❶ Do not do drugs!

這是一個「表示忠告」的祈使句。句子原本的主詞"you"被省略，原句應為
"You do not do drugs!"（你不要吸毒！）。

❷ Please go reach out for help!

這是一個「表示請求」的祈使句。此類句子一般不需要主詞，因為在使用這樣
的句子時，通常說話的一方是對著一個特定的對象在說這句話（如在文章中，
小勞勃道尼是對著使用毒品的人說的）；如："Please turn off the radio!"（請
關掉收音機！），說話者和聽話者彼此都知道句中需要做關掉收音機動作的這
個人是誰。

 Practice Time ★

Q1：道尼說：「停止使用毒品！」

_____.

Q2：道尼說：「嗑藥前請想想你的家人。」

_____.

Q1 Ans：Downey said, "Stop using drugs!"

Q2 Ans：Downey said, "Please think about your family before using drugs."

Unit 07
感嘆句

> How different I am! I discovered that being a little bit different actually sets you aside in show business; it makes you special. You always try to turn your **❶**negative into a **❷**positive.

—— Jay Leno 傑•雷諾

（我是多麼與眾不同！我發現有點與眾不同事實上能讓你在演藝工作中展露頭角，讓你變得特別。你總要試著將你不好的一面轉為正向的一面。）

❶ negative [`nɛgətɪv] **n** 負面　**❷** positive [`pɑzətɪv] **n** 正面

　　"How different I am!"（ 我是多麼與眾不同！）雖然是以疑問詞"how"做為句首的句子，但這個並非是個疑問句，而是「感嘆句」。那麼，到底此類疑問句做為句首的句子是如何形成感嘆句的呢？

Grammar Show

　　感嘆句"Imperative Sentence"是用來表達對某事或某物的驚嘆。通常以"How"或 "What"起首。要注意感嘆句雖然以"How"或 "What"起首，但與疑問句一點關係也沒有。此外，感嘆句的句尾需以驚嘆號（！）結尾。

❶ 以"How"起首的感嘆句：**How + 形容詞 (副詞) + (主詞 + 動詞) !**

　　例 It's 37 degrees today! How hot! 今天是攝氏 37 度，超級熱！

例 How adorable the baby is! 這個嬰兒多可愛呀！

例 How beautifully Mary can sing! Mary 唱歌唱的多麼好呀！

2 以"**What**"起首的感嘆句：**What + a/an + 形容詞 + 主詞!**

例 What a tall building! 多麼高的大樓！

例 What a gorgeous dress you are wearing! 妳穿的洋裝真漂亮！

例 What an honest girl she is! 她是多麼誠實的一個女孩！

3 句中含有 "**so**"的感嘆句：**主詞 + 動詞 + so + 形容詞 (副詞) .**

例 My sister can type so fast! 我的妹妹可以打字打得很快！

例 Maria is so polite! Maria 非常有禮貌！

例 His brother is so mature now! 他的弟弟現在已經非常成熟了。

4 句中含有 "**such**"的感嘆句：**主詞+ 動詞 + such + a/an + 形容詞 +主詞.**

例 She is such a thoughtful lady! 她是一個很體貼的小姐！

例 This is such a terrible story! 這是一個非常糟的故事！

例 We are such a great team! 我們是一個非常厲害的團隊！

例 It is such a wonderful day! 今天是多麼美好的一天！

Life Story

The popular American late-night talk show, *The Tonight Show,* host Jay Leno may not be as famous as Oprah Winfrey in Taiwan. However, in America, his story inspires many people and he has become a household name. People who know his background always say, "**❶**How impressive his story is!"

Leno started at the show 20 years ago and has held the record for the longest running host ever since. His accomplishments include interviewing President Barack Obama and having reached ratings of over five million viewers a night. Behind the scenes, he has actually suffered from dyslexia since he was a child. Instead of acting negatively, he learned to see dyslexia as a motivator. He worked harder than other people and was willing to wait long hours for an audition. He has never asked for sick leave during the time he hosted the show and thus was named "the hardest working man in show business" by his colleagues. Leno has proved that it is possible for people to achieve their goal if they show great perseverance. **❷**What a guy!

也許美國受歡迎的深夜談話節目《今夜秀》的主持人傑・雷諾在台灣的名氣不如歐普拉響亮。但是在美國，他的故事啟發了很多人，他的名字也成為了一個家喻戶曉的名字。知道他背景的人們總是說：「他的故事是多麼的令人敬佩啊！」

雷諾在 20 年前開始主持這個節目，並且由此擁有最長的主持記錄。他的成就包含訪問過美國總統歐巴馬，以及曾經達到每晚有五百萬觀眾的收視率。在螢光幕後，他其實自小就因為閱讀障礙所苦。他並沒有表現消極，而是學著將閱讀障礙視為動力。他比其他人更努力工作，並且願意長時間的等待試鏡。在主持期間，他從沒有請過病假，因此他的同事稱他為「演藝圈最認真的男人」。雷諾證明了如果人們有堅忍的毅力，他們就有可能達成他們的目標。多棒的一個人啊！

- accomplishment [ə`kɑmplɪʃmənt] 🅝 成就 ・ motivator [`motɪvetə] 🅝 動力

Sentence Show ★

❶ How impressive his story is!

這個感嘆句句是依照了"How+形容詞 (impressive) +主詞 (his story) +動詞 (is)"的文法。倘若以"What"做為此感嘆句開頭，則句子需調整為"What an impressive story he has!"

❷ What a guy!

使用"what"為開頭的感嘆句文法規律一般為"What+ a/an+形容詞+名詞+主詞 +動詞"，但其中的形容詞及最後的主詞、動詞均可省略；本句即是此三者省略 後的形式。"What a guy!"、"What a woman!"，這類的句型是很常見的口語 句型，常用於讚賞某人。

 Practice Time ★

Q1：雷諾是多麼棒的一個人啊！（請用 What 開頭）

_____.

Q2：雷諾的故事是多麼的發人深省啊！（請用 How 開頭）

_____.

Q1 Ans：What a great man Leno is!

Q2 Ans：How inspired Leno's story is!

Unit 08
主語與述語

> The first ①step is you have to say that you can.
> —— Will Smith 威爾 • 史密斯

（第一步是你必須說你辦得到。）

❶ step [stɛp] **n.** 步驟

　　一個句子可分為「主語」和「述語」。主語為句子的主詞，即本句中的"the first step"；述語則為其後描述、修飾主語的部分，即"is you have to say that you can"。詳細的說明和例句，請看下個部分。

Grammar Show

　　通常來說，一個句子可以分為「主要部份」，即「主語」(Subject) 和「描述部分」，即「述語」(Predicate)。

　　所謂主語，就是句子的主詞（主角部分），而主詞通常是指「名詞」，「代名詞」，「名詞子句」，「動名詞（片語）」和「不定詞（片語）」。述部（描述主角的動作或狀態的部分）為動詞，也可能可含有受詞、補語或修飾語。請牢記一個觀念：一個完整的句子，必有一個主詞和一個動詞。

例 My sister likes coffee.

　　我的妹妹喜歡咖啡。

　　（"My sister"是這個句子的「主語」，而 "likes coffee"則是句子的「述語」，用來描述說明我的妹妹喜歡咖啡）

例 The dog at the front door barks so loudly at strangers.

在前門的狗對陌生人如此大聲地吠叫。

（ "The dog"是這個句子的「主詞」，而 "at the front door"則是「修飾語」，用來修飾前面的主詞 "the dog"，所以 "the dog at the front door"形成一個完整的主語。其後的 "barks so loudly at strangers "，"so loudly"是副詞用來修飾前面的動詞 "barks"，而 "the stranger"則為動詞片語 "barks at"的受詞，所以動詞+副詞+受詞在這裡則形成一個完整的「述部」，來補充說明前面的「主部」）。

例 Swimming in the morning is good for health.

晨泳對健康有益。

（ "Swimming in the morning"「動名詞片語」是這個句子的「主詞」，而 "good for health"則是「補語」，用來補充說明前面的主詞 "swimming in the morning"，所以這是一個有主部 "swimming in the morning"及述部 "is good for health"所形成的一個完整句子。）

在大致了解主語與述語後我們會再進一步討論句子的樣貌。我們常說的五大句型，最大的差別就是在「述語」的部分，請讀者之後再探討五大句型的時候，可以思考：動詞是否為及物或是不及物動詞，還有沒有受詞或補語？

Life Story

"There is so much negative imagery of black fatherhood. I have got tons of friends that are doing the right thing for their kids, and doing the right thing as a father—and how come that's not as newsworthy?" This was quoted from one of Will Smith's interviews. Even in today's society, race prejudice and discrimination still exist. Therefore, since he started acting, [1]Smith has kept passing positive messages to people. [2]He tries to speak his points of view about black America, and how he feels about black men. Meanwhile, he often chooses roles that black men should play in their lives with their children and in their lives with their women.

Throughout life there will be people who make us mad, disrespect us or treat us badly. While facing these situations, this comic actor suggests we let God deal with it instead of growing hate in our heart and letting hate consume us eventually.

　　「有許多關於黑人父親的負面印象。但我有超多黑人朋友對孩子們做正確的事，做一個父親該做的正確的事。為何這些沒有新聞價值？」這是威爾・史密斯在某次訪問中所說的一段話。即使在今日的社會，種族偏見及歧視依然存在。因此，自從他開始演戲，史密斯持續傳遞正面的訊息給人們。他試著說出他對美國黑人的觀點以及他對黑人的看想。同時，他總是選擇做好黑人在生活中與小孩及另一半相處的角色。

　　在生活裡，一定會有人惹我們生氣、不尊重我們，或是對我們不好。當面對這樣的情況時，這名喜劇演員建議我們讓把這一切交由老天爺作主，而不是在心中滋生怨恨，這樣怨恨終將會吞噬我們。

- newsworthy [ˋnjuzˏwɝðɪ] **adj** 有新聞價值的
- prejudice [ˋprɛdʒədɪs] **n** 偏見
- discrimination [dɪˏskrɪməˋneʃən] **n** 歧視
- consume [kənˋsjum] **v** 消耗
- eventually [ɪˋvɛntʃʊəlɪ] **adv** 最後

Sentence Show ★

❶ Smith has kept passing positive messages to people.

"Smith"是本句中的主詞,也是「單一主語」,其後的"has kept passing positive messages to people"為「述語」,也就是說明主詞(Smith)的動作。此處需注意動詞 "keep" 之後的動詞需使用"Ving"型式,而"passing positive messages to people"為該動作的受詞。

❷ He tries to speak his points of view about black America.

本句中的主詞是"he",同時也是「單一主語」,其後的"tries to speak his points of view about black America"為「述語」,說明主詞(he)的動作。不定詞片語"to speak his points of view about black America"則做為動詞 "tries"的受詞。

 Practice Time ★

Q1:威爾・史密斯很小心地挑選角色。

_____.

Q2:威爾・史密斯喜歡闡述他的觀點。

_____.

Q1 Ans:Will Smith chooses his characters very carefully.

Q2 Ans:Will Smith likes to express his points of view.

Unit 09
句子的基本要素

Life comes with many ❶challenges. The ones that should not scare us are the ones we can ❷take on and ❸take control of.

—— Angelina Jolie 安潔莉娜・裘莉

（生活中伴隨許多挑戰。那些嚇不倒我們的，就是我們可以承擔和控制的。）

❶ challenge [`tʃælɪndʒ] **n** 挑戰　❷ take on **ph** 承擔　❸ take control of **ph** 掌管

　　在上個單元，我們談到了一個句子必須具備「主語」與「述語」；即一定要有主詞和動詞。但倘若這裡只看第一個句子的主詞"life"和動詞"comes"時，"life comes" 會發現句子語意不詳，comes 什麼？所以需加上後方介系詞片語做補語來成為一個完整句子，且表達完整的意思。

🎬 Grammar Show ★

　　在認識句子的主要構造之後，接著就必須了解形成句子的主要元素有哪些，並使用這些要素組合成一個完整的句子。由前一單元的「句子的主語與述語」中，我們可以分析出一個句子的基本元素有四個：「主詞」、「動詞」、「受詞」和「補語」；其中「主詞」和「動詞」是不可或缺的主要元素，而「受詞」和「補語」則是可有可無，它們扮演的角色是讓整句話的意思更為完整。

例 Cynthia is a talented entrepreneur.

Cynthia 是位有天份的企業家。

（ "Cynthia"是這個句子的「主詞」，而 "is"則是句子的「動詞」，單只有 Cynthia is 本句話沒有意思，所以我們需要主詞補語"a talented entrepreneur 一個有天份的企業家"，來補充說明主詞 Cynthia，使語意更完整）

例 Kids like to run around in the park.

小朋友喜歡在公園跑來跑去。

（ "kids"是這個句子的「主詞」，而 "like"則是「動詞」，用來說明前面的主詞 "kids"的動作，而"不定詞片語 to run around in the park"則是 like 的受詞）

例 We made a cake for her birthday party.

我們為她的生日舞會做了一個蛋糕。

（ "we"是這個句子的「主詞」，而 "made"則是「動詞」表示「做」，單只有"We made 我們做" 看不出意思，所以我們需要一個受詞 a cake，表示「做蛋糕」， "for her birthday party"則為介係詞片語為副詞，修飾 made a cake）

例 What you just did is totally unacceptable.

你剛剛的所作所為是完全不可以被接受的。

（ "what you just did"這個名詞子句是句子的「主詞」，而 "is"則是「動詞」後接主詞補語 "totally unaccepted"）

 **Life Story** ★

On August 23rd 2014, ❶Angelina Jolie married Brad Pitt in France. She was once accused of being the reason for the divorce of Brad Pitt and Jennifer Aniston. However, over the years, there is only fondness, instead of hatred, people have grown to love her. She has been voted as "the world's most beautiful woman" by various magazines. Moreover, she was appointed as Special Envoy of the United Nations High Commissioner for Refugees (UNHCR) after years of dedicated work with refugees.

❷Jolie is also an award-winning actress, filmmaker and philanthropist. Nevertheless, these impressive titles are not the reasons that make her a role model. It is her words of wisdom that inspire many people. For example, while knowing most people are busy finding their Mr. or Ms. Right, Jolie has her own viewpoint on the matter. She said, "We come to love not by finding the perfect person, but by learning to see an imperfect person perfectly."

2014 年 8 月 23 日安潔莉娜・裘莉與布萊德・彼特與法國完婚。她曾經被指控為是布萊德・彼特和珍妮佛・安妮斯頓離婚的主因。然而，這些年來，人們對她只有越來越多喜愛，而沒有憤恨。她被許多不同的雜誌票選為「世界最美麗的女人」，此外，在多年致力於難民工作後，她被指派為聯合國難民事務高級專員辦事處的特別大使。

裘莉同時也是個獲獎的女演員、電影製作人和慈善家。然而，這些令人印象深刻的頭銜並不是她成為模範的原因。她智慧的言語激勵了許多人。例如，當她知道許多人忙於找尋自己理想的另一半時，她對這件事有自己的看法。她說：「我們談戀愛並不是要找完美的人，而是要學習如何看到不完美的人完美的一面。」

- accuse [əˋkjuz] **Ⅴ** 指控
- hatred [ˋhetrɪd] **ⁿ** 憎惡
- philanthropist [fɪˋlænθrəpɪst] **ⁿ** 慈善家
- fondness [ˋfɑndnɪs] **ⁿ** 喜愛
- refugee [ˌrɛfjʊˋdʒi] **ⁿ** 難民

Sentence Show ★

❶ Angelina Jolie married Brad Pitt in France.

這個句子為一個簡單句型，首先看到主詞為"Angelina"，過去式動詞"married"，以及受詞"Brad Pitt"，說明 Jolie 要嫁的人是誰。最後的介系詞片語"in France"，則說明兩人結婚的地點在哪。

❷ Jolie is also an award-winning actress, filmmaker and philanthropist.

這也是個主詞動詞完整的句子。主詞"Jolie"，動詞"is"；但光（「裘莉是。」）這樣句意無法完整，故加上名詞片語"also an award-winning actress, filmmaker and philanthropist"做為主詞"Jolie"的補語。

 Practice Time ★

Q1：安潔莉娜・裘莉是布萊德・彼特的妻子。

_____.

Q2：安潔莉娜・裘莉看起來總是令人驚艷。

_____.

Q1 Ans：Angelina Jolie is Brad Pitt's wife.

Q2 Ans：Angelina Jolie always looks stunning.

Unit 10
句子的 5 種形式

" *I have never been cool. And I don't care.* "
—— *Celin Dion 席琳•迪翁*

（我從來都不酷。而我也不在意。）

　　上面兩個句子分別顯示了兩種不同的句型。"I have never been cool."是「主詞+ 不完全不及物動詞+主詞補語」句型；句中的主詞補語補充說明主詞 "I"從來沒有的是「酷」"cool"。第二個句子則屬於「主詞+ 完全不及物動詞」句型，即動詞"care"之後不需再加任何受詞或補語，句子的意思就很完整了。

 **Grammar Show** ★

　　根據句子的「動詞」不同，英文的常見見五大句型可分為以下：

❶ 「主詞+ 完全不及物動詞」＝S + V

★ 「不及物動詞」 即不需補語也不需受詞，語意便可完整的動詞，如: grow, happen, tremble…

　例 The tree **grows.**

　　樹生長。

　例 This just **happened.**

　　事情就這樣發生了。

2 「主詞+ 不完全不及物動詞 + 主詞補語」= S + V + C

「不完全不及物動詞」指不需受詞，但需要補語來讓意思完整的動詞，如：

think, sound, smell, become, beV···

例 Dinner **smells** delicious.　晚餐聞起來很好吃。

例 She **is** my sister.　她是我姊姊。

例 She **has become** a mature lady.　她已經變成一位成熟的女士了。

3 「主詞+ 完全及物動詞 + 受詞」= S + V + O

「完全及物動詞」後只需受詞，但不需補語，如：**write, learn···**

例 My brother is **writing** an email.

我哥哥正在寫一封 email。

例 Mark doesn't **eat** seafood at all.

馬克完全不吃海鮮。

4 「主詞+ 不完全及物動詞 + 受詞 + 受詞補語」= S + V + O + C

「不完全及物動詞」為同時需要受詞與補語的動詞，如：**elect, keep···**

例 He **forced** his employees to sign the contracts.

他強迫他的員工簽下合約。

例 You should **keep** your mouth shut.

你應該保持沉默。

5 「主詞+ 授與動詞 +間接受詞+直接受詞」= S + V + I.O. + D.O.

「授與動詞」如：**give, take, bring**，需要兩個受詞，間接受詞 I.O.（多為
「某人」）通常在前，而直接受詞 D.O.（多為「某物」）通常在後。

例 The teacher **gave** me a lesson on English grammar.

老師給我們上了一課英文文法。

例 Alex **brought** his girlfriend roses.

艾力克斯買了玫瑰花給他女友。

 **Life Story** ★

If you are fascinated by the movie *Titanic,* you should recognize the main soundtrack *My Heart Will Go On* from the movie. This song was recorded by the Canadian singer Celine Dion, who is renowned for her technically skilled and powerful vocals.

Unlike other celebrities, you hardly ever read gossip or scandals about Dion on page six. She married her manager husband René Angéli, who is 26 years older than her, in 1994 and had three kids. Compared with her career, she enjoys being a mother more. She said, "I love performing, but I never really liked show business. My success is my family. I want to be more successful as a mother." To protect her kids, ❶she keeps her family life private. What also makes her different from other famous people is the way she handles her stress. She admits there are some days that she feels low. ❷Some people do drugs at that time. As for her, she buys shoes.

如果你對電影《鐵達尼號》很著迷,你一定知道它的主題曲《我心永恆》。這首歌的主唱人是以歌唱技巧,以及有力的嗓音著名的加拿大歌手席琳‧迪翁。

　　和其他的名人不同,你很少在娛樂版讀到席琳‧迪翁的八卦或醜聞。她在 1994 年時,嫁給了大她 26 歲的經紀人雷尼‧安杰利,並生了 3 個孩子。比起她的事業,她更享受當一位媽媽。她說:「我喜歡表演,但我永遠也不會喜歡演藝圈。我的家庭就是我的成就。我想要成為一個成功的媽媽。」為了保護孩子,她從不曝光她的家庭生活。而其他讓她有別於大部分名人的地方,則是她處理壓力的辦法。她坦承有低潮的時刻,有些人可能就會嗑藥;但對她來說,她會買鞋子。

- fascinate [`fæsn͵et] **V** 迷住　● vocal [`vokl] **n** 演唱(通常為複數)
- scandal [`skændl] **n** 醜聞　● page six **ph** 娛樂版　● stress [strɛs] **n** 壓力

Sentence Show ★

❶ She keeps her family life private.

這個句子是一個「主詞+不完全及物動詞+受詞+受詞補語」的句型。句中 "she"為主詞，動詞"keep"屬於一個不完全及物動詞，故需要受詞"her family life"與受詞補語"private"。此外，受詞補語"private"為形容詞，補充受詞"her family life"的狀態。

❷ Some people do drugs at that time.

這個句子是一個「主詞+完全及物動詞+受詞」的句型。句中"some people"為主詞，動詞"do"屬於一個完全及物動詞，也就是說，不需要任何補語，但需要有受詞在其後，故此處"do"之後接受詞"drugs"。

 Practice Time ★

Q1：席琳‧迪翁花了很多錢。

_____ .

Q2：人們發現席琳‧迪翁很有才華。

_____ .

Q1 Ans：Celin Dion spends a lot of money.

Q2 Ans：People have found Celin Dion very talented.

Unit 11
名詞子句--疑問詞帶領、that 帶領

❝Who cares what people think, just believe in yourself.
That's all that ❶matters.❞

—— Britney Spears 布蘭妮‧斯皮爾斯

（誰在意人們怎麼想，只要相信你自己。這是唯一重要的。）

❶ matter [`mætɚ`] **V** 要緊

　　"what people think" 是一個名詞子句，在小甜甜布蘭妮的這句話中，當為動詞care的受詞。名詞子句的功能就和名詞一樣。

Grammar Show

　　名詞子句，顧名思義，就是可當作名詞來用的子句。或許這聽起來有點抽象，那麼，我們換個方式說，名詞子句就是「以子句方式所呈現的名詞」，也就是在句中還是做為「名詞」的功能。共有三大類，本單元先討論兩大類。分別是「疑問詞帶領的名詞子句」（即間接問句）及「that 帶領的名詞子句」。

❶ 疑問詞帶領的名詞子句（間接問句）

　　將「直接問句」 為「間接問句」時，此「間接問句」即為「疑問詞為首的名詞子句」。「間接問句」＝疑問詞＋主詞＋動詞。

　　-- 做為「主詞」時:

例 **How he survived the air crash** is still a puzzle.

　　他如何從空難存活至今仍是一個謎。

★　名詞子句當做為「主詞」時，視為「第三人稱單數」，故需使用「單數動詞」"is"。

-- 做為「受詞」時:

例 I want to know **who the man is.**

　　我想知道那個男人是誰。

-- 做為「補語」時:

例 I am not sure **where Mrs. Jackson is.**

　　我不確定 Jackson 太太在哪裡。

❷　that 帶領的名詞子句

由 **that** 帶領的名詞子句，語意清楚時可以省略 **that**，然而假如 **that** 在句首時一定不能省，或是需使用虛主詞**"It"**。

-- 做為「主詞」時：

例 **That** Vincent is lazy is true.

例 **It** is true **that** Vincent is lazy.

　　Vincent 很懶惰是事實。

-- 做為「受詞」時:

例 I guess **that** Ruby is not coming.

　　我猜 Ruby 不會來。

★　that 為首的名詞子句常接在「動詞」"guess", "think", "believe"等字之後做為動詞的受詞使用，而 that 可省略。

-- 做為「補語」時:

例 I am afraid **that** Mr. Green is going to be late.

　　恐怕 Green 先生將會遲到。

★　「關係代名詞 that」為首的名詞子句常接在「be 動詞+形容詞」"be afraid", "be happy", "be sure"之後做為受詞補語。

Life Story

❶If you are around thirty now, you should know who Britney Spears is. Or at least, you might have heard her *Baby One More Time* and *Oops!... I Did It Again* when you were a teenager. Both title tracks achieved huge success and broke international sales records. She became the most popular teenage solo artist at the time. Everyone saw her as a rising star of the music industry.

However, in 2007, her much-publicized absurd behavior sent her career into hiatus. She once escaped from are rehabilitation center for-drug addicts and then shaved her head with electric clippers at a hair salon the following night. ❷Seeing Britney's ridiculous behavior, the public was so sure that she would never be able to regain her fame and position. To everyone's surprise, not only did she pull herself together but she also released several hits afterwards. Therefore, some talk show hosts sometimes cite Britney's story to encourage people. "If Britney Spears made it through 2007, you can make it through today."

　　如果你現在 30 歲左右，你應該知道誰是小甜甜布蘭妮。或者至少當你還是青少年時，你可能聽過她的《愛的初告白》以及《愛的再告白》。這兩張同名專輯獲得了巨大的成功，也打破了世界的銷售記錄。她也成為當時最受歡迎的青少年個人歌手。大家視她為一顆音樂界新堀起的新星。

　　然而，在 2007 年時，常被報導的脫序行為幾乎讓她的事業中斷。她曾經逃離吸毒康復中心，隔天晚上便於一家美髮沙龍剃光自己所有的頭髮。布蘭妮的所作所為讓大眾相信，她是永遠不可能回復她的名聲和地位了。但讓每個人驚訝的是，她不止重新振作，還在之後發行了幾首熱門歌曲。因此，一些脫口秀主持人偶爾會使用布蘭妮的故事來鼓勵人們。「如果小甜甜布蘭妮能渡過她 2007 年的難關，那麼你就可以渡過你今天的難關。」

● impression [ɪmˈprɛʃən] **n** 印象　　　● catch sb's eyes **ph** 吸引某人的目光

Sentence Show ★

❶ If you are around thirty now, you should know who Britney Spears is.

句中"who Britney Spears is"（誰是小甜甜布蘭妮）是「疑問詞帶領的名詞子句」，且在本句作為 know 的受詞。

❷ Seeing Britney's ridiculous behavior, the public was so sure that she would never be able to regain her fame and position.

本句主詞為"the public"，「that」帶領的名詞子句做為"was so sure"的主詞補語，說明大眾很確信的是「布蘭妮無法回到過去的名聲和地位了」。

 ## Practice Time ★

Q1：她不知道小甜甜布蘭妮在 2007 年做過什麼。

_____.

Q2：可以確信的是小甜甜布蘭妮已經學到了教訓。

_____.

Q1 Ans： She doesn't know what Britney Spears did in 2007.

Q2 Ans： That Britney Spears has learned her lesson is certain. /

　　　　　　 It is certain that Britney Spears has learned her lesson.

Unit 12
名詞子句--if / whether 帶領

Real ➊integrity is doing the right thing, knowing that nobody's going to know ➋whether you did it or not.

—— Oprah Winfrey 歐普拉・溫芙蕾

（真正的正直是做正確的事，即使知道將沒有人會知道你是否做這件事。）

➊ integrity [ɪn`tɛɡrətɪ] n. 正直　➋ whether [`hwɛðɚ] conj. 不管

　　除了"that" 和疑問詞外，if/whether… (or not) 亦可用來做為連接詞，連接主要子句及附屬子句。if/whether 子句依照在句中的用途，又可分為名詞子句和副詞子句。本句中的 whether 子句可做為"know"的「受詞」，中文可翻譯為「你是否做了（正確的事）」，故屬於「名詞子句」。

Grammar Show

　　除了上個單元提到過的「以疑問詞首的名詞子句」外，另外一個常見的名詞子句，就是「以"if/whether"起首的名詞子句」了。「以"if/whether"起首的名詞子句」在句中可分別做為「主詞」、「受詞」或「補語」，中文多譯為「是否」。

➊ 做為「主詞」時

例 **Whether you make it to the final is very important.**

你是否可以進入總決賽是非常重要的。

★ 「whether 名詞子句」擺句首做主詞時，視為「第三人稱單數」，故需使用「單數動詞」。

★ 「whether 名詞子句」擺句首做主詞時，不可與"**if**"做替換：

例 **Whether she will join us (or not)** depends on you.

她是否會加入我們就視你而定了。(*NOT* ~~If depends on you.~~)

2 做為「受詞」時

例 No one cares **whether Bill will attend this meeting (or not)**.

沒人在乎 Bill 是否會出席這場會議。

★ 「Whether 名詞子句」做為受詞時，可與"**if**"做替換，如上句可改為：

No one cares **if Bill will attend this meeting**.

★ 使用否定敘述時，通常只可使用「whether 名詞子句」

例 Tell me **if May didn't go to Oxford**.

如果 May 沒去牛津的話要告訴我。

(*NOT* ~~Tell me whether May didn't go to Oxford.~~)

3 做為「補語」時

在 **be** 動詞後做為主詞補語。此時不可使用 "**if**"。

例 The question is **whether this typhoon will bring more rain**.

問題是這個颱風是否可以帶來更多的雨水。(*NOT* ~~The question is if this ty-phoon will bring more rain.~~)

亦可在形容詞後做為補語。此時不可使用"if"。

例 She is not sure **whether she will stay (or not)**.

她不確定她是否會留下。(*NOT* ~~She is not sure if she will stay.~~)

 **Life Story**

Oprah Winfrey is an American talk show host, media producer and philanthropist. She is best known for her self-titled and multi-award-winning talk show *The Oprah Winfrey Show*. As the supervising producer and the host of the program, she has over the years conducted interviews with hundreds of people and celebrities from all over the world. These people share their life stories, great experiences and their personal side, which totally entertain and enlighten viewers.

❶Whether you have watched The *Oprah Winfrey Show* is not important. ❷The important thing is if you learn anything from her words and spirit. As a public figure and professional host, she always sends a positive message to her audience. She once said, "Over the past twenty years when I hit rock bottom and was about to give up, I told myself that there is no lucky guy in the world. Luck is just a matter of good preparation, meeting the right opportunity."

　　歐普拉・溫芙蕾是美國脫口秀主持人、媒體製作人,以及一個慈善家。她最知名的是她獲獎無數的同名脫口秀節目《歐普拉秀》。身為一個監督製作以及節目主持人,多年來已經與來自世界各地的群眾和名流人士進行過訪談。這些人分享他們的生活故事、絕佳的經驗以及個人秘辛,而他們所說的話不僅娛樂,也感動了觀眾。

　　你是否看過《歐普拉秀》其實並不重要。重要的是,你是否從歐普拉的言語和精神學到了任何事情。做為一個公眾人物與專業的主持人,她總是傳遞正面的訊息給她的觀眾。她曾經說:「過去的 20 年來,每當我遭遇困境,即將要放棄時,我告訴我自己,世界上沒有幸運的人。幸運只是好的準備,遇上了適當的機會。」

- conduct [kən`dʌkt] **V** 引導
- entertain [ˌɛntə`ten] **V** 娛樂
- inside [`ɪn`saɪd] **n** 內幕
- enlighten [ɪn`laɪtn] **V** 啟發

Sentence Show ★

❶ Whether you have watched The Oprah Winfrey Show is not important.

本句中的 whether 子句為「名詞子句」，在句中做為「主詞」使用；中文可翻譯為「你是否看過《歐普拉秀》」。

❷ The important thing is if you learn anything from her words and spirit.

本句中的 if 子句亦為「名詞子句」，"if "可和"whether"代換使用。然而，if 子句此處在句中做為「補語」使用，中文可翻譯為「你是否從她的言語和精神中學習到什麼」。

 Practice Time ★

Q1：你是否為歐普拉的粉絲並不重要。

_____.

Q2：歐普拉正在電視上討論窮人是否應該繳稅的議題。

_____.

Q1 Ans： Whether you are a fan of Oprah Winfrey is not important.

Q2 Ans： Oprah Winfrey is discussing on TV the issue of whether the poor
should pay tax .

Unit 13
形容詞子句--關係代名詞

Everyone in Hollywood is so damn [1]skinny and you [2]constantly feel like you're not skinny enough. But I have "fat days" and I [3]accept the fact that I'm never going to be [4]rail thin.
—— Scarlett Johansson 史嘉蕾•喬韓森

（在好萊塢的每個人都是誇張的瘦，於是你時常會覺得自己不夠瘦。但我有胖的時候，而我接受我永遠不會像杆子一樣瘦的事實。）

❶ skinny [`skɪnɪ] adj 皮包骨的　❷ constantly [`kɑnstəntlɪ] adv 時常地

❸ accept [ək`sɛpt] V 接受　❹ rail [rel] n 杆子

　　史嘉蕾•喬韓森這句話的末尾出現了本單元的重點「關係代名詞"that"」，就讓我們來分析一下最後的這個句子吧！這句話原本為"I accept the fact."和"I'm never going to be rail thin."兩個句子，使用"that"代指"the fact"並連接兩個句子。"I'm never going to be rail thin."說明史嘉蕾•喬韓森接受的事實（"fact"）是什麼事實。

Grammar Show

　　關係子句，是指由「關係代名詞」所引導構成的「從屬子句」，在句中通常做為「形容詞子句」。這裡來看看幾個主要的關係代名詞的用法：

❶ **"who", "whom"**之前需有代表「人」的名詞；**"which"**之前需有代表「事物」的名詞。而**"that"**則可取代前三者使用

例 I like the girl **who/that** lives next door.

我喜歡住在隔壁的女孩。

例 Are you sure you know the man **whom/that** you were talking to?

你確定你認識剛剛跟你交談的男人嗎?

例 This is the window **which/that** my brother broke last week.

這是我弟弟上禮拜打破的窗戶。

2 **"which"**和**"who"**在所引導的子句中可做為主詞或受詞;但**"whom"**僅能做為受詞

例 She is a good mother **who loves** her children very much.

她是一個非常愛小孩的好媽媽。("who"在子句中做主詞,代指"she")

例 She is singing the song **which** was played last night in the concert.

她正在哼唱昨天演唱會的歌。("which"在子句中做主詞,代指"song")

例 These are the apples **which** I bought yesterday.

這些是我昨天買的蘋果。("which"在子句中做為動詞"bought"的受詞)

例 Bruce is a boy **whom** everyone loves.

Bruce 是個大家都喜歡的男孩。("whom"在子句中做為動詞"loves"的受詞)

3 在下列情況下,通常用**"that"**做關代

在序數詞 **(the first, the second,…the last)**、比較級與最高級之後,後面只能接 **"that"**。

例 Roy is **the last person that** I want to see.

Roy 是我最不想見的人。(不可用"whom")

例 Brushing my teeth is **the first thing that** I do every day.

我每天做的第一件事是喝咖啡。(不可用"which")

當"人"和"物"兩個名詞同在一起時,需使用"that"做為關代

例 For Mr. Brown, **his car and his daughter** are the two things **that** he loves the most in his life.

對 Brown 先生來說,車子和女兒是他生命中的最愛。

 **Life Story**

[1]In her latest film *Lucy*, Scarlett Johansson was cast as a woman who possessed psychic abilities from a special drug, which made her reach 100% of her cerebral capacity. In real life, people generally considered Johansson not only a sex symbol but also a smart woman.

In Hollywood, there might be some celebrities who like to sell their private life to the paparazzi in exchange for fame. As for Johansson, she values her privacy. Therefore, she claims that she will never exploit her personal life. Meanwhile, she also points out those tabloid magazines represent the downfall of our society and thus the public should stop buying them. Besides, she is serious about her job. [2]She never knowingly went into a film that she wouldn't pay to see, or portrayed a character that didn't challenge her. She always tries to find something that she can focus her energy on because for her this is the moment she feels the happiest.

在她的最新電影《露西》裡，史嘉蕾·喬韓森扮演一個因為一種神奇藥物而擁有超能力的女人，這個藥物令她的腦容量發揮到 100%。而在現實生活中，人們一般也認為喬韓森不止是一個性感的象徵，同時也是一個聰明的女人。

在好萊塢，也許有些名人喜歡將隱私賣給狗仔隊以交換名氣。但對喬韓森來說，她重視自己的隱私。因此，她宣稱她絕對不會利用自己的私人生活。同時，她也指出，八卦雜誌代表著我們社會的沉淪，因此，大眾應該停止購買。除此之外，她對工作也很認真。她從不會演出一個連自己都不願意付錢進電影院看的片子，也不會接沒有挑戰性的角色。她總是試著找出能夠讓她自己集中精力去做的事，因為對她而言，這是她覺得最快樂的時刻。

- capacity [kə`pæsətɪ] **n** 容量
- privacy [`praɪvəsɪ] **n** 隱私
- tabloid [`tæblɔɪd] **adj** 小報式的
- value [`vælju] **v** 重視
- exploit [ɪk`splɔɪt] **v** 利用

Sentence Show

❶ In her latest film *Lucy*, Scarlett Johansson was cast as a woman who possessed psychicabilities from a special drug, which made her reach 100% of her cerebral capacity.

本句第一個"who"的關係子句說明史嘉蕾‧喬韓森扮演的女人"a woman"是「因為特殊藥物而獲得超能力的女人」("who possessed psychic abilities from aspecial drug")；而後面的"which"關係子句則說明藥物所帶來的作用。

❷ She never knowingly went into a film that she wouldn't pay to see, or portrayed a character that didn't challenge her.

第一個"that"關係子句說明喬韓森不會接拍的電影是「她不會想付錢看的電影」("that she wouldn't pay to see")；第二個"that"關係子句則說明他不會演出的角色是「沒有挑戰性的角色」("that didn't challenge her")。

 Practice Time

Q1：喬韓森扮演一個住在台灣的美國女性。

_____.

Q2：喬韓森不喜歡那些總是編造故事的八卦雜誌（tabloid magazines）。

_____.

Q1 Ans：Johansson was cast as an American woman who lives in Taiwan.

Q2 Ans：Johansson doesn't like those tabloid magazines which always make up stories.

Unit 14
關係副詞

The beauty of a woman is seen in her eyes, because that is the doorway to her heart, the place where love resides.

—— Audrey Hepburn 奧黛麗‧赫本

（一個女人的美可以從她的眼裡看到。因為那是她心靈的入口，也是愛情駐足的地方。）

　　「關係副詞」，簡單的說就是「介系詞+關係代名詞」。這個句子出現了表示「地方」的關係副詞"where"，而它其實可替換成"in which"，也就是原句可改為"…the place in which loves resides."

Grammar Show

　　關係副詞，在句中的角色等同於「介系詞+關係代名詞」，而根據句中先行詞的不同，關係副詞主要可分為："when"、"where"、"why"。

　　由關係副詞所引導的句子，需為完整子句，其結構為「主詞 + 動詞 + 關係副詞 + 主詞 + 動詞 +（受詞/補語）」。

❶ 先行詞表示「時間」時，使用關係副詞 "when"，等同於 "at/on/in + which"

例 I know the time **when** the party starts.

　　我知道舞會開始的時間。（"when"等同於"at which"）

例 She is not sure of the time **when** the holidays end.

　　她不確定假期何時結束。（"when"等同於"at which"）

例 The year **when** you were born was memorable.

你出生的那年真是難忘的。

例 The day **when** the concert takes place is Friday.

演場會開演那天是週五。

2 先行詞表示「地點」時，使用關係副詞 **"where"**，等同於 **"at/on/in + which"**

例 Joe told me that he knew the location **where** the office is.

Joe 告訴我他知道辦公室的位置在哪。("where"等同於"in which")

例 This is the spot **where** he lost his wallet.

這裡是他遺失皮夾的地方。(where 等同於"in which")

例 The street **where** the parade begins is Songshou Rd.

遊行開始於松壽路。

例 The city **where** you live is nice.

你住的那個城市很好。

3 先行詞表示「原因」時，使用關係副詞 **"why"**，等同於 **"for + which"**

例 Paul didn't explain **the reason why** he was late for the meeting yesterday.

Paul 沒有解釋為什麼他昨天會議遲到了。("why"等同於 "for which")

Life Story

①Most people still remember the day when Audrey Hepburn was active during Hollywood's Golden Age. For all these years, she has been considered as a film and fashion icon. Her hairstyle shown in the movie *Roman Holiday* is still a classic today. Furthermore, she was ranked by the American Film Institute as the third greatest female screen legend in the history of American cinema.

As the most naturally beautiful woman of all time, Hepburn did have some ideas on how women should live their lives. Firstly, she said elegance is the only beauty that never fades. Clearly, Hepburn's public image and unfading beauty has explained to us what she meant. Secondly, for a woman to have beautiful eyes and lips, she should look for the good in others and speak only words of kindness. Finally, she encouraged women to pursue their dreams, and she expressed her own particular view about the definition of "impossible". She stated **②**the reason why nothing is impossible is because the word itself says "I'm possible".

奧黛麗・赫本活躍於好萊塢電影的黃金時代。這麼多年來,她都被視為是電影界和時尚界的代表人物。她在電影《羅馬假期》中的髮型至今仍是經典。此外,她也被美國電影學會列為美國電影史上最偉大的女演員第 3 名。

身為最具自然美的女性,赫本確實對於女性該如何生活有一些見解。首先,她說,優雅是唯一不會褪色的美。顯而易見地,她的公眾形象以及不朽的美貌已為我們解釋了她說這句話的意思。第二,要擁有美麗的眼睛和嘴脣,女性應該多看別人的優點,多說些好話。最後,她鼓勵女性勇於追夢,並且描述了她對於「不可能」三字的特殊見解。她說為什麼說沒有事情是不可能的,是因為「impossible(意:不可能的)」這個字本身就說明了「I'm possible(我是可能的)」。

- hairstyle [`hɛr͵staɪl] **n** 髮型　　● legend [`lɛdʒənd] **n** 傳奇人物
- cinema [`sɪnəmə] **n** 電影業　　● elegance [`ɛləgəns] **n** 優雅　　● fade [fed] **v** 褪去

Sentence Show ★

❶ Most people still remember the day when Audrey Hepburn was active during Hollywood's Golden Age.

在先行詞"the day"之後出現的"when"為表示「時間」的關係副詞,可以替換為"on which"。

❷ The reason why nothing is impossible is because the word itself says "I'm possible".

句中先行詞"the reason"之後出現的"why"為表示「原因」的關係副詞,可以替換為"for which"。

 Practice Time ★

Q1:布魯塞爾是奧黛莉・赫本出生的城市。

_____.

Q2:奧黛莉・赫本演《羅馬假期》那年是 1953。

_____.

Q1 Ans:Brussels is the city where Audrey Hepburn was born.

Q2 Ans:The year when Audrey Hepburn stared in *Roman Holiday* is 1953.

Unit 15
複合關係代名詞

> Honestly, I think we should be delighted people still want to read, be it on a Kindle or a Nook or whatever the latest device is.
>
> —— J. K. Rowling J. K. 羅琳

（老實說，我想我們應該高興人們仍願意閱讀，無論他們是使用 Kindle 或 Nook 的電子閱讀器，或是任何最新的設備。）

　　此句中的 "whatever" 稱為「複合關係代名詞」，可以代指「物」，亦等同於 "anything which"；故此句中的 "…or whatever the latest device is" 可改為 "…anything which the latest device is"。那　除了 "whatever"，是否還有其他的複合關係代名詞呢？

Grammar Show

❶ **"whoever"可代替人，並等同於 "anybody who"，在句中可做為「主詞」或「受詞」使用**

例 **Whoever/Anybody who** comes to Betty's birthday party should prepare a present.

任何參加 Betty 生日派對的人，都應該準備一份禮物。

例 I hate **whoever/anybody who** is rude.

我討厭任何無禮的人。

2 **"whichever"** 可代替人或物，等同於 **"any of which/who "**。此外，**"whichever"** 可指「同一類的人或物」

例 You can pick **whichever** book you want to read.

你可以挑選任何你喜歡的書來讀。

例 **Whichever** course you decide to take, you will need to study hard.

不管你決定選擇什麼課程，你都需要認真研讀。

3 **"whatever"** 可代替物，等同於 **"anything which"**

相較於 "whichever"，"whatever" 僅可代指「物」，但可指「不同類」的任何東西（"whichever" 用於代指同一類中的任一）。

例 Amanda's grandmother left a house, two cars and many famous paintings. **Whatever/Anything which** she inherited cost a great fortune.

Amanda 的祖母留下了一棟房子，兩輛車和許多名畫。她繼承的任何一項都值許多錢。（房子、車子和名畫都不是同一類的東西，而這些東西的任何一項都可用 "whatever" 代指）

3 **"whomever"** 則可代替人，等同於 **"anybody whom"**，僅能為受詞，不可做主詞。

例 I don't know **whoever/anybody whom** I can stay with.

我不知道我可以跟誰一起住。

★ Life Story ★

According to the 2008 *Sunday Times* Rich List, J.K. Rowling's fortune was estimated at £560 million, which made her the twelfth richest woman in the United Kingdom. ❶Whoever knows this information might not believe that she had once been living on hard times.

Seven years after graduating from university, Rowling was jobless with a dependent child. ❷She didn't even know whomever she could borrow money from. She stayed at several local café to write her first novel, *Harry Potter*, and finished in 1995. The book was highly praised by the public after being published and was adapted for the big screen afterwards. Looking back, Rowling concludes that perhaps failure was a good thing for her because she was then able to focus on the things which she is really into. If she had been successful in the past, she would never have had such determination to pursue her dreams. After all, hope will not be defeated as long as we always have faith.

根據 2008 年的《星期日泰晤士報富豪榜》，羅琳的財產估計總值約 5,600 萬英鎊，是英國第 12 位富有的女性。任何知道這個資訊的人，一定不會相信她曾有過一段困苦的日子。

從大學畢業七年後，羅琳沒有工作，並且還帶著一個嗷嗷待哺的孩子。她甚至不知道她可以向誰借錢。她待在當地的咖啡館寫她的第一本小說《哈利波特》並在 1995 年完成。之後，這本書獲得大眾高度的評價，更改編成了電影。回想過去，羅琳總結說，也許失敗對她來說是件好事，因為她便可以專心在她真正喜歡的事情上。如果她之前是成功的，她便永遠不會有決心追求自己的夢想。畢竟，只要我們長存信念，希望是不會落空的。

- fortune [ˋfɔrtʃən] n 財產
- dependent [dɪˋpɛndənt] n 受扶養的親屬
- determination [dɪ͵tɝməˋneʃən] n 決心
- estimate [ˋɛstə͵met] v 估計
- adapt [əˋdæpt] v 改編

252

Sentence Show ★

❶ Whoever knows this information might not believe that she had once been living on hard times.

"Whoever"代指「人」，在本句中做為「主詞」。此外，還可與 "Anyone who" 替換，表示「任何知道這個消息的人」。

❷ She didn't even know whomever she could borrow money from.

此句的"whoever"雖同樣代指「人」，但在本句中做為「受詞」使用；可與 "anyone who"替換，指的是「願意借錢給羅琳的人」。

 Practice Time ★

Q1：我有很多羅琳的書。你可以借任何一本你喜歡的。

_____.

Q2：你知道任何人有羅琳的書嗎？

_____.

Q1 Ans： I have many of Rowling's books. You can borrow whichever you like.

Q2 Ans： Do you know whoever has Rowling's books?

Unit 16
形容詞子句--限定與非限定

66 I had a friend who worked at a **①**hospice, and he said people in their final moments don't discuss their successes, awards or what books they wrote or what they **②**accomplished. They only talk about their loves and their regrets, and I think that's very **③**telling. 99

—— Brad Pitt 布萊德•彼特

（我有個朋友在安寧病房工作，他說人在臨終時不會談論他們所獲得的成功或獎項，也不會談論他們寫過什麼書或是有什麼成就。他們只會談他們喜愛的事物及他們的悔恨。我想這番話很發人省思。）

① hospice [ˋhɑspɪs] **n** 安寧病房　**②** accomplish [əˋkɑmplɪʃ] **V** 實現

③ telling [ˋtɛlɪŋ] **adj** 生動的

　　首先看到這句話中的關係詞"who"前面並沒有逗號，說明這是個「限定用法」。使用這個表達法說明布萊德•彼特有很多朋友，但他提到的這個朋友限定為是「在安寧病房工作」的那個朋友。在英文裡，這一小粒「逗號」可是會有很大的不同，不能隨便加也不可以都不加，我們一起來思考一下！

Grammar Show ★

1 在「限定」關係子句裡，關係代名詞前不加「逗號」

使用限定用法時，其關係子句裡的資訊不可或缺；換句話說，這個句子如果少了此關係子句，則句意或內容會不完整。

例 He is the man **who assisted me at the reception yesterday.**

他是昨天在櫃檯幫我的那個男士。(限定這個男士是「昨天在櫃檯幫忙我的那個人」，而不是其他人)

例 This is the tea **which my father likes to drink.**

這是我父親喜歡喝的茶。(限定說明這個茶是「我爸爸喜歡喝的」茶)

2 在「非限定」關係子句裡，關係代名詞前加「逗號」

使用非限定用法，關係子句的資訊只是補充說明；亦即，這個句子如果少了此關係子句，句意也不會受影響。

例 My teacher, **who is talking to Bryan,** is from America.

正在跟 Bryan 講話的是我的老師，他從美國來的。("who is talking to Bryan"只是一個資訊的補充，即使不加這個關係子句，聽話者還是知道說話者的老師從美國來。)

例 *American Idol*, **which I watch every Sunday**, is my favorite TV program.

我每週日都看的《美國偶像》，是我最喜歡的電視節目。("which I watch every Sunday"是一個補充資訊，即使沒有這個關係子句，聽話者也知道說話者喜歡的節目是《美國偶像》)

3 「限定用法」和「非限定用法」的使用規則

--關代"that"不可使用於非限定用法中。

--在限定用法中，當關代"which / that / who"做為代替受詞時，在句中可以省略；但使用非限定用法時，關代"which/whom"不可省略

Life Story ★

Although he has been described as one of the world's most attractive men, Brad Pitt doesn't think a person's look should be the first thing we concentrate on when we first meet a person. To him, the look is just a first impression and the best way to know a person is to talk to him. ❶There might be someone who doesn't catch our eye at the beginning, but we might find him attractive after talking to him. Therefore, Pitt concludes that the greatest actors sometimes aren't what we would call beautiful symbols.

Obviously, Pitt's look is not the only thing that makes him a popular worldwide celebrity. ❷He pays attention to many public issues and supports the ONE Campaign, which is an organization aimed at combating AIDS and poverty in the developing world. Meanwhile, together with his wife Angelina Jolie, they established the Jolie-Pitt Foundation, which aids humanitarian causes around the world.

雖然他被形容是世界上最性感的男人之一，布萊德‧彼特並不認為一個人的長相，是我們第一次見到某人時，最先注意的地方。對他而言，長相只是第一印象。認識一個人最好的辦法是和他聊天。也許有人一開始並沒有吸引我們的目光，但在交談後，我們也許會發現他吸引人的地方。因此，彼特總結說，最偉大的演員有時並不是那些被視為美麗象徵的人。

顯而易見地，彼特的長相並不是唯一讓他成為全世界受歡迎的名人的原因。他關注許多公共議題，並且支持「一活動」，該組織的目標為對抗未開發國家的愛滋和貧困問題。同時，他和他的妻子安潔莉娜‧裘莉一同建立了裘莉一彼特基金會，幫助救助全世界的人道項目。

● concentrate on **ph** 專注於
● catch sb's eye **ph** 吸引某人的目光
● impression [ɪmˋprɛʃən] **n** 印象
● symbol [ˋsɪmbl] **n** 象徵

Sentence Show ★

❶ There might be someone who doesn't catch our eye at the beginning, but we might find him attractive after talking to him.

此處的關係子句"who doesn't catch our eye at the beginning"說明了句中所指的"someone"身份「限定」為「一開始並沒有吸引我們的目光」的人。

❷ He pays attention to many public issues and supports the ONE Campaign, which is an organization aimed at combating AIDS and poverty in the developing world.

關係子句", which is an organization aimed at combating AIDS and poverty in the developing world"在這裡為「非限定用法」，因為句中已闡明布萊德‧彼特支持的是「一活動」，故後方的關係子句只是補充說明的作用。

 Practice Time ★

Q1：美國演員布萊德‧彼特今年 50 歲了。

_____.

Q2：這是布萊德‧彼特向安潔麗娜‧裘莉求婚的地方。

_____.

Q1 Ans：Brad Pitt, who is an American actor, is 50 years old this year.

Q2 Ans：This is the place where Brad Pitt proposed to Angelina Jolie.

Unit 17
副詞子句--跟時間相關

"You have to ❶embrace getting older. Life is ❷precious, and when you have lost a lot of people, you realize each day is a gift."

—— Meryl Streep 梅莉 • 史翠普

（你必須欣然接受變老這件事。人生太珍貴了，當你很多朋友不在了之後，你會了解每一天都是一份禮物。）

❶ embrace [ɪmˋbres] **V** 欣然接受　❷ precious [ˋprɛʃəs] **adj** 珍貴的

　　梅莉 • 史翠普這句話中的" when you have lost a lot of people"為一個表示時間的副詞子句，在句中只是充當一個副詞的作用，不能單獨存在，需有另一句主要子句"you realize each day is a gift"，才是一個完整的句子。

Grammar Show

　　副詞子句 ("Adverb Clause") 簡單來說，就是可以做為「副詞」使用的子句，為從屬子句。因為副詞子句的功能就像副詞一般，所以它可以用來修飾「動詞」、「形容詞」和「副詞」。一般而言，它在句中的角色也像副詞一樣，是可有可無的修飾語，即使句子少了它，也不會影響到主要的句子結構，而不同的附屬連接詞又可以引導出不同類別的副詞子句。現在，我們就先從與「時間」相關的附屬連接詞所組成的副詞子句來看吧！

❶ 與「時間」相關的附屬連接詞如

when, while, whenever, after, before, as soon as, as long as, by the time, until/till, once

❷ 副詞子句有時可放在主要子句之前（即句首），有時可放在主要子句之後（即句末），放在句首需要有逗號隔開

例 **Whenever** you need help, just call to let me know.

= Just call to let me know whenever you need help.

無論何時你需要幫助，就打電話告訴我。

❸ 時間副詞子句用來修飾「動詞」

例 I will go to the library **after I finish my lunch.**

在我結束午餐後，我會去圖書館。("after I finish my lunch"在這裡用來修飾動詞 "go"。)

❹ 時間副詞子句用來修飾「形容詞」

例 Sarah seemed very happy **as soon as she knew that John is visiting her.**

一知道 John 要來拜訪她，Sarah 看起來非常快樂。("as soon as she knew John is visiting her"在這裡用來修飾形容詞 "happy"。)

❺ 時間副詞子句用來修飾「副詞」

例 He runs so fast **when someone is chasing him.**

當有人在追他時，他跑的非常快。("when someone is chasing him"在這裡用來補充說明 "fast"這個副詞。)

Life Story

Nobody will object to the idea that Meryl Streep is one of the greatest film actresses of all time. After all, **❶Streep has received countless awards since the day she started her acting career.**

In fact, many people are impressed by not only the roles she plays but also the way she lives her life. **❷After some of her friends passed away, she formed a deeper appreciation of the finite number of years she has and wanted to make every day count.** Therefore, she no longer wastes time worrying about her skin or her weight. Instead, she integrates what she believes in into every single area of her life. She takes her heart with her to work and enjoys what she does. She once said, "The great gift of human beings is that we have the power of empathy." From this we can assume that Streep could resemble any character she has played except perhaps the mean boss from *The Devil Wears Prada*.

　　沒有人會對「梅莉・史翠普是有史以來最偉大的女演員之一」這個想法有異議。畢竟，從開始演戲，史翠普便獲得了無數的獎項。

　　事實上，很多人有印象的，不止是她演出過的角色，還有她生活的態度。在她的一些朋友過世後，她更珍惜有限的時間，並且要讓自己活著的每一天有意義。因此，她不再浪費時間擔心她的皮膚或體重。取而代之的是，她將她的信念融合在生活中的各個方面。她用心在她的工作上，並且享受她所做的事。她曾經說：「人類最偉大的天賦，是我們擁有同理心的能力。」從她這句話我們可以猜想，史翠普也許會和她所演過的某個角色相像，但其中絕不包含《穿著 Prada 的惡魔》電影裡的那個刻薄的老闆。

● objection [əbˋdʒɛkʃən] **n** 反對
● integrate [ˋɪntəˏgret] **v** 結合
● resemble [rɪˋzɛmbḷ] **v** 相像
● pass away **ph** 過世
● empathy [ˋɛmpəθɪ] **n** 同情

Sentence Show ★

❶ Streep has received countless awards since the day she started her acting career.

"Since the day she started her acting career"（自從開始演戲）為表示時間的副詞子句；需注意當時用"since"時，主要子句的動詞需使用現在完成式，如此句中的"has received"（已經獲得）。

❷ After some of her friends passed away, she formed a deeper appreciation of the finite number of years she has and wanted to make every day count.

句首的"after some of her friends passed away"（在她的一些朋友過世後）即為表示時間的副詞子句，說明主要子句的動作是在副詞子句發生的時間之後。

 Practice Time ★

Q1：在開始演戲之前，梅莉·史翠普是耶魯大學的學生。

_____.

Q2：史翠普曾與名叫約翰的演員同居過三年，直到他在 1978 年過世。

_____.

Q1 Ans：Before she started acting, Meryl Streep was a student at Yale University.

Q2 Ans：Streep lived with an actor named John for three years until he died in 1978.

Unit 18
副詞子句--條件、比較

I am ❶looking forward to influencing others in a positive way. My message is you can do anything if you just put your mind to it.

—— Justin Bieber 賈斯汀·比伯

（我期望以正面的方法去影響別人。我要傳達的訊息是，如果你用心，就可以成就任何事。）

❶ look forward to **ph** 期望

在這句名言中，「小賈斯汀」賈斯汀·比伯提到"you can do anything"（你可以成就任何事），但要如何能做到呢？就是" if you just put your mind to it"（如果你用心）；這個"if"開頭的子句即為表示「條件」的副詞子句。

Grammar Show

副詞子句，也可以用來表示「條件」或「比較」的句子，就是由表示「條件」或「比較」的從屬連接詞所引導的附屬子句，一定需要與另一個子句連接，語意才會完整。現在我們就先從與「表條件或比較」相關的附屬連接詞所組成的副詞子句來看吧！

1 與「條件」相關的附屬連接詞為

if (如果) , unless (除非) , suppose (假設), in case, even if, as long as (只要) …

例 **Unless we work really hard on this project,** we will fail this subject.

> 除非我們非常認真的執行這個專案，不然我們無法通過這個科目。(在「認真執行這個專案」的條件下，我們即可通過這個科目。)

例 **If Judy can stay with us,** our team will definitely win.

> 如果 Judy 可以留在我們這一隊，我們就一定會贏。(在「Judy 留下來」的條件下，我們即可贏的比賽。)

例 Mother left plenty of food in the refrigerator just **in case the typhoon comes.**

> 媽媽留下很多食物在冰箱，以防如果颱風侵襲。(在"the typhoon comes"的假設條件下，媽媽留下很多食物在冰箱。)

2 與「比較」相關的附屬連接詞為

than (比) , as…as (和…一樣) , not as (so) … as (跟…不一樣) …etc

例 Her painting skills are **much better than Lisa's**.

> 她的畫畫技巧比 Lisa 好太多了。

例 The UK is **not as big as the USA**.

> 英國不如美國國土那麼大。

 **Life Story**

In 2010, the song *Baby* became a worldwide hit and Justin Bieber, the singer of this song, also became a household name. His album *Believe* sold over 300,000 copies in the fist week of release. In just one year, Bieber became an international superstar and teen idol. ❶His success made fans believe they can pursue their dreams as long as they have faith and put their mind to it.

Sadly, since 2012, Bieber's image has been transformed from "boy-next-door" to "bad boy". ❷His reckless behavior has been discussed more often than his music recently. For example, he was accused of drunk driving in 2012 and then charged in Brazil with vandalism the following year. What's more, most Americans now approve of the idea of deporting Justin Bieber. Fast-growing fame may bring a lot of glamorous things to Bieber, but it also destroys him in some ways. Let's hope we will see the good old Bieber again one day.

2012 年時，《寶貝》這首歌成為了全球熱銷單曲，主唱者賈斯汀・比伯也因此成為了家喻戶曉的名字。他的專輯《相信》，在發行後一個禮拜，銷售量便超過了 30 萬張。僅僅一年的時間，比伯成為了國際巨星以及青少年偶像。他的成功讓粉絲相信，只要他們有信念，並且肯用心，就能追尋他們的夢想。

令人難過的是，從 2012 年開始，比伯的形象從「鄰家男孩」變成了「壞男孩」。近來，他魯莽的行為被討論的比他的音樂還要多。例如，他在 2012 年時被指控酒後駕車，而隔年則在巴西因為破壞公物罪被起訴。除此之外，現在很多的美國人同意將賈斯汀・比伯驅除出境的議題。快速成名也許為比伯帶來了許多好處，但也摧毀了他。讓我們期望我們有天能再見到原本喜愛的、善良的比伯吧！

- pursue [pɚˋsu] **V** 反對
- transform [trænsˋfɔrm] **V** 使改變
- deport [dɪˋport] **V** 放逐
- faith [feθ] **n** 信念
- reckless [ˋrɛklɪs] **adj** 魯莽的

Sentence Show ★

❶ His success made fans believe they can pursue their dreams as long as they have faith and put their mind to it

"as long as"（只要）通常連接一個表達條件的子句；所以這裡歌迷們相信可以追尋自己的夢想（"fans believe they can pursue their dreams"）的條件是什麼？就是"as long as they have faith and put their mind to it"（只要他們有信念，並且肯用心）。

❷ His reckless behavior has been discussed more than his music recently.

"more than his music"為帶有「比較」意味的副詞子句；句中比較賈斯汀的「魯莽行為」和「音樂」，前者比後者現在更被人討論。

 Practice Time ★

Q1：如果有一個好的經紀人，你也可以成為一個像賈斯汀一樣有名的歌手。

_____.

Q2：賈斯汀比他的朋友們更喜歡唱歌。

_____.

Q1 Ans：If you have a good agent, you can become a famous singer like Justin.

Q2 Ans：Justin likes singing more than his friends do.

Unit 19
副詞子句--方法、結果、狀態、程度

" I loved school so much that most of my classmates considered me a ❶nerd. "

—— Natalie Portman 娜塔莉・波曼

（我太愛上學了，以致於我大部分的同學認為我是一個書呆子。）

❶ nerd [nɜd] ⓝ 書呆子

在"so…that"的句型中，that 子句表示「結果」的副詞子句。如本句中，娜塔莉・波曼說"I loved school so much"（我太愛上學了），而此事導致的結果就是"that most of my classmates considered me a nerd"，她大部分的同學因此覺得她是書呆子。

🎬 Grammar Show ★

副詞子句也可以是以含有「方法」、「結果」、「狀態」與「程度」這些意思的從屬連接詞所引導的附屬子句。同時，使用這類副詞子句時，也一定需要與另一個子句連接，語意才會完整。現在我們就先從與「方法，結果，狀態和程度」相關的附屬連接詞所組成的副詞子句研究吧！

❶ 與「方法/狀態」相關的附屬連接詞為

so that, as if, in the way that, in order that (為了⋯；以便⋯) ⋯etc。

例 She is playing the violin **as if she is a professional.**

她現在小提琴拉得宛如專家一般。（她拉琴的狀態像專家一般。）

例 Ian described the situation in the way that he saw it.

Ian 描述當時的狀態描述的栩栩如生，就好像他在現場一般。(伊恩描述的狀態好像他在現場一般。)

2 與「結果/原因」相關的附屬連接詞為

because (因為) , since (因為) , as (因為) , given that (因為) , for (為了) , now that...etc

例 Their sales performance is getting better because they have invested so much money on product improvement.

他們的銷售漸漸好轉，因為他們在產品改良上投資了很多錢。

例 Since you are unable to answer, perhaps I should ask Lisa.

因為你沒辦法回答問題，或許我應該問Lisa。

例 I told him to leave, for I was very busy.

我告訴他先離開，因為我很忙。

例 Cindy enjoying the job now that she's got more responsibility.

因為承擔了更多的責任，Cindy很喜歡這工作。

3 與「程度」相關的附屬連接詞為

as…as (跟…一樣) , not as (so) …as (沒有跟…一樣) …etc

例 His contribution to this company is not as much as mine.

他在這家公司的貢獻沒有跟我一樣多。

例 I don't play the piano as much as I used to.

我彈鋼琴沒有彈的跟我以前一樣多。

例 Children come to visit their parents as often as they can.

孩子們盡可能多去探訪他們的父母親。

 **Life Story**

In Hollywood, many celebrities give up studies for the screen. For example, *Jobs* star Ashton Kutcher decided not to go on doing his bio-chemical engineering program at the University of Iowa. Hugh Grant, an Oxford grad, even gave up a potential career as an art history professor. However, for Natalie Portman the jump between Hollywood and academia worked the other way around.

To start with, Portman was different from other kids. She was more ambitious and serious than them. ❶She worked really hard as if she already knew what she liked and what she wanted. Later, even though she was chosen to play the leading role of a teenage mother in *Where the Heart Is*, Portman set her heart on pursuing her bachelor's degree in psychology at Harvard University. She said, "I don't care if college ruins my career. I would rather be smart than a movie star." For this reason, ❷she did not act for the next four years in order that she could concentrate on her studies.

在好萊塢，很多名人為了螢光幕工作放棄了學習。例如主演《賈伯斯》的艾希·頓庫奇決定不再繼續進行在愛荷華大學的生化工程課程；而牛津大學畢業的休·葛蘭甚至放棄了可能當上美術史教授一職的機會。然而，對娜塔莉·波曼來說，在好萊塢和學術界之間，她做了另一個選擇。

打從一開始，波曼就不同於其他的孩子。她比她們更有野心、更認真。她總是非常認真，就好像她已經知道自己喜歡的是什麼，以及想要的是什麼。之後，即使她已經被選為飾演《女孩第一名》中未成年母親的這個主要角色，波特曼仍下定決心至哈佛大學研讀心理學學士學位。她說：「我不在乎大學是否會影響我的事業，我寧願做一個聰明人，而不是一個電影明星。」因為這個理由，她在其後的四年停止接戲，也因此能夠更專心的學習。

● pursue [pɚˋsu] **V** 追求　　　● bachelor [ˋbætʃələ] **n** 學士

Sentence Show ★

❶ She worked really hard as if she already knew what she liked and what she wanted.

"as if"（就像）子句可用來表示方法或狀態；這裡"as if she already knew what she liked and what she wanted"修飾主要子句"she worked really hard"，說明她這麼努力工作的狀態就像是她已經知道她喜歡以及想要的是什麼。此外，"as if"亦可使用"as though"等代替。

❷ She did not act for the next four years in order that she could concentrate on her studies.

"in order that"（也因此）子句用來表示結果；副詞子句"in order that she could concentrate on her studying"修飾主要子句"she did not act for the next four years"，說明她接下來四年沒有演戲因此可以專心學習。

 Practice Time ★

Q1：即使很多名人放棄學業，娜塔莉・波曼仍然選擇讀大學。

_____.

Q2：娜塔莉・波曼會說希伯來語，因為她是猶太人。

_____.

Q1 Ans：Even if many celebrities gave up studies, Natalie Portman still chose to go to college.

Q2 Ans：Natalie Portman can speak Hebrew, because she is Jewish.

Unit 20
副詞子句--簡化成分詞片語

"
Stick to the classics, and you can't ever go wrong. When seeing fabulous old ladies on the street, I realize it's because they are probably wearing really classic items that they've had for years and years. I think if you find something that suits you, you should just stick to it. "

—— Alexa Chung 艾里珊•鍾

（堅持於經典服飾，然後你就永不會出錯。當我在街上看到年長的美麗女士時，我發現也許是他們正穿著他們擁有多年、非常經典的單品。我想如果你發現某樣適合你的東西，你應該執著於它。）

　　這句話將原本的副詞子句"when I see fabulous old ladies on the street…"簡化為分詞片語"when seeing fabulous old ladies on the street…"的方式。怎麼變的呢？請看下面變化方法，掌握原則就很簡單囉。

Grammar Show

　　為了讓句子更簡潔少冗言，有時我們會簡化子句成分詞片語。當從屬連接詞 when（當）、while（在……的時候）、if（如果）、unless（除非）等等所引導的副詞子句中，如果主詞與主要子句的主詞相同時，該副詞子句就可簡化為分詞片語。

步驟一：確認主詞相同。並刪除副詞子句的主詞

步驟二：主動用現在分詞（**V-ing**）；被動用過去分詞（**V-p.p.**）

　　　　be 動詞改為 **being**。

步驟三：刪除連接詞（連接詞為了句意清楚可保留）

例 When you see a doctor, you should listen carefully.

當你去看醫生，你應該要注意聽。

→When seeing a doctor, you should listen carefully.（省略相同主詞 you，see 為主動改為現在分詞 seeing）

→Seeing a doctor, you should listen carefully.（省略連接詞 When）

例 Because this classroom was abandoned for a long time, it is full of dirt.

這間教室已經被廢棄很久，所以佈滿灰塵。

→ Abandoned for a long time, this classroom is full of dirt.（省略副詞子句中的相同主詞 this classroom，並將主要子句的 it 改為 this classroom。was abandoned 為被動故改為過去分詞 abandoned。省略連接詞 Because。）

例 After I had finished my composition, I went to the movies.

寫完我的作文之後，我出門看電影。

→After having finished my composition, I went to the movies.（省略相同主詞 I，had finished 為主動故改為現在分詞 having finished）

→Having finished my composition, I went to the movies.（省略連接詞 After）

★ 若要表示「否定」，則將 not 加在分詞的前面。

例 Not knowing how to do it, she decided to have a break.

不知道如何做這件事，她決定先休息一下。

 **Life Story**

[1]Being a girl who is very into fashion, you must be familiar with an England IT girl — Alexa Chung. She was born to a Chinese father and an English mother. Chung started her modeling career at the age of 18. Since then, she has become – as people in fashion say– "a thing". She is the person you often see sitting on the front seat of shows during Fashion Week. Girls around the world trawl online galleries to see what she is wearing and how she is wearing it.

In fact, Chung's career path was not always promising. [2]After working as a model for four years, she found herself developing a "distorted body image" and "low self-esteem". Therefore, she began to take a fashion journalism course which she had always wanted to do. Because of her persistence and passion for fashion, the magazine *Vogue* noticed her and provided her an opportunity to write a column. Today, Chung is not only a fashion icon but also a successful woman whose sales have topped a billion.

做為一個喜歡時尚的女孩，你一定知道英國的女孩流行指標艾里珊·鍾。她的父親是一位中國人，而母親是英國人。她在 18 歲開始模特兒事業。從那時起，她成為了時尚業所稱的「指標」。她是時尚週期間，你常會在秀場前排看到的人。全世界的女孩都在網上搜索她的照片，為的是看她穿什麼和怎麼穿。

事實上，鍾的事業並不是一直都這麼順遂。在當了四年的模特兒後，她覺得自己發展出「扭曲的體型美感」以及「低落的自尊」。因此，她開始學習時尚記者課程，而這也是她以前一直想做的。因為她的堅持以及對時尚的熱情，*Vogue* 時尚雜誌注意到了她，並提供她一個寫專欄的機會。今天，鍾不止是個時尚偶像，還是個產品上市銷售額達十億的成功女企業家。

- trawl [trɔl] **V** 搜尋
- distorted [dɪs`tɔrtɪd] **adj** 扭曲的
- self-esteem [ˌsɛlfəs`tim] **n** 自尊
- column [`kɑləm] **n** 專欄

Sentence Show ★

❶ Being a girl who is very into fashion, you must be familiar with an England IT girl — Alexa Chung.

句中分詞片語"Being a girl who is very into fashion"是由副詞子句"If you are a girl who is very into fashion"簡化而來。因為主要子句和副詞子句的主詞均為"you"，故可以做此簡化動作。

❷ After working as a model for four years, she found herself developing a "distortedbody image" and "low self-esteem".

句中分詞片語"After working as a model for four years"是由副詞子句"After she worked as a model for four years"簡化而來。因為主要子句和副詞子句的主詞均為"she"，故可以做此簡化動作。

 Practice Time ★

Q1：在當了多年的「時尚指標」後，艾里珊・鍾對這個頭銜覺得厭倦。

_____.

Q2：當她開始模特兒事業時，並沒有預期後來會這麼成功。

_____.

Q1 Ans： After being an IT girl for many years, Alexa Chung is tired of the title.

Q2 Ans： (When) Starting modeling, she didn't expect to be so successful later.

Unit 21

時態一致與特例

"Come out" is so funny to me because I have never been in.

—— Adam Lambert 亞當・藍伯特

（對我來說，「出櫃」是個有趣的詞，因為我從來沒有進去過。）

　　一般而言，主要子句和從屬子句的時態是一致的，如："She likes cats because they are cute"（她喜歡貓，因為牠們很可愛），時態說明「她喜歡貓」是一個事實，而「因為牠們很可愛」也是一個常態性的事實。但此處兩個子句的時態不一致，"Come out" is so funny to me"「簡單現在式」表示對亞當藍伯特來說，「出櫃」這個詞很有趣是個「事實」，because 子句"because I have never been in"使用了「現在完成式」，說明他對自己是個同志的身份「從以前到現在」的狀態一直是開放的態度。

Grammar Show

　　在大部分的情況下，主要子句和附屬子句的動詞時態會是一致的；但在某些情況下，兩者時態會有不一致的情況。就讓我們來看看時態使用的規則吧！

❶ 當主要子句的時態為現在式和未來式時，附屬子句的時態可依所要表達的情況而使用不同的時態

　　例 Marco **says** that he is sick.

　　Marco 說他在生病。（表示兩個動作同時發生）

例 Marco **says** that he **was** sick.

Marco 說他之前生病了。（表示生病是一個過去動作）

例 Marco **says** that he **will be** sick.

Marco 說他之後會生病。（在當下預言之後會生病）

例 Marco **will say** that he **is** sick.

Marco 之後會說他在生病。（表示兩個動作同時發生）

例 Marco **will say** that he **was** sick.

Marco 之後會說他那時在生病。（表示生病是一個過去動作）

2 當主要子句的時態為過去式時，附屬子句大多使用過去式相關時態（如：簡單過去式或過去完成式）

例 Emily **said** she **would come.**

Emily 說她會來。

例 We **noticed** that the music **had stopped.**

我們注意到音樂已經停止了。

★ 當主要子句的時態為過去式，而附屬子句的時態則為現在式時，通常是表示「事實或真理」。

例 The teacher **told** us that honesty **is** the best policy.

老師曾告訴我們，誠實為上策。

3 當主要子句為未來式時，如果附屬子句為含有"**when**", "**until**", "**before**", "**after**"等表時間的附屬子句時，此時附屬子句的時態不可使用未來式

例 Mother **will** call us when dinner **is** ready.

媽媽會在晚餐準備好的時候叫我們。(*NOT* ~~Mother will call us when diner will be ready.~~)

4 使用"**as if**", "**If only**", "**It's time**"等表達法時，通常與過去式搭配

例 He talks **as if** he **knew** everything.

他說的好像他什麼都懂。

Adam Lambert was the runner-up on the eighth season of *American Idol*. He came to prominence during the show and was considered as the odds-on favorite at the time. Therefore, people were surprised when the final result of the competition was announced.

❶It was assumed that his sexuality was the main cause. Photos of him kissing another man were exposed before the season finale. Comments became controversial after Lambert confirmed the photos were his. Later, he admitted that he was gay in an interview with *Rolling Stone* magazine. Although many people questioned his decision to reveal his sexuality, Lambert knew he had made the right choice. He said, "I am proud of my sexuality." Lambert concentrated on his music despite these mixed opinions. His first album has sold nearly two million copies worldwide. Furthermore, he has received numerous awards and nominations since then. ❷Lambert proved to us that the effort we put into our career is the only thing that matters.

　　亞當・藍伯特是第八季《美國偶像》的亞軍。他在比賽中展露頭角，並在當時被認定為冠軍的人選。因此，當最後的比賽結果被宣佈時，許多人都感到非常驚訝。

　　許多人都猜想，是藍伯特的性向造成這個結果。在最後一集播出前，他和一名男性親吻的照片被揭露出來。在藍伯特確認照片中的人確實是他本人後，評論呈現兩極化。之後，他在與《滾石》雜誌的專訪中，承認自己的同志身份。雖然很多人質疑他坦誠性向的這個決定，但藍伯特知道自己做了正確的決定。他說：「我對自己的性向很驕傲。」儘管有各方的意見，他還是專注於自己的音樂。他的首張專輯在全世界有將近兩百萬的銷量。此外，從那時起，他也獲得了無數的獎項和提名。藍伯特向我們證明了，我們在工作上所付出的努力，才是唯一要緊的事。

- runner-up ph 亞軍
- odds-on ph 熱門人選
- prominence [ˋprɑmənəns] n 聲望
- sexuality [ˌsɛkʃʊˋælətɪ] n 性向

Sentence Show ⭐

❶ It was assumed that his sexuality was the main cause .

這個句子中，主要子句和附屬子句時態一致，均為「簡單過去式」，這也是常見的時態搭配。主要子句說明「在比賽當時的猜想」，附屬子句說明「當時的猜想是他的性向導致這樣的比賽結果」。

❷ Lambert proved to us that the effort we put into our career is the only thing that matters.

此句中主要子句為「簡單過去式」，但是附屬子句是「簡單現在式」。當附屬子句所要呈現的是一個真理（「我們在工作上所付出的努力，才是唯一要緊的事」）時，便會使用這樣時態不一致的句子形式。

 *Practice Time* ⭐

Q1：人們相信藍伯特會贏得比賽。

_____.

Q2：藍伯特告訴觀眾他是同志。

_____.

Q1 Ans：People believed that Lambert would win the competition.

Q2 Ans：Lambert told the audience that he is gay.

Unit 22
主詞動詞一致

❝Success is the best revenge.❞
—— Kanye West 肯伊 • 威斯特

（成功是最好的報復。）

　　此句的動詞為單數形式的動詞"is"，這是因為本句的主詞"success"（成功）是一個「不可數名詞」，故其後所接的動詞必須是單數形式。

Grammar Show

　　在使用英文時，需注意主詞與動詞的一致；然而，有些主詞很難看出到底需使用單數動詞或複數動詞。那麼，到底該如何判別呢？

1 **主詞是單數，動詞需使用單數動詞**

　　--主詞是單數名詞

例 **Lydia is** a good student. **She studies** hard.

　　Lydia 是個好學生。她讀書很認真。

　　--主詞是兩個或兩個以上的單數名詞，但表示的是一個概念

例 **The actor and film producer**, Mr. Lee, **has** won the prize.

　　身兼演員和電影製作人身份的李先生贏得了獎項。

--兩個或兩個以上單數主詞由"and"連接，且用"each"，"every"，"no"等字修飾時

例 **No boy or girl likes** the new coach.

沒有男生或女生喜歡新來的教練。

--「不定詞」、「動名詞」、「名詞片語」或「名詞子句」當主詞時

例 **Jogging is** a good exercise.

慢跑是一個好的運動。

2 主詞是複數，動詞需使用複數動詞

--主詞是複數名詞

例 These **books are** very interesting.

這些書很有趣。

--主詞表達的是一個全體的概念

例 **The rich donate** more money.

有錢人捐獻更多錢。

3 視主詞情況使用單複數動詞

--使用"all", "some", "most"等修飾「不可數名詞」時，用單數形動詞；修飾「可數名詞」時，用複數形動詞

例 Some **money is** left on the table.

一些錢被留在桌上了。

例 Some **girls are** from Spain.

一些女孩是從西班牙來的。

--"There be...", "Here be..."等句型中的動詞形式需與其後的名詞一致

例 There **are** a lot of **people** in the square.

有很多人在廣場上。

例 There **is** a lot of **information** you should know.

有許多你需要知道的訊息。

--"Either…or", "Neither…nor"句型的動詞需由最近的主詞決定

例 Neither Cindy nor I **am** coming.　我或 Cindy 都不會來。

例 Neither Cindy nor you **are** coming.　Cindy 或你都不會來。

 **Life Story** ★

¹The news about Kanye West being voted as Man of the Year is not really a new one. As in the singer's own words, he is "the greatest entertainer of our generation." With a statement like this, it is easy to assume Mr. West is an arrogant man. However, with 12 Grammys and record sales that exceed 20 millions, he has his reasons to back up his confidence.

In Taiwan, people who are not interested in rap music may have only heard his name from the extravagant wedding he had with the reality TV show star Kim Kardashian. In fact, West wasn't born rich. He has worked very hard to reach today's status. ²Giving up is the last thing he will do. He always thinks big and makes no secret of wanting to be the biggest star in the world. Just like he once said, at the end of the day we will see him as a legend no matter we like it or not.

肯伊・威斯特獲得「年度最佳男性」的新聞其實不是頭一回了。套一句他自己的說法，他是「我們這個年代最了不起的演藝人員」。聽到這樣的話，很容易就會覺得威斯特先生是個驕傲的人。然而，12 座格萊美的成績及超過 2 千萬的唱片銷售量，他確實擁有自信的理由。

在台灣，對饒舌音樂沒有興趣的人，也許是從他和真人實境秀明星金・卡達珊的奢華婚禮知道他的名字。事實上，威斯特並非出生顯貴，他非常努力才達到今天的地位。放棄，是他最不想做的一件事。他的想法總是很遠大，並且不會隱藏他想成為世界超級巨星的想法。就像他曾經說的，不管我們喜不喜歡，未來我們都會把他當做傳奇人物。

- entertainer [ˌɛntəˋtenə] **n** 表演者
- generation [ˌdʒɛnəˋreʃən] **n** 世代
- assume [əˋsjum] **V** 假想
- exceed [ɪkˋsid] **V** 超過
- extravagant [ɪkˋstrævəgənt] **adj** 奢侈的

Sentence Show ★

❶ The news about Kanye West being voted as Man of the Year is not really a new one.

本句的主詞為句首的名詞"news"。這個字的字尾雖有"s"，但它是一個「單數名詞」，故其後必須使用「單數動詞」"is"。和"news"一樣字尾有"s"，但屬於「單數名詞」的還有"the United States"及"physics"等。

❷ Giving up is the last thing he will do.

此句的主詞為「動名詞片語」"giving up"。而動名詞或動名詞片語做主詞時均被視為「單數」，故其後必須使用「單數動詞」"is"。

 Practice Time ★

Q1：肯伊・威斯特和他的妻子都是名人。

_____.

Q2：Green 一家人都是肯伊・威斯特的粉絲。

_____.

Q1 Ans：Both Kanye West and his wife are celebrities.

Q2 Ans：The Greens are all fans of Kanye West.

Part 4

語態與語氣

Unit 01
被動語態的構句

❝**①Gossip** is called gossip because it's not always the truth.❞

—— Justin Timberlake 賈斯汀•提姆布萊克

（八卦之所以被叫做八卦，是因為它不是真的。）

① gossip [`gasəp] **n** 八卦

　　這次我們一反往例，先從中文翻譯看起。「八卦之所以『被叫做』八卦」，句中這個「被…」的動作語句，是「被動語態」主要概念，即此動作的發生並不是主動發生的。那麼，這種被動語態該如何構句？又有什麼注意事項呢？

🎬 Grammar Show

❶ 語態 "**Voice**"是指句子中的「主詞」跟「動詞」之間的關係。如果主詞是動作（動詞）的「發起者或是執行者」，則這個句子的語態為「主動」；如果主詞是動作（動詞）「接受者或承受者」，則這個句子為「被動」。

❷ 當動詞是「及物動詞」時，主動的語態才可以轉換成被動語態，也就是說，並非所有的主動語態皆可以轉換成被動語態。被動語態的基本構句為：「動詞接受者+ be 動詞 + 過去分詞 (p.p.) + by + 動作發起者」。現在我們就從主動語態來看如何把句子轉換成被動語態。

例 These talented artists turned turn this shabby garage into a beautiful gallery.（主動語態）

這群有天份的藝術家把這破爛的車庫轉換成美麗的展覽館。

This shabby garage was **turned** into a beautiful gallery **by** these talented artists.（被動語態）

這破爛的車庫被這群有天份的藝術家轉換成美麗的展覽館。

例 This programmer developed this useful application to help people in need.（主動語態）

這位程式設計師研發這有用的應用程式，幫助有需要的人。

This useful application was **developed by** this programmer to help people in need.（被動語態）

這個有用的應用程式是由這位程式設計師所研發，用來幫助有需要的人。

★ 當動詞為「不及物動詞」時，主動語態不可轉換成被動語態。

Ryan arrived home safely last night.（主動語態）

Ryan 昨晚安全的回到家。(*NOT* ~~Home was arrived by Ryan safely last night.~~)

3 被動語態使用的時機

----該行為動作的人不知道或不重要時。

例 My laptop **was stolen**.

我的筆電被偷了。（被誰偷了不知道）

例 The new hospital **was completed** last week.

上週新的醫院完工。（是誰做的不重要）

----當從上下文中可得知做該行為動作的人或事物。

例 I **was born** in 1980.

我出生於 1980 年。（大家都知道，我是我媽媽生的，所以動作執行人省略）

----常用在科技論文上。一般學術寫作或口語較少使用。

Life Story

❶If you have read Justin Timberlake's profile, you will know the reasons why he is called "the busiest man in the music industry". He is not only a singer but also a producer, actor and businessman.

Timberlake first appeared on the television show *Star Search* at the age of 11 but achieved his fame after being cast as a member of *The Mickey Mouse Club* the following year. While some people assumed Timberlake must have not enjoyed his teenage years as much as his peers did, he claimed that his teenage years were exactly what they were supposed to be. He said people all have their own path, and it's just up to them to walk it. He never regrets the path he chooses. ❷He was often seen with different girls by the public before he settled down two years ago. However, up till now, he and his wife, Jessica Biel, are still happily married.

　　如果你有讀過賈斯汀・提姆布萊克的個人檔案，你就會知道為什麼他被稱為「樂界最忙碌的男人」。

　　提姆布萊克在 11 歲時首次於電視節目《尋找明星》中露面，但直到隔年成為米奇俱樂部的一員後才成名。然而有人猜想提姆布萊克一定沒有像他的同輩一樣享受過青少年時光，但他認為自己的青少年時光就應該是這樣。他說每個人有自己的路，而這是由他們自己決定是不是要走這條路。他從未後悔過自己所選的路。在他結婚之前的兩年，他時常被人們看到和不同的女孩們在一起。然而，直到現在，他和他的妻子潔西卡・貝兒仍然維持愉快的婚姻關係。

- teenage [ˋtinˏedʒ] **adj** 十幾歲的
- suppose [səˋpoz] **V** 猜想
- settle down **ph** 成家過安定生活
- peer [pɪr] **n** 同輩
- path [pæθ] **n** 路徑

Sentence Show ★

❶ If you have read Justin Timberlake's profile, you will know the reasons why he is called "the busiest man in the music industry".

本句被動語句為"he is called 'the busiest man in the music industry'";從使用被動形式"is called"（被叫做）我們可以知道「樂界最忙碌的男人」這個稱號是別人給提姆布萊克的,而不是提姆布萊克自己取的。

❷ He was often seen with different girls by the public before he settled down two years ago.

此句有 2 個需要留意之處:（1）被動形式為"was seen"（被看見）;（2）要說明被動式的動作是誰做的,需使用"by+做動作者"（如此處"He was often seen…by the public."，表示是人們看見了提姆布萊克）。

 Practice Time ★

Q1：賈斯汀‧提姆布萊克的音樂被全世界的人喜愛。

_____.

Q2：賈斯汀‧提姆布萊克的婚姻在 2012 年被報導。

_____.

Q1 Ans：Justin Timberlake' music is loved by people all around the world.

Q2 Ans：Justin Timberlake's marriage was reported in 2012.

Unit 02
被動的時態

"I was ❶*bullied* until I ❷*prevented* a new student from being bullied. By ❸*standing up for* him, I learned to stand up for myself."

—— Jackie Chan 成龍

（我以前曾被霸凌，直到我阻止了一個新學生被霸凌。從起身捍衛他，我學會了捍衛我自己。）

❶ bully [`bʊlɪ] ▼ 欺侮　❷ prevent [prɪ`vɛnt] ▼ 阻止　❸ stand up for ph 捍衛

　　上句中的"I was bullied"文法形式為"be 動詞+p.p."，是一個被動式的語態。此外，此句中的 be 動詞使用了過去式，表示「被霸凌」這件事是發生在「過去」，現在沒有人會（也沒有人敢）欺負成龍了。

Grammar Show

　　被動語態根據時態的不同，也會有不同的變化與構句。以下是較常使用到的被動時態。

❶ 被動簡單式：主詞 + be 動詞 + 過去分詞

　例 His application is **rejected** due to insufficient supporting documents.

　　他的申請被拒絕了，因為沒有足夠的輔助文件。(簡單現在式)

例 Kevin **was punched** by his friend because of the girls.

Kevin 昨天因為女孩們的問題，被他的朋友揍了。(簡單過去式)

2 被動完成式：主詞 **+ have/has/had been +** 過去分詞

例 His application **has been rejected** due to insufficient supporting documents.

他的申請已經被拒絕了，因為沒有足夠的輔助文件。(現在完成式)

例 Kevin **had been punched** by his friend before he had a chance to explain.

Kevin 在有機會做解釋之前，已經被他的朋友揍過了。(過去完成式)

3 被動進行式：主詞 **+ be** 動詞 **+ being +** 過去分詞

例 This skyscraper **is being built** by the laborers.

工人們正在建這棟摩天大樓。(現在進行式)

例 The novel **was being written** by Lily when the editor decided to change its title.

編輯決定更換書名的時候，這本小說正由 Lily 負責撰寫。(過去進行式)

4 被動未來式：主詞 **+ will + be +**過去分詞

例 This prisoner **will be released** next week.

這個囚犯下個禮拜將會被釋放。(未來式)

例 The novel **will be published** by the end of this month.

這本小說將會在這個月底被出版。(未來式)

Life Story

Jackie Chan is a billion dollar box office success. People enjoy watching his screen persona. In real life, Chan's personal life has received almost the same attention. For example,❶ he was reported having an affair with an actress by the tabloid press in 1999. Later in 2006, he upset the audience of Jonathan Lee's Hong Kong concert because he jumped up to the stage and disturbed the singer's performance.

Although some people may find Chan's behavior unacceptable, ❷they still can't deny the fact that he has been recognized as the most famous martial arts actor in the West since Bruce Lee. Chan was born in poverty and started to work at an early age. To achieve today's fame, he put a lot of effort into his work such as spending time practicing martial arts and learning English. "I never wanted to be the next Bruce Lee. I just wanted to be the first Jackie Chan," he said.

成龍是票房保證。人們喜歡看他在電影裡的演出。現實生活中，他的私生活也獲得了同樣的關注。例如，他在 1999 年時，被八卦媒體報導與某個女星發生婚外情。而 2006 年時，他因為跳上舞台，擾亂歌手李宗盛在香港的演唱會而惹惱了觀眾。

雖然有些人可能無法接受成龍的行為，但他們仍無法否認，在李小龍之後，成龍已成為西方最有名的武術明星。成龍出生貧寒，並在幼年時便開始工作。為了達到今日的名聲，他在工作上付出了很多的努力，比如花時間練習武術動作以及學習英文等。他說：「我永遠也不要做下一個李小龍，我只要做第一個成龍。」

- affair [əˋfɛr] **n** 外遇
- disturb [dɪsˋtɝb] **v** 妨礙
- poverty [ˋpɑvɚtɪ] **n** 貧窮
- upset [ʌpˋsɛt] **v** 使生氣
- concert [ˋkɑnsɚt] **n** 演唱會

Sentence Show ★

❶ He was reported having an affair with an actress by the tabloid press in 1999.

此句的結尾說明事件的發生時間為 1999 年（過去），故後面的被動式"was reported"（被報導）使用了過去式的形式。另外，"by the tabloid press"則說明了動作的進行者為「八卦媒體」。

❷ They still can't deny the fact that he has been recognized as the most famous martial arts actor in the West since Bruce Lee.

這裡的被動語態使用的是「現在完成式」"has been recognized"，因為句中所要表達的是「在李小龍之後」，成龍「一直被認為是最在西方最有名的武術演員」。

 Practice Time ★

Q1：成龍昨天被看見和他的兒子在一起。

_____

Q2：成龍的最新電影將於明年上映。

_____

Q1 Ans：Jackie Chan was seen with his son yesterday.

Q2 Ans：Jackie Chan's latest movie will be released next year.

Unit 03

假設語氣--純條件式和必為事實

If you spend too much time thinking about a thing, you will never get it done.

—— Bruce Lee 李小龍

（如果你花太多的時間在想一件事，你將永遠不會動手去做。）

李小龍此句話使用了「純條件」的假設語態，表達的是對未來的設想。"If you spend too much time thinking about a thing"（如果你花太多的時間在想一件事），而實際上這個情況還沒有發生，而倘若發生了，可能的結果就是主要子句的"you will never get it done"（你將永遠不會動手去做）。

 Grammar Show ★

本單元與 Unit4 將討論假設語態的使用法。首先，先來看看本單元標題的「純條件的假設語態」以及「必定為事實的假設語態」。

1 純條件的假設語態 (First Conditional)：**"If+ 主詞+現在簡單式動詞，主詞+will/won't+原形動詞"**

此種假設語態用於假設未來可能發生的事；if 子句雖使用現在簡單式動詞，但表達的是「在未來可能發生的情況或行動」，而主要子句則表示的是「事情的結果」。

例 If Mike **gets up** at 10, he **will miss** the school bus.

如果麥克十點才起床，他會錯過校車。（說話者假設如果麥克十點才起床（實際上這件事還未發生），他將會錯過校車。）

★ 亦可將主要子句與 if 子句位置調換：主詞+will/won't+原形動詞+ if+主詞+現在簡單式動詞。但使用此句型時，if 之前不需要有逗號。

例 Mike **will miss** the school bus if he **gets up** at 10.

★ 主要子句的 will/won't 亦可更換為 can/may/should 等其他助動詞，但通常此類助動詞僅出現在主要子句，而不會在 if 子句中

例 ~~If Mike~~ ~~will get up~~ ~~at 10,~~ he will miss the bus. (X)

★ 當 will 出現於 if 子句中時，多為請求的狀況：

例 If you **will** just wait a second, I will find the file for you.

如果你可以等我一下，我會將文件找給你。

2 必定為事實的假設語態 (Zero Conditional)："**If+ 主詞+現在簡單式動詞，主詞+現在簡單式動詞**"

此種假設語態用來表達所敘述的事通常為「事實」。

例 If you **want** to be a doctor, you **have** to pass the qualification for the job.

如果你想成為醫生，你必須通過資格審查。（要當醫生必須通過資格審查）

★ 亦可將主要子句與 if 子句位置調換：「主詞+現在簡單式動詞+ if +主詞+現在簡單式動詞」但需注意使用此句型時，if 之前不需要有逗號。

例 You **have** to pass the qualification for the job **if** you **want** to be a doctor.

 **Life Story** ★

[1]If you are a fan of martial arts, you should know the name Bruce Lee. He started to learn martial arts at the age of 16 and later worked as a Hong Kong action movie actor, martial artist and instructor. Although Lee died in 1973, he is still widely considered as one of the most influential martial artists of all time. Fans today still like to quote his line from the movie *Fist of Fury,* "We Chinese are not the shame of Asia."

In fact, most people are not only impressed by Lee's excellent martial arts skills but also his words of wisdom. He used to encourage people to conquer their fears and challenge themselves. He once said, "**[2]**If you always put limits on everything you do, physical or anything else, it will spread into your work and into your life. There are no limits. There are only plateaus, and you must not stay there, you must go beyond them."

如果你是一個武術迷,你會聽過李小龍的名字。他在 16 歲時開始學習武術,並在之後成為香港動作片演員、武術家和武術指導。雖然李小龍在 1973 年逝世,他仍被廣泛地視為古往今來最有影響力的武術家之一。粉絲們今日仍喜歡引用他在電影《精武門》中的台詞:「我們中國人不是東亞病夫!」

事實上,很多人不止是被李小龍精湛的武術技巧所打動,也為他智慧的話語所折服。他以前常鼓勵人們克服自己的恐懼,挑戰自己。他曾說:「如果你總是對自己做的事設限,不管是身體上的限制或其他,這種限制將會擴散到你的工作及生活。『限制』是不存在的,只有『停滯』。而你不能保持著停滯的狀態,你必須超越它。」

- martial arts **n** 武術
- quote [kwot] **v** 引用
- conquer [ˈkɑŋkɚ] **v** 克服
- limit [ˈlɪmɪt] **n** 限制
- plateaus [plæˈto] **n** 沒有進步的停滯期

Sentence Show ★

❶ If you are a fan of martial arts, you should know the name Bruce Lee.

這句話的文法是「純條件」的假設語態。由本例判斷，作者並不知道讀者是否是武術迷，但是知道如果有武術迷的話，就會知道李小龍的名字。

❷ If you always put limits on everything you do, physical or anything else, it will spread into your work and into your life.

這句話也是使用了「純條件」的假設語態。If 子句中的「如果你總是對自己做的事設限，不管是身體上的限制或其他」是作者假設可能發生的情況，而主要子句則說明可能出現的結果是「這種限制將會擴散到你的工作及生活」。

 Practice Time ★

Q1：如果你喜歡李小龍，你會知道他是一位美籍香港人。

_____.

Q2：李小龍說：「如果你是一個聰明人，就也能從某個蠢問題中學習。」

_____.

Q1 Ans： If you like Brue Lee, you will know he is a Hong Kong American.

Q2 Ans： Bruce Lee said, "If you are a wise man, you can also learn from a foolish question."

Unit 04

假設語氣--與現在和過去事實相反

" *If it wasn't hard, everyone would do it. It is the hard that makes it great.* "

—— Tom Hanks 湯姆‧漢克斯

（如果事情不難，那麼每個人都可以做。就是困難讓事情美好。）

　　此處第一句話使用了「與現在事實相反」的假設語態，表示湯姆‧漢克斯所描述的這個情況是他的想像，並非是真實情況。那麼，這種「與現在事實相反」的假設語態該如何使用？與其他情況的假設語句又有何不同呢？

Grammar Show

　　現在讓我們來看看另外兩種假設語態：「與現在事實相反的假設語態」以及「於過去事實相反的假設語態」。

❶ **與現在事實相反的假設語態 (Second Conditional)：If+ 主詞+過去簡單式動詞，主詞+would / wouldn't+原形動詞**

此種假設語態用於表達某事為「想像或非真實的」，與現在事實相反的情況。

例 If Michael Jackson **were** alive today, he **would be** about fifty-five years old.

如果麥克傑克森現在還在世，他差不多要 55 歲了。（這個句子想像麥克傑克森還在世的情況，但實際他已經過世了）

★ 亦可將主要子句與 if 子句位置調換：「主詞+ would / wouldn't +原形動詞+ if+主詞+現在簡單式動詞。注意使用此句型時，if 之前不需要有逗號」

例 Michael Jackson **would be** about fifty-five years old if he **was** alive today.

★ 主要子句的 would / wouldn't 亦可更換為 could / might / should 等其他助動詞，但通常此類助動詞僅出現在主要子句，而不會在 if 子句中

★ 當主詞是 I / he / she / it 時，if 子句的 be 動詞過去式為 were，不是 was。

例 If I **were** you, I wouldn't go out with that man.

　　如果我是你，我不會跟那男的約會。

2 與過去事實相反的假設語態 (Third Conditional)：「If+ 主詞+had p.p. , 主詞+would / wouldn't have + p.p.」

此種假設語態用於表達某事「在過去並未發生」，與過去事實相反的情況。

例 If the team **had won** the match, it **would have got** through to the final.

　　如果那個團隊贏得了這場比賽，就可以進入決賽。（但那個團隊輸了比賽）

★ 亦可將主要子句與 if 子句位置調換： 「主詞+ would / wouldn't have + p.p.+ if+主詞++had p.p.」。注意使用此句型時，if 之前不需要有逗號

例 The team **would have got** through to the final if it **had won** the match.

★ If 子句中不可使用 would have，但主要子句的 would / wouldn't 亦可更換為 could / might / should 等其他助動詞

 **Life Story**

It would be difficult to ask a person to name the best Tom Hanks' movie. After all, Hanks has already been cast in several hits, including *Forrest Gump*, *Apollo 13*, *Saving Private Ryan* and *You've Got Mail*.

In fact, Hanks went through some ups and downs at the beginning of his acting career. He made his debut in the 1984 film *Splash,* and then his career began to take off after playing the leading role in the fantasy comedy *Big* in 1988. Unfortunately, both his career and the box office were disappointing over the next four years. ❶Some people would feel depressed and stop trying if they were in Hanks' situation. However, Hanks climbed back to the top again with his washed-up baseball legend turned manager character in the movie *A League of Their Own*. He once mentioned this period of failure in an interview. He admitted it was a difficult time, but he never thought of quitting. We should be really grateful that Hanks didn't give up! ❷If he had at the time, we would never see his wonderful acting now.

要讓某個人說出湯姆・漢克斯最棒的一部電影是很困難的。畢竟，漢克斯已出演過許多的熱門影片，如：《阿甘正傳》、《阿波羅 13》、《搶救雷恩大兵》、《電子情書》等。

事實上，漢克斯在演藝生涯初期曾經歷過事業的高低潮。他在 1984 年電影《美人魚》中首次登上大螢幕，而在 1988 年的奇幻電影《飛進未來》中擔任男主角後，事業漸入佳境。不幸的是，他的事業和票房在其後的四年都令人失望。當某些人處於漢克斯的情況時，他們可能會覺得心情低落並停止努力。然而，漢克斯在演出《紅粉聯盟》中的那個原本是落魄的明星棒球員後成為球隊經理的角色後，重回事業的高峰。他曾在一次面談中提及那段失意的時光。他承認那是段難熬的日子，但他從未想過放棄。我們應該慶幸漢克斯沒有放棄！要是他當時放棄了，我們現在就看不到他精湛的演技了。

● take off `ph` 突然大受歡迎　　　● washed-up [ˋwɑʃˋʌp] `adj` 被淘汰的

298

Sentence Show ★

❶ Some people would feel depressed and stop trying if they were in Hanks' situation.

「有些人可能會心情低落並停止嘗試，如果他們處於漢克斯的情況」，「與現在事實相反」的假設語態表示這句話描述的是個理論上的情況，是作者自己的想像，實際上沒有人處於漢克斯的情況下。

❷ If he had at the time, we would never see his wonderful acting now.

這句話也是使用了「與現在事實相反」的假設語態。「如果他當時放棄演戲」是作者想像的情況，並非真實發生，即實際上漢克斯當時並沒有放棄，所以我們現在仍然可以看到他的演出。

 Practice Time ★

Q1：如果湯姆・漢克斯放棄演戲，他的人生會變得完全不一樣。

_____.

Q2：如果湯姆・漢克斯是位歌手，就不會演出那些熱門大片。

_____.

Q1 Ans： If Tom Hanks gave up acting, his life would be totally different.

Q2 Ans： If Tom Hanks were a singer, he would not be able to star in those blockbusters.

Learn Smart! 041

跟著大明星學英文文法
Learning English Grammar
with Hollywood Stars

作　　　　者／蘇瑩珊
封　面　設　計／高鍾琪
內　頁　排　版／菩薩蠻數位文化有限公司

發　　行　　人／周瑞德
企　劃　編　輯／徐瑞璞
校　　　　對／陳欣慧、饒美君、陳韋佑
印　　　　製／大亞彩色印刷製版股份有限公司
初　　　　版／2014 年 12 月
定　　　　價／新台幣 349 元
封 面 圖 片 出 處／2011 (c) Eva Rinaldi, the photo "Hugh Jackman" is provided under CC
BY-SA 2.0 Generic at flickr.com. Change has been made. 2014 (c) Hot Gossip Italia, the photo
"Angelina Jolie e Brad Pitt si sono sposati: le nozze in Francia il 23 agosto" is provided under CC BY 2.0
Generic at flickr.com. Change has been made. 2010 (c) David Shankbone, the photo "Cameron Diaz
Tribeca Shankbone 2010" is provided under CC BY 2.0 Generic at flickr.com. Change has been made.
2011 (c) Philip Nelson, the phote "Lady GaGa - Monster Ball - Nashville, TN" is provided under CC
BY-SA 2.0 Generic at flickr.com. Change has been made.
出　　　　版／倍斯特出版事業有限公司
電　　　　話／（02）2351-2007
傳　　　　真／（02）2351-0887
地　　　　址／100 台北市中正區福州街 1 號 10 樓之 2
E　　m　　a　　i　　l／best.books.service@gmail.com

港 澳 地 區 總 經 銷／泛華發行代理有限公司
地　　　　址／香港筲箕灣東旺道 3 號星島新聞集團大廈 3 樓
電　　　　話／（852）2798-2323
傳　　　　真／（852）2796-5471

國家圖書館出版品預行編目（CIP）資料

跟著大明星學英文文法 / 蘇瑩珊著. -- 初版. -
臺北市：倍斯特，2014.12
　　面；　公分. -- (Learn smart! ; 41)
ISBN 978-986-90883-4-3(平裝)
1.　英語 2.語法

805.16　　　　　　　　　　103022881

Simply Learning, Simply Best!

Simply Learning, Simply Best!